Extreme Justice

by
Linda Kistler

AuthorHouse™
1663 Liberty Drive
Bloomington, IN 47403
www.authorhouse.com
Phone: 1-800-839-8640

© 2009 Linda Kistler. All rights reserved.

No part of this book may be reproduced, stored in a retrieval system, or transmitted by any means without the written permission of the author.

First published by AuthorHouse 7/1/2009

ISBN: 978-1-4389-9771-1 (e)
ISBN: 978-1-4389-9773-5 (sc)

Printed in the United States of America
Bloomington, Indiana

This book is printed on acid-free paper.

This is for Jim and Steve

Prologue

He sauntered unannounced into her class, interrupting the morning lecture.

"Is this Organization Behavior, course M301?" he asked, handing her a slip of paper.

"Yes, it is." The professor glanced at the form, noted the dean's signature approving the student's admission to her course.

"And you are. . ." She regarded him over half-glasses.

"John Lombardo is the name," he replied, eyes scanning the classroom, relishing the attention his entrance created. "And you must be Abby Prescott."

"Correct. I'm professor Prescott," she said coolly. "Let me remind you that this course began ten days ago, and you're already fifteen minutes late today. Please don't make it a habit."

The class snickered, amused at the new student's cool reception.

She silently handed him a course syllabus and waved him to an empty seat.

"See me in my office after class," she directed, waiting as he tossed his ski jacket on the floor and slowly settled into his chair.

Elbows resting on the lectern, she gazed out the window at a stormy platinum sky and the white-capped Atlantic surf in the distance. The January nor'easter predicted for the Maine coast would be upon them before evening.

She resumed her lecture.

Chapter One

It was nearly noon when Abby Prescott's new student barged into her fourth floor office without bothering to knock. Engaged in a telephone conversation, she silently waved him to a seat.

He eased into the chair beside her desk and glanced around the professor's well appointed office in the Reid University School of Business. Tall, with fashionably cut gel-spiked dark hair and olive skin, Lombardo's otherwise handsome Italian features were marred by a weak mouth and ferret-like hazel eyes. Heavily developed abs rippled beneath his logo-emblazoned golf shirt and dual barbed-wire prison tats circled his bulging biceps. Overall, he projected a slightly menacing air.

"Let me call you back, Jen. I've got a student in my office."

She hung up, rooted through the pile of loose papers on her desk and retrieved the student's class admission form. She reviewed the form silently.

"Mr. Lombardo, please tell me why you registered for Organization Behavior at this late date," she began. "The deadline for adding a course passed a week ago. Despite the deadline and the fact that you've already missed five lectures, the dean has approved your admission into this class."

Eyebrows raised, he stared at her belligerently. "The admissions people already gave me grief about this," he grumbled. "I'm not looking for another lecture from you, Abby. Do I need an excuse from home because I missed a few classes?"

Taken aback, she was silent for a moment. "An excuse won't be necessary," she said finally. "By the way, my students are expected to address me as professor."

"All right, if that's the way you want it, professor," he said sarcastically. "And why don't you just call me Lombardo?"

"Fine. Lombardo it is," she smiled faintly.

She leaned forward, hands resting on her closed laptop computer.

"I'm curious," Abby persisted, "why did you enroll so late?"

"Actually, I was on vacation in the Caribbean with my parents. I didn't get to campus until late last night," he responded with a smirk. "How do you like my tan?"

"Nice."

"In case you don't recognize my name," he continued, "my father is Robert Lombardo, chairman of the board of trustees at this university." He tossed a business card on the desk. Abby glanced at it, noted a Manhattan address.

She waited for him to continue.

He leaned back in his chair. "If you really want to know, I'm a transfer student from New Jersey," he explained less belligerently. "My academic records were submitted more than a month ago, way before Christmas and my vacation. I was late for class today because the registrar hadn't bothered to evaluate my records."

"I see."

"The fact is, I shouldn't even be in your course," he continued.

"Really. Why is that?"

"I already took Organization Behavior at Alliance Community College last semester."

"And what was your grade in the course?"

He shrugged. "I think I got a C," he said noncommittally. "This morning the registrar said I need to take the course again. Are all the administrators at this university such assholes?"

"The registrar was following standard academic procedure. Reid University doesn't accept advanced courses from a community college," Abby explained evenly.

"That's a bunch of crap."

She ignored his outburst. "You should earn an easy A since it will be your second time through the material. "You have the syllabus," she continued. "The course requirements are detailed; that includes buying the textbook. I suggest you head over to the bookstore and pick up a copy."

"Why?" he protested. "I just told you I already took this course at Alliance."

"Buy the book, Lombardo," she directed firmly, "and start studying the material. You're already four chapters behind. Friday's assignment is Chapter Five. I've scheduled a ninety-minute examination covering the first five chapters next Monday. You've got work to do."

"I'll ace your exam, no problem," he sneered.

"Let me give you some advice," she said, beginning to lose patience. "I don't care whether you took a similar course at some community college.

You are required to take the course again, university rules. And no one aces my course without investing a significant amount of time and effort."

Lombardo flew out of his chair, fists clenched, his face suddenly an angry mask. He loomed over her so closely she smelled stale alcohol on his breath.

"Not a problem, professor."

She drew back. "That's all for now. If you have questions about the syllabus, send me an email. I'll respond within twenty-four hours." She turned to the papers on her desk.

He grabbed his backpack and left her office, closing the door none too gently.

Although Abby had encountered her share of aggressive students in the past, for reasons she later could not articulate, her heart began to race as adrenaline surged through her body. She felt edgy, uncertain how she would handle this wise guy. She finally tagged Lombardo as a wealthy, spoiled young man, perhaps marginally qualified for admission to the university and dismissed the incident from her mind.

An acknowledged expert in her field, Abby Prescott had earned the respect of students and faculty alike. Indeed, last year students voted her the outstanding professor in the School of Business.

Tall and slim with short dark hair peppered with grey, Abby had come to love teaching at Reid University. This was her first full-time academic position following graduation from Harvard Business School's doctoral program. In a few months she would learn whether her academic experience, the strong support of faculty colleagues, plus five years as a highly paid management consultant would earn her tenure as an associate professor at one of the most prestigious universities in New England.

She swiveled her chair and gazed out the window as throngs of students, bundled in ski jackets and jeans against biting wind and January cold, hurried across Founders Court toward the Student Center and lunch.

Chapter Two

Abby walked down the hall to the office of her friend and colleague, Jen Carpenter.

"Remember I mentioned a new student who wandered into my OB class a couple weeks ago?" she began.

Jen looked up from her laptop. "Yes, vaguely. Why don't you fill me in on the details."

"His name is John Lombardo and he enrolled late. He has a bad attitude that's already beginning to irritate me. I don't understand why the dean allows students to enroll ten days after classes have begun," she grumbled. "He transferred from some no-name community college in New Jersey, and claims he's already taken an Organization Behavior course," she went on.

"Sounds like your semester is off to an interesting start," Jen laughed. "Tell me more about his bad attitude."

"We got off on the wrong foot from the time he walked into class," Abby sighed. She glanced at her watch. "Can you join me for lunch in half an hour? I'll tell you the whole story."

*   *   *

The two women leaned into a biting February gale whipping across Founders Court and entered the Student Center. Surrounded by a hundred raucous students, they worked their way along the cafeteria line, exchanged a few words with the friendly cashier and paid their bill. Seated at a small table near two-story glass windows, they glanced at the white-capped Atlantic that lay below the deserted flagstone terrace. Recorded music blasted across the room, challenging attempts at conversation.

"Now," said Jen, a professor of management, "tell me more about your problem student. He's apparently made a strong impression."

Abby cautiously tested her clam chowder. "Apparently, Lombardo's father is chairman of the university's board of trustees. I suspect daddy may have exerted some influence in getting him into the university.

"Because the dean signed his admission slip, I had to allow him to stay in my class. To make matters worse, he is becoming disruptive and aggressive in class."

"What do you mean?" Jen asked more seriously.

"You know I hate students strolling into class after I've begun my lecture. This guy is consistently late for class, loves to make an entrance, to draw attention to himself. He is a perfect example of the self-absorbed X-Generation student."

"That doesn't sound especially serious. Surely you can straighten him out on that score."

"Unfortunately, he also displays signs of aggression; the class is beginning to fall apart," Abby admitted ruefully.

"Good luck to him. He won't have an easy time with your course, whether he took a similar course elsewhere or not. And his father's position certainly won't influence you."

"I just finished grading my first exam," Abby revealed abruptly.

"How did he do?"

"He not only failed the test, he had the lowest grade in the class. And my first exam is always the easiest one of the semester."

"If he can't pass your first exam, he clearly didn't learn a lot in that community college course," Jen observed.

"This isn't the first time you've had a disruptive student in your class," she reminded her. "We all occasionally have to deal with them. Obviously, most of our students are here to learn; with tuition and board running more than $50,000 a year, mom and dad want their money's worth."

"I can't explain exactly why, but Lombardo is beginning to bug me," Abby confessed.

"What exactly is so troublesome?" Jen asked, probing for more concrete reasons.

"It's strange—hard to describe. Basically, he challenges me, constantly draws attention to himself, tries to take control of the class. He interrupts other students in mid-sentence, insists on dominating the discussion. I'm no psychologist, but this guy clearly has control problems."

"What do you mean, he challenges you?" Jen asked.

"He keeps interrupting, wants to debate me on the content of my lectures. If he were brilliant, I might tolerate a bit of arrogance."

"Interesting," Jen said. "Now, I'm curious. After lunch let's check his background on the academic information system."

They deposited their trash in the bin, stacked their trays and headed across the wind-swept campus to the business school.

*   *   *

"Look at this," Abby pointed to the screen on her laptop computer. "Lombardo attended Adirondack Academy in upstate New York. Based on his date of birth, it took him twenty years to earn a high school diploma."

"I know something about Adirondack," Jen remarked. "The school combines a philosophy of strong discipline with the latest teaching techniques for students with learning disabilities. Perhaps his parents couldn't deal with him, so they shipped him off to private school."

She leaned over Abby's shoulder, examining John Lombardo's personal data. She pointed to the screen. "This is interesting. His home address is one of those posh New Jersey bedroom communities. I'm sure our board chairman is from around New York City."

Abby closed the personal data screen and brought up the student's admissions data and academic records.

"Look," Jen pointed to the information displayed. "Based on his SAT scores and his record at Adirondack, he doesn't appear to meet our normal admission standards. We rarely admit transfer students in the January semester, especially from an obscure community college. I'll bet he's a legacy admission to Reid."

"Probably," Abby agreed. "Let's check the other colleges he attended." She scrolled down the computer screen. "One in Oregon and two in New Jersey. Still, he has only accumulated enough credits to earn an Associate Degree from a community college. Not an impressive academic performance for someone twenty-five years old."

"Exactly," Jen said.

"If I don't crack down on him, I'm afraid his behavior will ruin the class for the other students, not to mention aggravating me." She closed the password-protected academic information system. "I can't allow a student to hijack my class," she said grimly.

"You can handle this wise guy," Jen said sympathetically.

* * *

Three weeks later Abby invited Lombardo to her office after the morning lecture. She walked silently beside him as they left the classroom and took the elevator to her fourth floor office.

"Please sit down." She waved him to a chair opposite her desk and closed her office door to ensure privacy.

Hands on his hips, he remained standing while she seated herself at her desk.

Abby gazed up at him. "You were especially disruptive in class today," she began calmly. "You're not the only student in this class, you know. When others want to offer opinions you constantly interrupt and try to dominate the discussion. Your behavior is rude and unacceptable; several students have complained. I want you to stop disrupting the class."

Lombardo glared down at her.

"Sit down," she pointed to the chair, her voice rising.

He dropped his backpack onto the floor and slouched insolently into the chair, stretching his long legs under her desk.

"I know more about Organization Behavior than anybody in the class, including you," he mocked. "That's why I have to speak up. I need to correct your mistakes."

Abby laughed aloud. "That's amusing, Lombardo. When you've earned a DBA in Management, have five years' consulting and six years' teaching experience, you can challenge me. Right now, your job is to listen and learn."

She leaned forward. "Sometimes a little knowledge is a dangerous thing. Earning a mediocre grade in Organization Behavior at a community college doesn't make you an expert. You failed the first examination two weeks ago. In fact, you had the lowest grade in the class."

Lombardo suddenly leaped to his feet and thrust his clenched fist in her face.

"Professor, my new goal in life is to get you," he snarled, his face an ugly mask.

"What exactly do you mean by that remark? Are you threatening me?" Abby asked, stunned. He didn't respond, grabbed his backpack, and left her office, slamming the door behind him.

Hands shaking and clammy, Abby's heart rate soared as adrenaline surged through her body. She slumped in her chair, struggling for control. Moments later, she cautiously opened her office door and looked down the hall. Her problem student had disappeared.

She locked the door and returned to her desk, fighting to still her racing heart. What had prompted the violent outburst? Did her relatively mild reprimand set him off? Or was it the fact that she had laughed at him? Had John Lombardo actually threatened her, or was she imagining it?

She gazed out the window at scores of bustling students, backpacks slung over their shoulders and jackets zipped against the raw February wind. In the late morning sunshine, she watched wind-driven surf pound the rocky cliffs in the distance. The familiar scene helped to calm her.

She needed to talk to someone, to get advice on how to deal with what was escalating into a serious behavior problem in her class. She locked her office door and walked down the hall.

Jen Carpenter looked up from her laptop.

"Are you all right? You look like you could use a cup of coffee."

"I really need something a little stronger," Abby responded wryly. "Let me tell you what just happened in my office." She seated herself on the sofa and related her confrontation with Lombardo.

* * *

"You took exactly the right approach with him," Jen said supportively. "If he's disrupting your class, put a stop to it now. And you were wise to set the record straight privately in your office. No need to set him off in front of your class. Did he acknowledge that his behavior is unacceptable?" she asked, concealing her concern.

"No, and this latest confrontation probably won't solve the problem. He's clearly not accustomed to taking criticism. I wonder whether he has problems with female authority figures," Abby mused, searching for a reason to explain her student's behavior.

"Lombardo said something rather strange just before he left my office," she confided reluctantly.

"Go on," Jen urged.

"He said his new goal in life is to get me," Abby laughed shakily. "It wasn't so much what he said as how he behaved."

"Walk me through every detail." Jen was deliberately calm.

"He completely lost control, went ballistic when I laughed at his comment about correcting my mistakes. He leaned over my desk and shook his fist in my face. Then he said, and these are his exact words, 'my new goal in life is to get you.'"

"What do you think he meant by that remark?" Jen asked quietly.

"That's the problem," Abby shrugged. "I don't know. Perhaps he's challenging me on knowledge of my subject matter. Of course, I've forgotten more about how organizations behave than he will ever know. He'll wait a long time to catch me in a technical mistake."

"Did you feel physically threatened by his remark?"

"Not exactly. He didn't touch me, grab my arm, or do anything overtly physical. But it's disconcerting to have a student shake his fist in my face."

Embarrassed, she rose to leave. "I'm sorry to bother you with my discipline problem. It's probably nothing."

"It's not a bother," Jen assured her. "You clearly were shaken when you walked in here. Are you feeling better now?"

"I'm fine. I'll go home after my afternoon class, fix myself a stiff drink and forget about John Lombardo. He probably was just blowing off steam, angry about failing the exam. And he clearly didn't appreciate my criticism of his behavior."

"You may want to discuss the problem with the dean," Jen suggested.

"The dean is the last person I want to discuss this with. I'm coming up for tenure in another month. I can't afford to have the dean think I can't handle my students."

"Fair enough. You don't need a student problem complicating his evaluation of your performance.

"Perhaps this isn't the time to point out that you've already gained some notoriety on campus with your support of the proposed liquid natural gas terminal north of Bar Harbor," Jen changed the subject.

"Speaking of the LNG terminal issue," Abby said, relieved the conversation was moving in another direction. "I hope you'll listen to my reasons for supporting it."

"Of course I'll listen to your reasons," Jen said. "However, that LNG terminal proposal is a political hot potato in this state, even more controversial than developing a windmill farm off Cape Cod in Massachusetts. President

Smythe has publicly opposed the LNG terminal on environmental grounds and the board of trustees agrees with him."

"What is your position on the project?" Abby challenged her friend.

"I haven't taken a position."

"I'm not the only faculty member supporting the terminal, you know," Abby reminded her. "Rick Stewart over in Environmental Sciences consults with the European group that's negotiating to build it. I've gotten to know him because he's leading the public relations efforts locally."

"I know Rick is way out front on the issue. Of course, he earned tenure and promotion last year. He can publicly support just about anything he wants. He can't be fired for his views on the project because he has tenure.

"You're in a different situation, Abby. You don't have tenure protection and you're supporting a project that the president, the board of trustees and half the citizens of Maine oppose."

"I can speak out on any issue I want," she retorted defensively.

"Of course, we all have the right to speak," Jen said patiently. "I'm only advising you to be cautious and avoid controversy until you get tenure."

"Are decisions at this university so political that I could be denied tenure because I support a project the president opposes?" Abby asked, incredulous.

"Frankly, yes," Jen replied evenly. "You are surprisingly naïve. I've been involved in tenure decisions on this campus for more than a decade. Trust me, the process is unbelievably political."

She checked her watch. "I have a suggestion. After classes this afternoon, let's head down to Portland and have a drink and dinner at a nice restaurant. Rob is out of town for a few days, and I hate eating alone. You can forget about your problem student and I'll explain how the tenure process really works at Reid University."

"Great idea," Abby smiled. "Meet you here around five o'clock. If you drive, I'll have not one, but two martinis."

Chapter Three

"Do you remember three years ago when Rick Stewart applied for tenure?" Jen asked after they were seated and had placed their drink orders.

"Vaguely. Wasn't he rejected that time?" Abby glanced around the crowded restaurant with its spectacular view overlooking the Portland Light.

"Yes. I served on the university committee that year," Jen recalled, "and there was a real battle over Stewart's application. The controversy focused squarely on his consulting activities with the oil and gas industry and his support for a proposed LNG terminal site that would be located only a few miles from campus. That site was rejected, largely because our president spearheaded the opposition."

"Now I remember," Abby said, reaching for a breadstick. "The NIMBY effect—not in my backyard—was behind that rejection."

The women paused while the waiter served their drinks.

"Granted, that was a major reason. And now the same Dutch company has proposed another site north of Bar Harbor, the site you support, Abby. I understand the company wants to build an offshore terminal and pipe the natural gas onto Indian land for distribution throughout New England."

"Right. I support the offshore project because it's in a remote location and addresses many of the security concerns. Besides," she reminded Jen, "Rick Stewart earned tenure last year, so his support for the terminal didn't ruin his application after all."

"True. But he lost two years of salary increases, and he had to resubmit his credentials and go through the entire process a second time."

"You've been on the Tenure and Promotion Committee for the past few years, haven't you?" Abby asked.

"Yes. Although the deliberations are supposed to be strictly confidential, nothing remains secret on this campus. I'll tell you exactly what happened three years ago if you promise to keep this conversation between us. You need to understand the political nature of the tenure and promotion process because you will be facing it yourself in a couple months."

"I'm all ears," said Abby, settling back in her chair.

Jen signaled the waiter for another round of drinks and prepared to take Abby back to three years earlier when Rick Stewart failed in his first attempt to win tenure and promotion at Reid University.

* * *

Spring, 2006. Horizontal sheets of rain swept across Founders Court, washing away the final traces of sand encrusted snow banks bordering the broad sidewalks, exposing vast expanses of dead, brown grass. The depressing landscape was relieved only by towering balsam firs swaying in the fury of a strong nor'easter.

Mitchell Billings, vice-president for academic policy, strolled into the trustees' conference room twenty minutes late. Switching on the ornate chandelier, he waved the six members of the Tenure and Promotion Committee to seats around the massive mahogany conference table. He made a show of cordially greeting each member of the committee, shaking hands with the men, leaning over the women possessively, exuding the false camaraderie for which he was quietly ridiculed behind his back. Committee members pulled folders and papers from briefcases, preparing for the afternoon's business.

He settled his heavy frame into the leather chair at the head of the table.

"I call this meeting of the Tenure and Promotion Committee to order," he began formally. "Let me apologize for being late. Lunch with our chairman of the board of trustees ran longer than expected."

"How exciting," Jen Carpenter whispered behind her hand to Sidney Orenstein, seated beside her. Committee members barely concealed their annoyance with the vice-president's habitual tardiness.

The full professors assembled around the table comprised the core faculty leadership of Reid University, and the Tenure and Promotion Committee was the most powerful faculty committee on campus. Under the tight-fisted leadership of the president and academic vice-president, the administration exercised rigid control over promotion and tenure decisions, setting up an irreconcilable conflict with senior faculty who believed those important decisions should rest solely with the faculty's elected committee representatives.

Billings fingered the stack of papers in front of him, and then looked around the table. "Our principal order of business today is to evaluate the candidates for tenure and promotion to the rank of associate professor. As is customary with this process, although I chair the committee, I will cast a ballot only in the unlikely event that a tie vote occurs with respect to a particular candidate.

"I assume each of you has reviewed the materials submitted by the candidates?" he inquired.

"Great," Jen muttered sarcastically. "Now he wants to know whether we've done our homework."

Sidney smiled. "Relax, it's going to be a long afternoon," he whispered. Jen's impatience with bureaucratic processes was well known; this meeting would test both her patience and her stamina.

"We will begin the proceedings by introducing ourselves," Billings said, continuing established tradition. "Please also identify yourself, your school and department and years of service to the university."

He nodded to his left.

"John Campbell, School of Environmental Sciences. This is my first year on the committee. I'm a professor of marine biology. I joined the faculty ten years ago."

"And I'm Jen Carpenter, School of Business. This is my third year on this committee. I've been a faculty member for nineteen years."

She glanced to her right.

"Sidney Orenstein, Chair of the Chemistry Department in the School of Environmental Sciences. I've also served on this committee for several years. I joined the university fourteen years ago."

He nodded to the woman across the conference table.

"Alice Matthews, Sociology Department, School of Humanities. This is my first year on the committee. I've been a faculty member here for the past nine years."

She turned to the colleague seated next to her. With her left hand she reached under the table and gently squeezed a chunk of Leslie Jarvis' groin. Smiling innocently, she awaited his reaction.

He grinned broadly. "I'm Leslie Jarvis, History Department, School of Humanities. I last served on this committee a decade ago. You might say I'm back from purgatory." The committee's only African-American, he joined in the general laughter greeting his remark.

The vice-president glared and gestured toward the next person.

"I'm Dan Roberts, Department of Chemical Engineering in the School of Environmental Sciences. I'm new to this committee. I joined the faculty eight years ago as a tenured full professor."

"Thank you." Billings glanced at his notes.

"Now I believe we're ready to hear from the president." He lifted the handset on a side table and touched an extension button.

Chapter Four

Roger Smythe, third president of Reid University, entered through a side door from his private office. Seating himself beside his chief academic administrator, he greeted the faculty, each of whom he had personally appointed to the committee.

The most prestigious of the many faculty committees at the university, appointment to the Promotion and Tenure Committee was a coveted assignment, restricted to tenured full professors with exemplary records of service to the university. Although Smythe consulted with his academic deans and vice-president before finalizing his selections, he alone shaped the committee, selecting a cross section from the university's many academic disciplines. He included a mix of outstanding classroom professors and researchers, appointing a few female faculty members and one African-American in order to avoid accusations of discrimination.

When he was elected to lead the university nearly a decade ago, Smythe faced a highly politicized atmosphere, one in which outstanding teaching, research and service to the university were not consistently rewarded. He reduced, but could not completely eliminate, the political influence of prominent alumni and politicians. Through faculty appointments and promotions, he carefully implemented a strategy that reflected his personal vision of excellence. His long-term objective was to lead the university toward national and international prominence in environmental and marine science. He gazed around the table, pleased with his choices.

"Let me thank each of you for agreeing to serve on this important committee. To those who served in the past, welcome back. To our new members, welcome.

"As is customary, I want to personally set out the committee's charge. All of you are familiar with the criteria for tenure and promotion to the various academic ranks from assistant to full professor.

"This afternoon you will evaluate candidates for tenure and promotion to the rank of associate professor."

He leaned forward, hands folded on the table.

"I'm sure you share my conviction that granting lifetime tenure to a faculty member is the single most important decision a university makes. Your recommendations are critical to the university's future and to achieving our mission as the leading marine and environmental sciences university in the country. Your decisions today will directly influence our growth and development for decades to come.

"Together with evaluating each candidate's teaching, research, and service to the university, you also must assess the character and professional promise of each candidate," he reminded the committee. "Our graduates must be prepared for professionally challenging and personally satisfying careers that contribute to society at large."

"Blah, blah, blah," Jen whispered under her breath. Orenstein smiled.

The president paused, sifting through his handwritten notes. He gazed around the table, making eye contact with each committee member.

"I cannot emphasize too strongly the importance of your work during the next few days. Be assured that I will consider your recommendations very carefully as I complete my own evaluations and present my decisions to the board of trustees for their approval.

"Thank you for agreeing to serve on this committee," he concluded. "I leave you in the capable hands of the vice-president." He gathered his notes and left the conference room.

Members settled back in the soft leather chairs, the candidates' curriculum vitae (detailed summaries of their professional accomplishments) and supporting documentation stacked in neat piles in front of them. Over the past several weeks individual members had invested many hours evaluating the applications and preparing written assessments of each candidate's strengths and weaknesses.

Following lengthy discussion, the committee would reach a final decision to recommend or not to recommend each applicant for tenure and promotion to the rank of associate professor. The meeting would proceed, interrupted only by a short break for the sandwiches and drinks provided by campus food services.

Chapter Five

An hour later, the committee turned to the application of Dr. Richard Stewart, a controversial assistant professor in Environmental Sciences. Assistant professors normally sought promotion and tenure during their sixth year of service to the university. Stewart, in an unusual move, had applied for tenure and promotion only three years after joining the faculty.

Faculty seeking early tenure faced a difficult challenge. They were subjected to intense scrutiny because the committee's decision was necessarily based on service over a limited period of time. The Tenure and Promotion committee rarely supported an applicant for early tenure and promotion.

"Let me summarize Dr. Stewart's credentials." Billings opened the thick folder in front of him.

"He has undergraduate degrees in both Environmental Sciences and Chemical Engineering from Cornell University. He then earned his PhD in both disciplines from MIT six years ago, apparently completing the dual program with great distinction. Three years ago several senior MIT faculty strongly recommended him for a position here at the university. He has industrial experience, having spent three years in the oil and gas industry before joining the faculty."

He slowly leafed through the documents in the folder.

"The file also contains a number of current letters strongly endorsing Stewart for promotion," he remarked.

"His student evaluations are extraordinary," he said, glancing at a summary of several years' evaluations. "Apparently, he's a superb classroom teacher. His department chair offers a glowing testimonial to his teaching and communication skills. He seems to have established a fine rapport with just about everyone."

Jen raised an eyebrow and nudged Sidney. Both were familiar with Rick Stewart's relationships with students. He frequented the local bars, hanging out with students, treating them to beers, playing video games and pool into the early morning hours. His reputation as a fun loving, approachable faculty member was enhanced by his exploits as an experienced private pilot. His full beard, youthful appearance and insistence that students address him by his first name encouraged a familiarity that some older faculty quietly criticized.

"I have some reservations about his publications, however. Stewart has published only ten papers in refereed environmental science and engineering journals," Billings frowned.

"He has also published one article in *Scientific American* relating to safety concerns surrounding the transportation and distribution of natural gas."

Billings looked around the table. "We are all aware of the controversy surrounding that issue in Maine," he said drily. "*Scientific American* is a fine publication for the scientifically literate masses; in my view, however, it doesn't qualify as a scholarly journal." He laid the article aside and continued leafing through the stack of papers.

"In addition to his publications, I see that Stewart has presented fifteen papers at international and national environmental and engineering conferences, mostly focused on liquefied natural gas safety issues."

He regarded the committee over the half-glasses perched low on his nose.

"I must say this vita is quite comprehensive. Stewart even cites a television commercial in which he touted the benefits of clean natural gas. You may recall the commercial was in response to the controversy over efforts to construct an LNG terminal not far from this campus. Thanks to the objections of our president and others, that effort failed. Of course, the proponents simply moved farther north to a site near the Canadian border."

Jen and several others around the table smiled at the reference to a year-old controversy.

"Those of you who viewed Stewart's commercial will doubtless recognize the setting," Billings continued. "A commercial video crew filmed that TV spot in the large lecture theater here at the university—without administrative knowledge or permission, I might add.

"What you don't know is that Stewart received a written reprimand as a result of that indiscretion. University policy prohibits the use of its facilities for private advertising of any kind."

He continued plowing through the papers. "Apparently, Professor Stewart didn't believe the reprimand merited inclusion in his documentation. Not surprising," he concluded drily.

"The committee will disregard this reference to his television appearance. Advocating for the natural gas industry in an advertisement is not appropriate scholarly or community service activity within our guidelines for promotion and tenure.

"Overall, I suppose one might conclude that his research shows promise, although the number of refereed publications is clearly less than I would expect from a faculty member seeking early tenure.

"Finally, I note that Stewart lists consulting activities with Randjumpp, Ltd. I believe that company is seeking a suitable location for a large offshore pipeline and terminal here in Maine. He also lists consulting arrangements with several natural gas utilities in the northeast."

He closed the folder.

"I believe that summarizes the essentials of his vita."

Billings looked around the table. "Who would like to begin the discussion?"

Alice Matthews raised her hand. "I've studied this application very carefully. Let me offer my assessment right now—I most definitely oppose Rick Stewart for tenure at this time." She sat back and folded her arms under her ample chest.

"That was certainly brief and to the point," the vice-president smiled. "Would you like to elaborate?"

"This may take a few minutes," she warned.

Billings nodded, looking forward to a lengthy tirade on the evils of the oil and gas industry. Alice's strident opposition to Stewart would put his supporters on the defensive.

"First," she raised an index finger, "this is his only academic appointment and he has just three years of service to the university. A faculty member should be nationally recognized in his field in order to receive tenure. Clearly, Rick Stewart demonstrates neither the experience nor the professional stature to merit tenure.

"Second, his work in the natural gas industry, specifically his present activities on behalf of Randjumpp, the Dutch conglomerate, is not appropriate professional activity for a faculty member. In fact, that justifies denying him tenure," she ran her fingers through her graying blond butch cut.

"Stewart is essentially a shill for the gas industry," she continued. "He's either being quoted in the newspapers or on television practically every week touting the need for an LNG terminal in Maine. And all of you know where I stand on that issue."

Laughter erupted around the conference table.

She forged ahead. "His publications record is marginal. It focuses almost entirely on the natural gas industry, a money-grubbing bunch of crooks out to rip off the people of Maine and around the country.

"Finally, we all know he hangs out with students in the Student Center and in local bars. Given our students' binge drinking habits, his behavior is inappropriate to say the least. I believe faculty members should have limited social interaction with students," she sniffed, nostrils flaring.

"Thank you," Billings said. "Your opinions on the gas industry, and particularly the LNG component, while shared by many of us, are not directly relevant to this discussion.

"Dr. Stewart is an environmental scientist and a chemical engineer. His professional involvement in the industry is not surprising. Further, the president is strongly committed to supporting and growing the university's programs in environmental science. Of course, he and the trustees oppose building an LNG terminal anywhere in Maine."

He turned to Sidney Orenstein. "What is your assessment of this candidate?"

Sidney paused, his fingers aligning the files in front of him. He chose his words carefully.

"I intend to support Rick Stewart," he began. "That is, unless the committee presents convincing arguments to the contrary." He glanced toward Alice Matthews.

"Let me explain," he continued. "First," he said, adopting Alice's approach, "he has superb teaching evaluations from his students and his department chair. My own informal feedback from the student grapevine convinces me that he is a master teacher.

"His file contains very supportive letters from former professors and advisors at MIT and also from prominent executives of major companies. These companies are developing essential domestic gas and oil facilities that will fuel this country's economic development, particularly in light of the war and turmoil in the Middle East. He is a recognized expert in his field and I expect his contributions to continue for many years."

Sidney looked around the table. "I need not remind the committee that academic custom and common practice permit faculty to consult one day per week during the academic year. We are expected to engage in research and consulting during the summer months. Many members of this committee, myself included, actively consult with companies around the country. We are rewarded for that work, professionally and financially.

"Consulting with private companies like Randjumpp is essential for Stewart to remain current in his field. Further, his students benefit from his consulting when he brings industry issues, like the need for more LNG supplies in New England, into the classroom. He has already built a formidable professional reputation.

"I see no reason to penalize a young, obviously talented faculty member for engaging in approved activities which bring prestige to the university. His consulting is a positive factor in my evaluation.

"Alice," he looked across the table to the sociologist, "while I share some of your concerns about the oil and gas industry, our personal views are irrelevant in assessing Rick's suitability for tenure.

"Now about your final comment. His association with students is a private matter. We all recognize that relationships between faculty and students have changed in the past decade. Informality in the classroom and social interaction with students is the norm. And I assume you and your colleagues in sociology also meet with students outside the classroom."

Alice frowned but did not interrupt.

"It's no secret that my wife and I often entertain students in our home," he continued. "Given the appalling quality of food services on campus, my students appreciate a good home-cooked meal occasionally. Life in the university's residence halls can be depressing.

"Let's be fair, if he spends time with his students, whether on campus or in a local bar, Stewart's interaction with his students is commendable—part of their collegiate experience. After all, he's only about ten years older than many of them.

"He has a wife and two small children. I doubt very much that he spends all of his leisure time in local bars. In fact, I've often seen him in the gym playing pickup basketball games with other faculty and students."

"What is your recommendation, Sidney?" Billings tried to move the proceedings along.

"I support Rick Stewart for tenure and promotion to associate professor. He has met or exceeded the academic criteria for tenure. I consider him a valuable addition to our faculty," he concluded.

There was a moment of silence around the conference table; finally, Leslie Jarvis raised his hand.

"I'll be brief. I cannot support Stewart for tenure and promotion at this time because his application is premature. Indeed, I consider his audacity insulting. He isn't ready for a lifetime academic appointment here or elsewhere for that matter. He has only a few years' experience in industry and is just completing his third year as an assistant professor. Moreover, his research record lacks depth and substance.

"As for his student evaluations, I hope the committee will disregard them—we all know he's an easy grader.

"It is apparently necessary to mention another aspect of his relationships with students, given his support by some members of this committee," he said, looking across the table at Sidney.

"Several of us have become aware that Rick has had personal relationships with at least two female students."

"Stop right there, Leslie," Sidney interrupted. "This is a tenure evaluation, not an inquisition into a faculty member's personal life. You are making a very serious allegation. And this is not an appropriate forum for such a discussion."

He turned to Billings for support. "Unfounded allegations such as this have no place in these deliberations," he said heatedly. "If we seriously consider rumors involving personal behavior, we could face legal action in the future if our discussion becomes public knowledge."

"I agree with Sidney. Let's focus on our academic assessment," the vice-president ordered, sidestepping an ethical and political controversy.

"I can't believe Leslie made that comment," Jen whispered to Sidney. "He has openly flaunted his own sexual relationship with Alice while maintaining a home with his male lover. What a hypocrite."

"Does anyone else wish to speak on Rick Stewart's candidacy?"

Jen raised her hand. "I'd like to offer a few comments."

"Of course."

"I hardly need to emphasize the quality of his academic credentials, nor the high level of his consulting activities. Business school professors, along with engineering and science faculty are encouraged—indeed expected—to consult while engaging in scholarly research.

"Granted," she continued, "he is well paid for his work with the gas industry. Incidentally, I understand he's been influential in bringing generous contributions to the university from several oil and gas companies.

"Finally, in some respects it's still an 'old boy' network out there, particularly in old line utilities. I'm personally aware of Rick's success in placing some of our top female engineering graduates in the largest utility companies along the East Coast. He has opened doors for our graduates that were closed in the past."

She paused, reviewing her notes, and then glanced around the table at her colleagues. "I'm also concerned that some committee members may have allowed their personal biases to cloud their professional judgments. We owe Rick Stewart and every other candidate an objective, unbiased evaluation."

Leslie Jarvis's fingers drummed impatiently on the conference table. Jen glared across the table and paused.

"Finally," she resumed, "he has assembled an extraordinary research record. According to his vita, he has personally brought more than $3 million in research funds to the university during the past three years. Federal agency reviews of his research are superb. Clearly, he is one of the top researchers on this faculty. He should be commended for his success."

She folded her hands and looked around the table. "Let me summarize my assessment." She raised her hand and began to count. "His students, science and engineering colleagues, and former professors at MIT enthusiastically support him. His research record is nationally and internationally recognized. He consults in his field and helps our students land jobs in the oil and gas industry. He's been active on numerous department and university committees." She turned to Billings. "I believe he has earned tenure and promotion to the rank of associate professor. The committee should support him unanimously."

In the silence that followed, the vice-president sensed it was time to call for a vote.

"Is the committee ready to vote?"

Hearing no objection, he distributed three-inch squares of paper and directed each committee member to record a simple yes or no vote. Members voted, folded their ballots and passed them forward to Billings, who tallied them.

"I count three yes votes and three no votes," he reported, stacking the scraps of paper in a neat pile. "In the event of a tie, I am required to cast the deciding vote.

"I vote no," he announced without hesitation, gathering up the scraps of paper. "I will report to the president this committee's decision not to recommend Richard Stewart for tenure and promotion to associate professor."

"Will you also report that the vote was a tie, and that you cast the deciding vote, as required by our committee rules?" Sidney asked quietly.

"Indeed, I shall do precisely that," Billings responded, glancing at his watch. "It's 6:30. Let's break for dinner. We'll reconvene promptly at 7:30."

* * *

"I think he expected that tie vote," Sidney remarked to Jen and Dan Roberts as they left the trustees' room. "He didn't waste any time casting his negative vote."

"He cut off discussion and I didn't get a chance to speak," grumbled Dan, the only engineering professor on the committee. "Obviously, I would support Rick. At least he could have invited me to speak. Now, word will get around that I didn't support one of my colleagues."

Dan turned to Jen. "Should I advise Rick to appeal this vote to the president directly?"

"No," she said decisively. "Roger Smythe won't promote him now. Billings delivered that message with his tie-breaking negative vote.

"I'm confident Rick will earn tenure in another year or two. He needs to be patient."

* * *

Jen and Abby were among the few remaining diners in the restaurant when Jen finished recounting the details of Rick Stewart's failed attempt to win tenure three years earlier. Their waiter had cleared their dishes and brought coffee more than an hour ago.

Dinners finished and the restaurant about to close, the women split the bill and left, strolling along the waterfront to Jen's car.

"That's quite a story, Jen. I had no idea that tenure and promotion decisions were so political," Abby confessed.

"It's all about politics," Jen said emphatically.

"Rick Stewart's case is only one example. Granted, he finally earned tenure and promotion last year, but only because the faculty who opposed him earlier were not reappointed to the committee. Through his appointments, the president completely controls promotion recommendations.

"This is an example of Roger Smythe's manipulation of the faculty through committee appointments. Remember, the faculty can only recommend; the president's decisions on promotions are the only ones that matter. The board of trustees always rubber stamps his recommendations.

"Please keep our discussion confidential," Jen went on. "I'm hoping to be appointed to the Tenure and Promotion committee this year. I intend to be your advocate on the committee."

"I really appreciate your support," Abby said. "This conversation never happened. My lips are sealed."

Jen unlocked the car and slid into the driver's seat. Before turning the key in the ignition, she regarded her younger colleague. "Now, will you please promise not to openly campaign for the LNG project until your tenure and promotion decision is approved by the president?"

Abby threw up her hands. "All right, I get the message. I'll be quiet, but only until I get tenure."

Jen smiled to herself as they reached the interstate and headed home. Abby could be headstrong at times, and the stakes were high. Her career at Reid depended on earning tenure during the next few months.

Chapter Six

One morning in early March Jen Carpenter strolled down the hall to Abby's office.

"The personnel committee of the School of Business met this morning to evaluate your application for tenure and promotion," she reported.

"Don't keep me in suspense. Did they recommend me or not?"

"Congratulations, Abby. Of course, your colleagues unanimously recommended you," she smiled warmly. "Remember," she cautioned, "this is just the first hurdle on the way to final approval by the board of trustees. Your application is very strong; approval was a no-brainer. The committee needed only an hour to reach a decision. The official memo will be in your mailbox this afternoon."

Abby rose and hugged her colleague. "What a relief! Thanks for not keeping me in suspense."

Jen laughed. "This is one time I enjoyed chairing a committee."

"Now, what happens next?"

"As chair, I'll forward the committee's recommendation to the dean. I'm confident he will enthusiastically support your application. Next month your application, along with the endorsements of the committee and the dean will be forwarded to the university Tenure and Promotion Committee.

"Incidentally, the president just appointed me to serve on that committee. I'm equally confident you'll be approved at the university level. Then the entire package goes to the president."

"The process seems to take forever," Abby said.

"Almost," Jen agreed. "Remember, the president's decision is the only one that really counts. He is the reason I asked you to tone down your support for an LNG terminal."

"I still think supporting the terminal shouldn't influence my tenure decision. The terminal makes perfect economic sense," Abby said stubbornly.

"The merits of the project are irrelevant," Jen said, exasperated. "Please don't challenge the president on his pet issue.

"Realize that to the outside world our president is a warm, distinguished academic leader. Within the university, we know better. He's a dictator who makes the final decision on every tenure and promotion application. Faculty recommendations and even the dean's support are essentially meaningless. Your future is in his hands."

"So much for faculty influence in tenure decisions," Abby said wryly.

"That's the reality of the situation. Deal with it, if you want to survive and prosper here.

"To be fair, the president has some very good arguments for opposing an LNG terminal anywhere in Maine," Jen said, returning to Abby's favorite issue.

"Granted, his focus is on environmental issues," Abby said, "but his reasons are parochial—he's ignoring the larger economic implications."

"I don't disagree. Nonetheless, his environmental and security concerns are real, and many people agree with him. You've aligned yourself on the opposite side of a hot button issue that's polarizing people all over New England. And Roger doesn't look favorably on people who challenge him.

"I hear you've been discussing the issue with students in your classes," Jen continued, touching on a sensitive subject.

"What's wrong with discussing a major business issue in my classes?" Abby asked defensively. "A terminal is potentially a $900 million project that will bring jobs and tax revenues and all sorts of economic benefits to the region. Besides, what I discuss in my classes is a matter of academic freedom. I can discuss whatever I want."

"I'm not suggesting you avoid the issue. Just soften your image on the matter," Jen said. "After you've earned tenure, you can speak out on all sorts of controversial issues without risking your career."

"You still haven't told me where you stand on the proposed terminal," Abby challenged her.

"I haven't made up my mind. Granted, the economic benefits are obvious. However, I can't simply dismiss the legitimate security concerns. The terminal would be an obvious terrorist target. In an accident, it would become an environmental disaster impacting our fishing interests and tourism, industries that are essential to Maine's prosperity. There are sound arguments on both sides, Abby.

"You're a business professor, not an environmental scientist," she reminded her. "Aside from you and Rick Stewart, the faculty are lining up solidly behind the president in opposing the proposal. You're way out on a limb."

Abby tossed her head defiantly. "I promised you at dinner the other night that I'd tone down my public activities. Believe me, after I get tenure, I'll be speaking out and working hard supporting the project."

"For now, please be restrained when you discuss the project, especially in your classes," Jen pleaded. "Lay out the arguments on both sides. After all, the university has special academic expertise in marine studies and environmental sciences. Surely you understand the need for caution, especially now that you know why Rick Stewart was rejected for tenure a few years ago."

"But he earned tenure last year and I'm a lot less outspoken on the issue than he."

Jen shook her head, frustrated. "Rick obviously supports the project—he earns substantial consulting fees from the gas industry. That's how he maintains his lifestyle. And it's a very flashy lifestyle, especially in the past few years.

"Why give the president a reason to deny you tenure because you're not a team player? Like it or not, your support for the terminal project will factor into his decision. Be patient. Play the political game for a few more months until tenure decisions are announced."

Jen glanced at her watch. "I've got a one o'clock class and I need to pick up my notes," she said, turning to leave Abby's office.

"Rob and I have invited a few faculty and spouses for dinner tomorrow night. The LNG project doubtless will be discussed and you can judge for yourself how senior faculty feel about it. Please join us," she invited, "and bring along a friend if you want."

"Thanks. I'll bring a couple bottles of wine and come alone."

Chapter Seven

Shortly after midnight, debate on the proposed offshore LNG terminal reached fever pitch in Jen and Rob Carpenter's living room.

"Granted, New England desperately needs more natural gas supplies and a terminal several miles offshore north of Bar Harbor seems like a viable and relatively secure option. The project would provide jobs for people who lost their paychecks when the shipyard closed," Rob concluded.

"Exactly. I couldn't have said it better myself." Knees tucked under her chin, her empty wineglass on the coffee table nearby, Abby reclined on the Oriental rug, pleased that at least one person was persuaded tonight.

"The uproar on environmental and security grounds is nothing more than the NIMBY effect. Environmentalists and property owners managed to kill several terminal proposals, just like they're fighting hard to stop the windmill farms proposed off Cape Cod. The same environmentalists will oppose every site wherever it's proposed," she declared.

Hoarse from the evening's verbal battles, she would not give up. "The environmentalists say they understand the need for increased energy sources, but they only talk the talk. They never get around to walking the walk.

"The economy will stagnate if more energy is not delivered to New England. Our high tech businesses continue to migrate to less expensive places like Texas and the South, not to mention outsourcing our manufacturing base and service jobs to India and China."

"Wrong," Alice Matthews spoke up. "Everyone recognizes the need for additional energy resources, but we need solutions that don't endanger the environment, the fishing industry and Maine tourism. And of course an LNG terminal will be a prime terrorism target. Don't forget, this proposal introduces complex technology on an offshore platform and transfers natural gas for miles under the ocean."

"You're a sociology professor. What do you know about complex engineering issues?"

"You've got no more expertise on technical issues than I," Alice retorted hotly, not about to be challenged by a junior faculty member. "It doesn't take a techie to worry about committing to untested technology in an area that experiences severe weather at least six months of the year. We need the energy supplies during the winter months, precisely when the seas and weather patterns are at their worst.

"Let Louisiana and Texas take gas from the Gulf, refine it and pipe it north. They've been doing it for years," she concluded.

"You are absolutely wrong," Abby responded angrily. "Don't say the technology can't be done safely in the Atlantic, it's in place right now in the Gulf of Mexico, which is subject to violent hurricanes. Have you forgotten Katrina? Our storms just occur at different times of the year. The risk is the same."

"I'd expect you to oppose this project, Alice, just like you fought the wind farm off Cape Cod. Anything that helps the region grow economically will always be opposed by knee-jerk liberals and pseudo-environmentalists," Abby said grimly. "Mark my words, an LNG project for northern New England ultimately will be approved. Get used to the idea and deal with it."

She stopped, glanced around the room at senior faculty who were openly delighted with the confrontation. She had gone too far.

"It's definitely time for me to go," she said abruptly, gathering her empty wine glass and heading for the kitchen.

"Thanks Jen and Rob, for great food and stimulating conversation." Jen accompanied her friend to the front door. "Obviously, this is a hot button issue. You probably didn't change many opinions tonight. I suspect we'll be arguing about the terminal a year from now."

"Sorry about confronting Alice. I didn't mean to wreck your party," Abby apologized.

Jen laughed. "On the contrary, you were the life of the party. You made your points and held your own against the veterans. Faculty love debating hot issues."

She handed Abby her raincoat, opened the door and watched her dash through a cold February downpour to her car.

Chapter Eight

"My problem student's behavior is becoming more disruptive by the day," Abby reported over a brown bag lunch in Jen's office. "My little talk with him a couple weeks ago apparently made no impression.

"Even the class is fed up with Lombardo and I don't blame them," she continued. "This morning the student sitting next to him asked to move to another seat."

"Really? You haven't said much about him recently. I assumed the problem was under control." Jen raised an eyebrow. "How did you handle the situation?"

"Of course, I said that was fine. Lombardo now is surrounded by empty seats. And last week several students came to my office complaining about his disruptive behavior. They blame me for not controlling him. Frankly, I don't know what to do."

Jen had listened sympathetically to the litany of escalating behavior problems in Abby's class since the semester began in January.

"You can't let this problem continue," she said finally. "And the stress you're experiencing may be affecting your other classes. Worse, the problem could influence your tenure application. If students complain to the dean that your class is out of control, it could affect his recommendation."

"God, I hope students don't go directly to the dean," Abby frowned.

"It wouldn't be the first time," Jen said. "How is Lombardo doing academically?"

"Terrible. He flunked my second midterm exam last Wednesday. His average on the two exams is less than fifty percent. He needs sixty percent to pass the course and I doubt that he can pass with only the final examination and a major research paper remaining."

"You really need to discuss this problem with the dean," Jen said decisively. "Would you like me to come with you? I can back up your side of the story."

"I don't want to discuss this with Cory Howard," Abby said flatly. "If he decides I can't control my class, it could put the kiss of death on a positive tenure recommendation from him."

"That is a risk," Jen conceded.

"What about Lombardo's behavior in his other classes? What is his schedule?"

"Let's take a look."

Jen opened her laptop and with a few keystrokes pulled up Lombardo's schedule. Staring at the screen, she said, "Apparently, your student is enrolled in a course in International Finance with Conor Kelley, plus a survey course with Rick Stewart in Environmental Sciences and an American Lit course with Jack Andrews in Humanities.

"Conor has a reputation as a challenging professor, Abby. Let's see whether your problem student has been disruptive in his class."

"Okay, but I want to keep all inquiries within the business school. I'd rather not admit to Jack Andrews or Rick Stewart that I'm having a problem with a student," Abby said.

*　*　*

Conor Kelley, senior professor of finance, greeted the two women cordially, puzzled by their unexpected visit.

"Conor, I believe one of my students also has a class with you. His name is John Lombardo," Abby began. "Can you tell me how he's doing in your class?"

"Sure, let me check." He turned to his computer and accessed his class rosters.

He scrolled down the roster. "He's enrolled in my afternoon International Finance class," he said. "As I recall, he's not very talkative, doesn't contribute much to class discussion. Finance apparently isn't his favorite subject."

"Would you mind telling me his grades?"

"No problem." He accessed a screen listing his students' current grades and moved the cursor down the screen. "It looks like he would squeak by with a D if I had to assign a grade now. Of course, we have a final examination next month along with a major financial analysis project that's due at the end of the course. Students work in teams to analyze the financial situation of an international company. That project is worth thirty percent of the final grade."

Kelley leaned back in his chair. "I recall recently that a couple of students on Lombardo's team—female students—complained about him.

They said he avoids meetings and is refusing to contribute to the project. However, despite conflicts with his team, he can pass the course if the project grade is high enough.

"Tell me, Abby, why are you interested in this student?" he asked quizzically.

"Lombardo exhibits very different behavior in my Organization Behavior class," she responded reluctantly. "He tries to dominate the discussion, interrupts me during lectures to argue issues he knows nothing about and is generally disruptive. Even the students are fed up with him.

"His disruptions are ruining the class for the other students and for me," she admitted finally.

"Interesting," Conor said. "He displays quite the opposite behavior in my class. Why don't you throw him out? If his behavior is that bad, you have an obligation to the other students to get the class back on track," he advised.

"I've been teaching here for six years and earlier at two other schools while I was finishing my doctorate. I've never removed a student because of a behavior problem. I hate to kick him out now. The dean is considering my application for tenure and promotion."

"I see," Conor nodded sympathetically.

He turned to Jen. "What are you recommending?"

"Initially, I thought Abby should speak to the dean about this student's behavior. Now I'm not sure. Your experience with him is completely different. Maybe he has problems dealing with women in authority positions, especially one who challenges his behavior," she speculated.

Conor shrugged, noncommittal.

"By the way, Lombardo's father is our current chairman of the board of trustees," Jen revealed after a pause.

"Really? That does present a delicate issue," Conor nodded.

"And his past academic record is suspect. He attended several colleges before finally earning an Associate Degree at a community college in New Jersey. He's a twenty-five year old undergraduate with a very different academic profile than most of our students," Abby said.

"That's certainly true," Kelley said. "Frankly, my assessment of this young man is that he's a little 'bent'—a bit weird. And perhaps he has issues with women, although I wouldn't go that far, based on my own experience with him."

"What do you recommend?" Abby asked.

He was silent for a few moments, thinking. "I think you should approach the dean and lay out your concerns," he said finally. "Cory Howard is fair; he'll listen. Ask him to administratively remove Lombardo from your class. Explain that his behavior is damaging the course for the rest of your students."

"I appreciate your advice. I need to think about this some more."

Walking back to Abby's office, Jen said finally, "Conor is right. You need to talk to the dean. This problem has gone on long enough."

"I'd rather not," Abby shook her head. "I should be able to deal with this on my own."

"Let me go with you and back up your concerns," Jen suggested.

"All right," she agreed finally. "I'll call for an appointment tomorrow."

Chapter Nine

They waited patiently in the dean's outer office. "Thanks for joining me," Abby said quietly.

"Don't thank me yet. We haven't accomplished our objective. By the way, did you decide to speak to Rick Stewart about his experience with Lombardo?"

"Yes. I finally stopped by his office yesterday afternoon. We had an interesting conversation. His Environmental Issues course has more than 200 students enrolled. Despite the large class size, Rick seems to know Lombardo rather well. Apparently, he actively participates in the class and often stops by his office.

"I asked Rick to check his grade," Abby continued. "He seemed genuinely surprised that Lombardo currently has a D in the course. I guess he doesn't pay much attention to his students' grades. He insisted there's no danger he will fail the course, despite the low grade."

"Given Rick's reputation as an easy grader, I'm not surprised," Jen laughed.

"My impression from our conversation is that Rick and Lombardo are buddies. I know Rick is friendly with students, but this seemed more than a casual faculty-student relationship. He mentioned spending time in the Athletic Center working out, playing hoops. And of course, I've noticed Rick hanging out with students in the Student Center."

"My husband hangars his plane at the Seal Point Airport," Jen revealed. "Last week Rob mentioned that Rick recently bought a twin-engine Cessna, a huge step up from the small plane he flew ever since he came to the university. His consulting business must be very successful these days."

* * *

Cory Howard personally opened his office door and ushered them into his private office. Jen and Abby seated themselves in leather chairs facing the dean across his massive mahogany desk, which was piled high with papers.

"Abby, I understand you have a problem you want to discuss with me. How can I help?" the dean asked.

Surprised at the tension she felt, Abby began. "A student in my Organization Behavior class is giving me problems. After dealing with him for almost two months, I'm requesting his administrative removal. It's the only solution to a problem that is ruining the class for the other students."

"Really, Abby." Howard leaned back, surprised. "This is the first time in years that a faculty member has asked me to administratively remove a student from a class. Most unusual. Tell me more," he directed, concerned.

Hands clasped in her lap, Abby prepared to offer her most persuasive arguments. "His name is John Lombardo. He enrolled in my class more than a week late back in January. You signed a form allowing him to register after the normal period for adding a class."

"Yes, now I remember that young man," Howard said. "Are you aware that he is the son of our chairman of the board of trustees?"

"Yes. He made sure everyone in the class also knew the connection," she said dryly.

"Can you describe the problem more specifically?" the dean asked.

Abby took a deep breath. "He objects to taking my course in Organization Behavior class because he completed the same course in a community college."

Howard regarded the two women, puzzled. "Our academic standards require Organization Behavior to be taken here. Students can't transfer it from a community college. Have you explained that to him?"

"Yes, more than once."

The dean shrugged. "Obviously, he needs to take the course. I assume he'll earn an easy A."

"Not exactly. He flunked the two mid-term examinations, and very likely will fail the course. Frankly, he knows little or nothing about the behavior of complex enterprises.

"My problem is with his disruptive behavior in class. He constantly interrupts my lectures, speaks out of turn, and ignores my efforts to control him. The other students are increasingly angry with him and expect me to control his behavior."

The dean frowned. "I must say, this is not the typical behavior of our students. How have you dealt with the distractions?"

"Initially, I listened patiently. Then I tried cutting him off when he rambled on, often without making much sense. I'd call on another student, ask for comments and try to continue the discussion.

"Recently, his disruptive behavior has escalated; he is aggressively interrupting other students who try to speak. Unfortunately, his behavior has become progressively worse in the past two weeks.

"I checked his academic records; there is nothing to indicate that he has an attention deficit disorder or ADHD problems. Frankly, I don't know how to control him. In many respects, he behaves like an out-of-control grade school child," she confessed.

"Lombardo is destroying the atmosphere in my class. I want him out of there," she concluded firmly.

"This is most unusual," the dean said noncommittally. "I'll need to discuss the situation with his other instructors, see whether this is part of a pattern or merely isolated behavior in your class.

"I sympathize with your frustration," he said after a pause, "but I cannot arbitrarily remove a student without more substantive reasons than you have offered. And I need to consider how to deal with his father."

Jen, who had listened silently during the exchange, joined the discussion.

"Cory, I'm not a psychologist. However, I've taught long enough to recognize that this student is a serious problem. He has poisoned the environment in Abby's class. Teaching and learning have become impossible.

"For whatever reasons, he has a major problem with Abby. Perhaps he can't deal with female authority figures. Maybe he has some sort of psychological problem.

"I reviewed his prior academic record with Abby. This student is twenty-five years old, has compiled a mediocre academic record at three other schools, and only recently earned an Associate's Degree from a community college in New Jersey."

"Let me take a look at his record myself." The dean turned to his computer and with a few key strokes opened Lombardo's record. He stared at the computer screen. "Granted, he is a good bit older than our average undergraduate." He tapped a few keys and brought up another screen. "His SAT scores are marginal." The dean shook his head. "It's possible the university admissions office was influenced by his father's position. He's probably a legacy admission," he said finally.

"I thought legacy admissions were discontinued years ago," Jen said.

"What is a legacy admission?" Abby asked, unaware of the term.

"In the past some highly selective schools like Reid University and the Ivy League schools admitted a few students whose parent or grandparent was an alumnus of the school. These alumni may have been generous donors or have contributed in some way to the prominence of the school. Legacy admissions, as they were called, often don't meet the strict admission requirements of the university. In recent years, the practice has decreased, although it hasn't completely disappeared."

With a final glance at his computer screen, he turned to Abby and Jen. "Your problem student clearly would not qualify for admission under our normal standards.

"He did manage to earn a community college degree," he pointed out. "However, fewer than five percent of our students are community college graduates. And those transfer students must meet the same high academic standards as our typical undergraduates."

He rose, signaling the end of the interview. "I'll do some additional checking on Lombardo's background and get back to you, probably in a week or two. Meantime, Abby, you'll just have to be more forceful in how you deal with his disruptive behavior."

"You won't remove him now? I have to wait another week or two?" Abby asked, dismayed.

"Please be patient," the dean said firmly. "I need to investigate your complaint further."

*   *   *

"Take it easy," Jen advised as they headed back to their offices. "Cory will do his own investigation. And his sources are better than ours. He'll find out whether the admissions staff was influenced by his father and he'll probably check with other professors about his behavior. I bet he'll even phone administrators at the other schools Lombardo attended.

"This will be over in a couple more weeks. Like every academic dean I've ever known, Cory survives because he's a politician. And if your problem student is the son of our chairman of the board of trustees, you can bet he will do a very thorough investigation."

"I can't put up with that student in my class one more day," Abby retorted.

"You don't have a choice. Deal with it."

Chapter Ten

"Good morning, professor. I'm Pete Byrnes, detective in our campus security office." The casually dressed man handed her a photo ID in a leather case.

Abby invited him into her office, closed the door and motioned him to a chair.

Tall and slim with curly brown hair and startling blue eyes, Pete Byrnes could easily pass as a graduate student or junior faculty member. In his late thirties, he mingled with the student population, unobtrusively monitoring the drug scene that thrived on the fringes of the campus.

"Chief Edwards has assigned me to investigate your concerns about a student in one of your classes, a Mr. John Lombardo." Byrnes reached into his briefcase and retrieved a thin folder.

"I don't understand. Why is campus security involved in an academic matter? I've already discussed my problem with Cory Howard, dean of the business school."

Byrnes smiled, searched through the folder and retrieved a sheet of paper. "I have a memorandum signed by president Smythe requesting an investigation of this student's activities since he arrived on campus in late January."

"Really?" Abby frowned.

"Two weeks ago you complained to your dean about this student's disruptive behavior in your class. Is that correct?" Byrnes gazed at her across the desk.

"Yes, that's true. In fact, his behavior has become even more disruptive since that meeting."

"I'm here to get more detailed information about your concerns," Byrnes continued. His tone was cool and businesslike, and Abby wondered how much he knew about her interview with the dean. She was dismayed that president Smythe was now aware of her problem.

Byrnes took out a note pad, glanced at his watch and began to write. "I'd like to ask you a few preliminary questions for the record."

"Go ahead."

"How long have you been a faculty member here at the university?" he smiled, trying to put Abby at ease.

"I'm completing my sixth year."

"Have you ever encountered a problem with student behavior in the past? Here or at other schools?"

"Never," she said sharply. "I have more than ten years' teaching experience here and elsewhere. This problem is a first."

"How do your students evaluate you?"

"That's easy," she laughed, beginning to relax. "Go online to Ratemyprof.com and check me out. You'll find that students consider me a demanding but approachable professor. On our own student evaluations, I rank as one of the best professors in the business school," she said, a touch of pride in her voice.

"I combine lectures and case studies in my classes, which encourages a lot of back and forth discussion with the students," she explained. "I've never had a problem controlling my students. Until now, that is."

Byrnes continued writing, and then made eye contact with Abby. "When did the problem with Mr. Lombardo first arise?"

"From the moment he walked into my class. He registered more than a week after the semester had begun. The first day he came to class he was fifteen minutes late, interrupted my lecture, and tried to dominate the discussion almost before he found a seat."

"Specifically, what types of behavior do you find disturbing?" he asked.

Abby sighed. "In the beginning he kept interrupting me, blurting out comments, asking questions without raising his hand. I was patient with him, since he'd joined the class late and had a lot of catching up to do.

"I tolerated his interruptions for a week or so, expecting him to settle down. He's chronically late—often walking into the room ten or fifteen minutes after I've begun my lecture. He brings the class to a complete halt, deliberately drawing attention to himself while he settles himself and takes out a notebook. His behavior has become progressively more disruptive.

"He delights in challenging me on the most minor points in my lectures; when we do a case study, he'll try to engage me in one-on-one discussions, excluding other students who also want to participate. The other students are increasingly annoyed by his aggressive behavior and superior attitude."

Byrnes continued to take notes, a hint of a smile on his face.

"This behavior may seem trivial to you," Abby said defensively. "You really need to be in the room to understand how disturbing it is, both to me and to the other students."

The detective eyed her. "I can sympathize, having taken some evening courses recently. I understand how aggravating the behavior you describe might be," he said, quietly supportive.

"You said he is aggressive," Byrnes continued. "What do you mean?"

"He has an attitude, and he's big—at least as tall as you—and he probably weighs over 200 pounds."

Byrnes consulted his notes and nodded. "That's an accurate description. I've noticed him around campus. He hangs out in the weight room at the Athletic Center. He may seem rather intimidating to you."

"I've had football and basketball players in my classes who are a lot more physically intimidating than Lombardo," she retorted, "and I've never had a problem before.

"This student is different," she went on more calmly. "It's difficult for me to articulate why I'm uneasy. Perhaps it's his slightly menacing manner combined with an absolute compulsion to dominate the class."

Byrnes continued taking notes without comment.

"I've asked the dean to remove him. He still hasn't responded to my request. And now president Smythe apparently is aware of my problem. Meantime, this guy continues to disrupt my class." She threw up her hands, disgusted.

"Obviously, the administration wants to respond to your concerns. I'm sorry it's taking so long," Byrnes said. He silently leafed through the documents in the folder on his lap.

He looked up. "Tell me, professor, do you feel physically threatened by Mr. Lombardo?"

Abby leaned back in her chair, surprised at the unexpected question. Finally, she shook her head. "I guess not."

"You don't sound especially positive about that. Let's discuss it a little more."

"Frankly, Lombardo is a bit of a wise guy, if you know what I mean," Abby confessed.

"Go on," Byrnes urged, his head down, writing rapidly.

"Actually, one day he made a strange remark in my office. Something about wanting to get me. I assume his aim is to embarrass me in front of the class, to catch me in some perceived error in my lectures."

"What did he say? Do you recall his exact words?" Byrnes asked.

"As best I can remember, he said 'my new goal in life is to get you.' I think those were his precise words."

"And you interpreted his comment to mean he wanted to embarrass you in some way?" Byrnes repeated, eyeing her closely.

"Yes. I asked him what he meant by that remark."

"How did he respond?"

"I don't recall exactly, except that he was angry. Then he left the office and slammed the door. Why do you ask?"

"No particular reason. It's just that your description of his behavior is rather imprecise, except for that last remark."

"Do you know something about this student you're not telling me?" Abby asked suspiciously.

"I'm not at liberty to discuss other aspects of this case because they don't involve you directly. I am, however, conducting a preliminary investigation of your student's behavior, including his activities at several other universities."

Abby leaned forward. "Please help me get this student out of my class," she pleaded.

"This isn't just about me. It's also about my students, who are furious with him. The class is an ordeal for the students, too. A few have actually asked me to throw him out of class. Unfortunately, I can't. The administration has to authorize that action. And the dean is taking his good old time responding to my complaint," she said bitterly.

"I understand your frustration, professor. Unfortunately, my investigation may take a week or two longer. Then it will be reviewed by my boss, Craig Edwards, before it's submitted to the president. That may take another week or so."

"By that time, the semester will be more than half over," Abby protested. "In the meantime, my students are becoming angrier, and I'm losing control of my class. This is ridiculous."

"Please be patient," Byrnes said calmly. "I'm working full time on this investigation, following several different lines of inquiry in addition to your concerns."

"I suspect the dean doesn't want to remove Lombardo because his father is chairman of the university's board of trustees," Abby confided angrily.

Byrnes smiled. "You may be right, but I still must ask you to be patient."

He shoved the folder into his briefcase and stood, extending his hand to Abby. "Thank you for your time. This discussion has been very helpful."

Abby walked him to her office door. "Will you get back to me after you submit your report to chief Edwards?"

"Yes. I'll tell you as much as I can about the larger investigation."

"Thank you, detective Byrnes."

"Please call me Pete."

Abby smiled. "And you may as well call me Abby. I suspect we'll be seeing more of each other in the days ahead."

Chapter Eleven

Abby wandered down the hall to Jen Carpenter's office one afternoon in late March.

"Any word from Cory Howard on your rogue student?"

"No," Abby shook her head. "That class will be the death of me yet," she sighed. "I dread walking into the classroom. No matter what I try, I can't shut Lombardo up," she fumed. "On more than one occasion, I've flat out told him to be quiet and let other students contribute their ideas. Then he sulks and fidgets in his chair like a third grader with attention deficit disorder. That class is becoming the class from hell."

"How are your other classes going?" Jen asked.

"They're fine, a relief in fact."

"Abby, you know the faculty supports your efforts to remove him. We all believe it's taking the administration much too long to take action."

"I appreciate the faculty support, but they don't have to deal with him. I keep hoping I'll wake up and realize this was just a bad dream."

"Have you heard from that campus security officer who interviewed you a few weeks ago? Has he finished his investigation?"

"Yes. Actually, Pete Byrnes phoned me yesterday to say he has turned in his report to his boss. Unfortunately, the chief still has to review it before it goes to the president. The administrative wheels grind slowly at this university."

"Pete has begun dropping by my office a couple of times a week to see how I'm holding up," Abby revealed with a smile. "It's like he's keeping watch over me. We're practically buddies now."

"So, you're on a first name basis. Do I detect some extracurricular interest in this fellow?" Jen teased.

Abby shrugged. "He is attractive, I must admit. But with my tenure decision coming up next month, the dean probably wouldn't be impressed if I start dating a campus cop. I'm already on Cory's radar screen because of Lombardo."

"There's no law against associating with staff members, although faculty are strongly discouraged from dating students."

"I could name at least one faculty member on this campus who violates that rule," Abby remarked. "I'm surprised you haven't seen Rick Stewart hanging around with Judy Perkins. She's in my class with Lombardo. I understand she works part time at the First Portland branch office near campus. She and Rick are quite openly carrying on an affair."

"I really don't want to know," Jen said, irritated. "I know Rick's wife, Sue, and their two kids. If he's carrying on an affair, it's disappointing."

"You know about Rick's work with Randjumpp," Abby continued, sipping her afternoon tea.

"Let's talk about the terminal project," Jen said, changing the subject. "Apparently, Rick's public relations campaign is paying off. Public opposition is beginning to fade.

"I've done my own research on the proposal, by the way. The offshore approach looks like a safer option than building an onshore terminal. At least the terminal will be several miles offshore and those huge LNG tankers won't be unloading directly in a Maine harbor.

"Obviously, the region needs more energy supplies," she continued. "Of course, the fishing industry is screaming that developing a terminal three miles out in the Atlantic will limit their access to major fishing grounds. And the security and environmental issues are a continuing concern.

"Although a lot of hurdles remain, you have finally convinced me that the project probably should be approved, not that my opinion really matters," Jen concluded.

"Great. Another supporter for the terminal," Abby smiled. "Even president Smythe appears to be backing off his public criticism, although the university still officially opposes the project."

Chapter Twelve

Spring, 2008. Five hundred feet above the village of Seal Point, Rick Stewart banked his Cessna 170 and lined up on final approach to the airport. Balancing a half eaten ham and cheese sandwich on his lap, he nudged the throttle back and reduced the airspeed. He gently eased the stick forward, scanned the instrument panel, set the flaps and relaxed. The single-engine craft touched down, skipped once, and settled onto the short macadam runway.

The sun was low in the west and air traffic was negligible on this late Friday afternoon in May. Stewart slowed, reversed direction and taxied briskly toward the private aviation hangar.

The area was virtually deserted as he maneuvered into spot 436 near the wooden chocks and tie-down ropes. Glancing out his side window, he watched Rob Carpenter, husband of Jen Carpenter and a prominent Portland attorney, inspect the tires and landing gear of his twin-engine Cessna 310.

Stewart would kill for a Cessna 310. All he needed was money, and lots of it. Around Seal Point only the doctors and lawyers could afford expensive planes, ones with flight ranges south to the Caribbean or the West Coast. Not that his 170 was a bad plane—it was just was too small to load up the family and head to a vacation spot. A twin-engine aircraft, even a used one, was way beyond his financial reach, despite efforts to generate extra cash from his consulting activities.

He shut down the engine, set the brakes, and gave the instrument panel and cockpit a final cursory inspection. Grabbing his overnight bag from the storage space behind the rear seat, he jumped to the ground and attached the tie-down ropes to the wing mounts. He nudged the wooden chocks into place around the tires, completed a cursory walk around inspection and headed toward the tiny office in the hangar.

Inside the building, Rick took out his flight log. With a ballpoint pen, he jotted down the date, his departure time from New Jersey, arrival time in Seal Point, and the flight's elapsed time.

"Hi, Rick. Have a good flight?" Rob Carpenter greeted Stewart cordially.

"Yes. Business trip to New Jersey the past few days. With the semester nearly over, I've landed a couple consulting contracts that will keep me busy over the summer."

"Sounds like you'll be logging more flight time."

"Right. One job is outside Newark; another is in Atlanta. At least my plane allows me to get home faster and without the hassle of flying commercial.

"What I would give for a Cessna like yours," Rick continued with a touch of envy. "I'll need a lot more consulting assignments before I can afford even a used 310," he laughed ruefully.

"It's the initial investment that hurts," Rob pointed out sympathetically. "After that, the operating costs aren't too bad. And you do a lot of maintenance on your own plane, don't you? That should keep your costs down."

"Yeah. That's one benefit of an engineering degree. I got my mechanic's certification while I was at MIT."

"By the way, congratulations on your tenure and promotion to associate professor. Jen was pleased your application was successful."

"Thanks. When I first applied two years ago, some knee jerk liberals on the committee managed to deep six my application. My involvement with the oil and gas industry and support for an LNG terminal here in Maine upset them. Fortunately, they weren't on the committee this year.

"The politics of tenure are brutal," he observed. "I owe a lot to your wife and Sidney Orenstein. Thanks to them, I was recommended unanimously this year. I'm glad it's over."

"I understand the tenure process is tough. In fact, Jen's tenure experience was also difficult," Rob confided. "She didn't get tenure the first time she applied. That led to one of those nasty academic battles she and other women on campus fought and finally won. In her case, sex discrimination was the issue. That was some years ago. Apparently things are better now."

They walked to the parking lot together. Rob unlocked the door of his Porsche Carrera and slid onto the black leather seat.

"Nice choice of wheels, Rob," Rick said, making no attempt to conceal his envy. "Maybe someday you'll give me a spin in that baby."

"Any time. And give me a call when you're ready to move up to a larger plane," he offered. "You can take a check ride in my plane."

Stewart watched Carpenter gun the Porsche out of the parking lot.

He walked to his battered and rusted Toyota Camry and tossed his bag onto the back seat. Damn, he swore, wheeling out of the airport and heading home, I'll be an old man before I can replace this pile of junk and own a decent plane.

His New Jersey consulting job paid $800 a day, a welcome supplement to his $150,000 annual salary as a young associate professor. Still, his credit card debt was increasing each month. Sue's expensive tastes and the needs of their two kids cost a hell of a lot more than his salary. At least there wouldn't be any more little Stewarts running around. The vasectomy solved that problem.

He swung south onto a secondary road, and moments later reached a quiet cul de sac lined with middle class homes two miles from the ocean. He punched the garage opener on the visor, waited for the door to rise and pulled in beside the leased Mercedes SUV.

Rick entered the kitchen of his spacious Cape Cod style home through the mudroom. Located in Seal Point's only upscale development, the colonials, capes and traditional homes were set on one acre landscaped lots. Home to many young professionals—attorneys, doctors, and university faculty—the development reeked of conspicuous consumption in Seal Point, an otherwise sleepy Maine coastal village.

"Anybody home?"

"In the family room," Sue yelled, as his two children ran to greet him.

Moments later he kissed his wife perfunctorily and slumped onto the leather sofa opposite the 50-inch plasma television set. Twisting the cap off a bottle of beer, he took a long deep swallow, wiped his hand across his mouth, and suppressed a burp. He reached for the TV controller and surfed the channels, searching for a Red Sox game.

"How did the job go?" Sue asked indifferently.

"Fine. Mother and Dad send their love. I stayed with them in Princeton Wednesday and Thursday nights."

Too bad his parents were in such good health, Sue mused. Rick wouldn't collect his legacy for years.

"What's new with them?"

"Same old, same old—golf and social crap at the club." He drained the beer and headed to the refrigerator for seconds.

"As a matter of fact, there's good news on the financial front," he said over his shoulder. "Dad finally made good on his promise to set up trust funds for Courtney and Stevie. We went over preliminary documents for a $300,000 fund for each kid."

"That's nice," Sue said a bit more enthusiastically. "Your salary barely covers our living expenses right now. At least we won't have to borrow to send the kids to college."

"The trusts are specifically designated for college expenses," Rick related. "Since dad is a financial guru, I figure those trusts will be worth a pile of dough ten years from now."

"Big deal," Sue said sarcastically. "A few hundred thousand is small change for your parents."

"Unfortunately, those trust funds won't solve our cash flow problems right now," Rick said.

"If you didn't have such expensive hobbies, like flying your own plane, we might be able to make ends meet," Sue said peevishly.

"Yeah, and you haven't found a clothing boutique or department store you didn't love," he shot back. "Do you realize we owe $25,000 on our credit cards right now? You charged almost a thousand bucks on the Visa card just last month. Damn, you and the kids must be the best-dressed people north of Portland!"

"Not true," Sue retorted angrily.

"I swear I'm going to cut your cards in half and throw them away. And how the hell could you run up a $500 bill at the club in one month? What do you do, pick up the tab for your girlfriends and their kids, too?"

"Will you guys quit fighting? We're trying to watch the game," whined Courtney Stewart, lying prone on the carpet in front of the TV. Tossing her long blonde hair from her face, the slim nine-year-old crawled over to the sofa and snatched the remote controller.

"Courtney, go to your room," Rick ordered, lunging for the controller and losing the contest. "You too, Stevie," he commanded, nudging his six-year-old son, sprawled on his belly beside his sister.

"Why do you think I bought televisions for your bedrooms? This TV is for adults."

The children ignored their father, suddenly absorbed in the baseball action on the screen. Rick surrendered, too tired to play enforcer. Lately, the kids seemed to win every battle.

"You're going to have to teach them some discipline," Sue chided.

"Fat chance. They don't listen to me. They take after you." The ongoing battle over disciplining the kids would never end.

A broad smile suddenly spread across his handsome face. "Actually, we do have something else to celebrate tonight."

Sue regarded him sullenly. "What? Did daddy dear cough up a few of his millions just for us?"

"No such luck," Rick retorted. "Fact is, I landed a major extension of my consulting assignment with Appalachian Pipeline in Atlanta. It'll keep me busy through August and pays $800 a day. Maybe we can start paying down some of those credit card bills."

"Great. I suppose that means more trips out of town."

"What say we celebrate a little later," he nodded toward the bedroom.

"Sorry, wrong time of the month. You should have thought of that last week. Oh, I forgot. You were out of town."

Wordlessly, Rick stalked from the family room, opened the refrigerator and chugged down a third beer as he sorted a stack of unopened bills and junk mail on the kitchen table. Minutes later he carried his overnight bag to the bedroom and closed the door.

Sue heard the shower running and waited another hour before putting the kids to bed and setting the alarm system. Rick didn't move when she slipped between the sheets of their king bed and turned out the bedside lamp.

Chapter Thirteen

He left the silent house the next morning, backed the battered Toyota onto the street, and set off through the slumbering neighborhood. Next week would be intense, crammed with twelve hour days preparing for the Atlanta consulting assignment. He needed to get started.

He eased up to the Dunkin' Donuts takeout window, windshield wipers slapping away the morning fog and light rain hanging over the village center. He flirted casually with the high school kid who handed out his coffee and crullers. Munching on his pastry, he drove past the stores lining Main Street and pulled up to the red light at the intersection of Route 1. Despite the rain, heavy weekend traffic was moving north on this late spring morning. He turned south toward the campus.

Thirty minutes later he swung onto the wide boulevard leading to the university entrance. He turned right onto the perimeter road that skirted three sides of the campus and reached the security gate at the main parking garage. Today, the gate was upright and unguarded. Summer school would not begin for another two weeks, and the normally crowded four story parking facility was nearly deserted.

He pulled into a space next to the elevators and stairwell. Leaving the car unlocked, he sprinted through the rain to the rear entrance of the Environmental Sciences building, a four-story complex housing environmental and marine science and engineering.

Despite the prospect of a long day of work, Stewart thrived on the relatively leisurely pace of life at Reid University. He didn't regret leaving the intensely urban and brutally competitive environment he'd endured at MIT during his graduate school years. Housing in Maine was far less expensive than in a major city, and he prized his spacious home on an acre lot not far from the ocean.

Stewart had grown to love the campus, generously endowed by the school's founder, a Maine entrepreneur and environmentalist. Situated on more than 200 acres of prime land overlooking the Atlantic, founder James Reid had donated the land and funds to design and build the first campus buildings twenty-five years ago.

Founders Court, dotted with majestic Norway pines and balsam firs, was the gathering place and heart of the campus. The university's spectacular contemporary architecture and striking coastal location were effective recruiting tools in attracting highly qualified faculty and students. A national reputation in environmental and marine sciences justified the $50,000 annual price tag for its undergraduate programs.

Finally earning tenure and promotion to associate professor earlier this month was a major milestone in Rick's career, a load off his back. Reid University would be his academic home and long-term base of operations. He planned to raise his family in Seal Point, the picturesque coastal village less than half an hour drive north of the campus.

Now he could aggressively pursue lucrative consulting assignments to supplement his university salary. Unfortunately, his paid consulting would cut into his research, an essential component for success in the academic world. Teaching duties would quickly become a secondary priority. Although he enjoyed working with students, it was a minor factor in reaching his next career goal, promotion to full professor. Reaching the highest academic rank was a long term objective, one that he hoped to achieve within the next five years.

Prospects for buying a new, larger plane, one with real distance capabilities, a larger house, and two new cars were on indefinite hold. Despite his parents' wealth, he couldn't expect his legacy in the foreseeable future. Sue's frequent boasts to acquaintances about the Stewart family wealth led his faculty colleagues to assume they were financially well off. Little did they know.

Rick unlocked his third floor office door, flipped the light switch, and lifted his laptop computer from his brief case. Glancing outside the window overlooking Founders Court, he could barely make out the ocean in the distance, shrouded in rain and fog. His voice-mail light flashed on the phone, and he listened impatiently to ten messages, including three from engineering colleagues congratulating him on achieving tenure and promotion to associate professor.

Settling down, he connected his laptop to his large flat screen monitor for ease of viewing, entered his password and accessed his email. More than a hundred messages jammed his mailbox. Deleting the obvious spam, he scrolled down the screen, searching for the document that managers at Appalachian Pipeline had promised to email from Atlanta two days ago.

He found the message, opened the document and noted the access codes to Appalachian Pipeline's internal computer network. Inserting the appropriate codes, he watched as a new mailbox on Appalachian's server popped into view. The mailbox already contained three technical documents he would need to begin his new assignment. A few keystrokes and the data he sought flooded his screen. He downloaded the files to his hard drive, saved them to his backup memory stick and began to work.

Immersed in his spreadsheets, he thrived on the technical challenges presented by the Atlanta utility. Five hours later he checked his watch. He needed cash for the weekend and the bank would close at one o'clock. Taking a break, he locked his office and strolled off campus to the local branch office of his Portland bank.

He entered the small lobby and recognized Judy Perkins, an older business student who had just completed his introductory environmental issues elective with an A. His student was seated at a desk in the loan department. He waited in line, reached a teller, and withdrew $500. Then he sauntered across the lobby and greeted the young divorcee with the great body.

"Hi professor," Judy greeted him warmly, inviting him to a seat beside her desk.

"Please call me Rick," he smiled, admiring her artfully concealed cleavage in her low-cut silk blouse.

"How can I help you today?" she asked, trying to combine a friendly tone and businesslike manner.

"I'd like to check on the outstanding loan balance on my plane. Can you help me with that?"

"Give me your ATM card and I'll access your account," Judy leaned toward him, reaching for the card. She tapped a few commands on the keyboard.

"Here's the loan data," she said, turning the computer monitor so both could view the screen. "Actually, your loan is current, monthly payments are on time and the principal balance is just over $25,000," she said. "Is there anything more I can do for you on this loan?"

"Actually, I'm thinking about trading up to a larger plane," he said. "Maybe a Cessna 310 or a twin-engine Beech. What are my chances of getting a bigger loan, given the rock bottom interest rates I keep hearing about? Or do I have to hit the Boston banks to finance a major purchase?"

"This office can authorize loans up to $1 million," she responded quickly. "Of course, I'd have to run a comprehensive credit check on you and your wife. Would you like me to begin the process?"

"Not yet. I'm just kicking tires to see what rates are available."

"That depends on your credit standing, of course," Judy said. "May I ask why you need a larger plane?" she went on, curious. "If you use your plane for business purposes, we may be able to offer you a commercial loan."

"If my consulting work is considered a business, then I guess a commercial loan would work."

"In addition to an application, we would need three years' tax returns to evaluate your cash flow."

"That sounds like a lot of paperwork," he frowned. "Why can't I use the plane as collateral and forget all those other details?"

"Sorry, the bank is required to evaluate a borrower's credit situation. Since the economic downturn, we're required to check the borrower's creditworthiness more carefully than in the past. However, given the loan details on your current plane. I can calculate the down payment you would need to buy a larger plane, assuming you trade in your current one." She tapped a few keys, stared at the monitor, and flashed him a smile.

"This looks promising, but I need to check your mortgage balance." Her fingers flew across the keyboard, and she paused as the data come up on the screen.

"Hmm. This screen displays your complete financial picture here at the bank. The mortgage on your house is more than $400,000. Your savings account has a $5,000 balance, and you've got less than $1,000 in your checking account after the withdrawal you just made. You are carrying a fair amount of debt, about $425,000, right now. Depending on the value of your home, we may be able to offer you a home equity loan."

"How much would you expect to pay for a new plane?" she continued.

"Actually, I'll be working on several new consulting contracts this summer. That savings account is going nowhere but up," he responded, dodging her question.

"Look, Judy," he smiled disarmingly, "I probably won't buy a plane this summer, anyway. I just wanted to get a feel for interest rates."

"On a commercial loan, the five-year rate is currently around seven percent," she said. "On the other hand, a personal loan, collateralized by a new plane, would run a bit higher. You may not have enough equity in your home for a home equity loan."

Rick was sorry he'd asked.

"How would you like a ride in my current plane?" he asked impulsively.

"Really?" She flashed him a dazzling smile. "I'd love a ride with you. A couple of vacation flights to Florida are the extent of my flying experience." She arched an eyebrow, flirting openly. "Just name the time and place."

"How about a quickie flight on Monday afternoon? The weather is supposed to clear by then," he suggested.

"What's a 'quickie' flight?" she asked innocently.

"It's like sex. You know, short and sweet," he said, watching her settle her gorgeous butt more deeply in the chair.

"So, how about it? We could take a flight in late afternoon after you get off work," he flashed his most persuasive smile.

"I suppose that can be arranged." She glanced at her manager's cubicle across the lobby. "I'll need to finish my daily activity reports on Monday before leaving. Is 5:30 too late?"

"Not at all. Meet me at the Seal Point Municipal Airport, north of here, off Route 1."

"I know where the airport is," Judy assured him.

He rose and pointed a finger. "Good. Monday afternoon, 5:30. Try not to be late," he ordered. "I can't fly after dark. We wouldn't want our quickie to be cut short, now would we?"

Chapter Fourteen

The huge red ball hung low in the southwest sky, filtered through late afternoon haze. Judy wheeled her leased Bimmer convertible through the unguarded chain link gate and braked to a stop near the tiny airport terminal.

Stewart watched silently from his car. Sue wasn't currently available for sex; Judy Perkins might make an interesting diversion. He beeped his horn and waved. Grabbing his flight logbook from the center console, he jogged toward her car.

"Hi. Have any trouble finding the place?"

"No problem." She smiled nervously, glancing around the nearly empty parking lot in the late afternoon sun.

"I've already taken care of the preflight chores. We're almost ready to go, and I promise to get us back before dark," he said, leading her through the deserted office to the tarmac in front of the small hangar.

"Glad you changed into more comfortable clothes," he said, admiring the way her slim figure filled the tight shorts and tank top that left nothing to the imagination. "You wouldn't want to mess up a business suit scrambling in and out of my plane. This time of year, shorts and tops are standard gear for recreational flying.

"You'll see in a moment why I want a larger plane," he continued. He led her toward his plane parked on the tarmac where he had left it three days before. "You can chalk up this flight to business prospecting for the bank. After all, I did inquire about a loan," he said half seriously.

He unlatched the cockpit door. "Watch your step," he warned. His hands circled her waist and he boosted her into the plane, deliberately brushing across her tight buns. He gathered the safety harness and set the shoulder straps across her chest, his arm casually touching her breasts as he secured the belt. She didn't resist. With a friendly pat on her shoulder, he closed the door.

He strolled around the plane and completed a cursory visual preflight inspection. Waving to her through the front windshield, he kicked away the wheel chocks, removed the tie down ropes and coiled them neatly on the tarmac. Opening the pilot's door, he crawled inside and strapped on his safety harness.

"Ready?" he smiled reassuringly.

"As ready as I'll ever be," she said nervously. "How long will the flight last?"

He checked his watch. "We've got about an hour before sunset. Is that long enough for you, or do your quickies take more time?" He leaned unnecessarily close to her as he flipped switches and prepared to start the engine.

"Mine usually don't take an hour," she retorted with a smile. "But I suppose I could extend it a bit, if you need a little help."

"Mine don't take long either. That's why I call them quickies," he kept the banter going.

"Here, let me help you with the mike and earphones. You'll need them so we can talk back and forth when we're airborne." He reached for the device draped over the wheel on the passenger side and positioned the earphones securely over her ears. Then, tilting her head back, he kissed her lightly on the lips. She responded with surprising passion. He drew back and gazed into her brilliant green eyes.

"Maybe we should just cancel the flight and proceed to the main event."

"Oh, no. I've been looking forward to this all afternoon," she smiled. "Let's go before you have to fly in the dark."

"Right. I wouldn't want to fly in the dark on our first flight." He smiled and placed the tiny microphone just below her lips.

Rick pressed the ignition button and started the engine. He hurried through his preflight checklist and then taxied to the west end of the runway. Suddenly focused and businesslike, he searched the sky for other aircraft. Satisfied, he eased the throttle forward and the plane slowly gathered speed.

Judy screamed delightedly as the plane lifted off and they climbed steeply toward the coast. Throttling back, he circled over the village, pointing out the tall steeple of the Unitarian Church rising above the town common. Route 1 and the Maine turnpike were clearly visible in the distance. Then he began a gradual ascent to five thousand feet.

When they reached cruising altitude, Rick turned south, pointing out the Reid University campus along the Atlantic. The tall buildings of Portland soon appeared on the horizon.

"It's really beautiful," said Judy, gazing down at the sparkling ocean and the handsome mansions dotting the shore. "I had no idea this could be so much fun. It's nothing like flying in a commercial airliner."

"Want me to demonstrate some exciting maneuvers—show you a stall or maybe a spin?"

"No!" she squealed.

He reached across and removed her headset. With one hand on the controls and the other behind her head, he drew her to him and kissed her deeply. She responded instantly, reaching over and boldly caressing his groin through his khaki shorts.

He banked and set a course for the Seal Point airport. They landed ten minutes later and Rick hurriedly secured the plane on the tarmac. In separate cars, they headed for a small motel just off Route 1 as darkness fell.

Chapter Fifteen

Summer 2008. A blanket of suffocating heat and humidity assaulted Rick as he left the Atlanta headquarters of Appalachian Pipeline Company. He patted the $5,000 check tucked in his shirt pocket, tossed his briefcase and jacket onto the back seat of the rental car and exited the industrial park, pausing to hand over the visitor's pass at the security shack. A quarter-mile later he wheeled onto I-85 and headed south toward DeKalb Regional Airport where his Cessna was fueled and ready to go.

Adjusting the air conditioning control to extreme cold, he tuned the radio to a local country rock station and settled back, smiling in anticipation of the next forty-eight hours. Sue and the kids would never learn the real purpose of his side trip to West Palm Beach, nor his liaison with Judy Perkins at his parents' oceanfront condo. He would call Sue tonight to explain that he was following up a consulting lead with a Florida gas company.

Since their initial sexual liaison in May, Rick's affair with the part-time university student and bank loan officer had reached fever pitch. He looked forward to forty-eight hours of nonstop fun and sex games. For the first time, they could indulge their passion without risking discovery. Rick would introduce Judy to several sophisticated pleasures not found in rural Maine. When they tired of sex, the South Beach discos offered an exciting diversion.

Two hours later, he radioed the control tower at Palmetto Regional Airport near Fort Lauderdale and received permission to land. He set the plane down, taxied to the private aviation area and parked in the rental spot he'd reserved the day before.

Judy greeted him in the pilot's lounge, having flown by commercial airline to West Palm Beach and picked up the rental car Rick had booked in her name. Completely absorbed in each other, they failed to notice that others observed their arrival with interest.

* * *

Judy's finger lightly traced figure eights on Rick's chest. "This condo is gorgeous," she said, glancing around the spacious master bedroom. "I guess the rumors that your family is wealthy are true."

"Yeah, my dad made a lot of money on Wall Street. Unfortunately, he's in very good health, so my legacy won't arrive for years. Meantime, I have to live on my salary and any consulting I can scrape up."

"When you were promoted, you must have gotten a big raise."

"Not really. The main benefit was earning tenure. That was after I'd been turned down earlier."

"I didn't realize getting tenure was such a big deal. Why weren't you promoted before? You're a terrific teacher. Doesn't that count for something? "

"The tenure and promotion process at the university is very political," Rick explained. "When I applied a couple years ago, some members of the committee blocked my promotion because they didn't approve of my consulting activities with the gas industry. It cost me two years salary increase, and was a major embarrassment because people knew I was turned down."

"Why would faculty oppose your consulting work? Everyone seems to do it," Judy pressed on, curious.

"Mostly professional envy," he replied. "I consult with the gas companies on technical problems and pipeline security. I also lobby for public support of additional LNG facilities along the east coast. I couldn't afford my plane or getaways like this without the extra bucks my consulting brings in.

"The university's resident liberals, Alice Matthews and Leslie Jarvis, railroaded me the last time," he rambled on bitterly. "They weren't appointed to the committee this year, and I was unanimously recommended. Now I have job security for the rest of my life."

"I took a sociology course with Alice Matthews last year," Judy remarked. "She was a pushover for a grade, but the course was boring and I hated her New York accent."

Rick fondled Judy's breasts. "Why not take another course with me next fall? My advanced course in Environmental Studies is very popular."

"That would be cool. Maybe we can have a little fun during your office hours," she giggled. "Promise you'll give me an A," she demanded half seriously.

"I need another beer," Rick said, avoiding any promises. He rolled over and headed for the kitchen. "Want one?" he asked over his shoulder.

"Sure."

He returned with two bottles and climbed back into bed.

"Let's get serious for a minute," he said. "I'm about ready to buy a bigger plane, probably a twin-engine used aircraft. Remember that I asked about interest rates when we first talked at the bank?"

"You already have a nice plane. Why do you want another one?"

"To take you to the Caribbean," he teased. "Seriously, I plan to expand my consulting work to Louisiana and even to California, two hot spots for LNG terminal expansion. I can't swing a new plane without another large bank loan. How about it? Know where I can get a good interest rate?"

"For a small finder's fee, I might be able to point you in the right direction," Judy said, not interested in talking business. She groped for signs of life between his legs.

He slapped her butt none too gently and reached for his watch on the bedside stand. "How about a quiet dinner at a little Italian café I know?" he suggested.

"Later, we can hit the disco scene in Ft. Lauderdale or drive down to South Beach. After that, I'll introduce you to something really special."

He rolled off the bed and padded across the heavy Berber carpet to the bathroom.

"Sounds like a plan. Beat you to the shower," she said, nudging him aside and stepping into the shower.

He closed the glass door, turned on the water, and began lathering her breasts.

*   *   *

Rick fumbled for the key, unlocked the condo door and caught Judy as she stumbled across the threshold into the entry hall. Together, they staggered to the bedroom and fell onto the bed.

"If folks at the bank could see me now," Judy giggled, "and who would have guessed that an upright college professor could be such a hot guy?"

"The evening isn't over yet." He glanced at the digital clock on the nightstand. "Actually, it's 3:30, too early to go for a jog, too late to go to sleep." He clumsily unbuttoned the back of her silk blouse.

"We've just begun to play. Time for a special treat I picked up in the men's room at the Black Voodoo. Hold on a minute," he reached across her body for his trousers lying on the floor.

She responded by climbing onto his back. Straddling him, her hands massaging his shoulders and neck, she leaned forward and bit his neck.

Focused on his search, he tossed his car keys onto the nightstand, retrieved his wallet and pulled out a small bag of white powder.

"Is that what I think it is?" she asked, leaning over his shoulder.

"It's not coke. This shit is a lot better than coke," he assured her.

He waved the packet in her face. "Baby, this is the latest and greatest, the best money can buy." Judy sprawled beside him, bleary eyes fixed on the bag of white powder.

"Remember that guy, Carlos, in the disco tonight? Short, dark hair, Hispanic."

She shook her head. "That place was loaded with dark-haired Hispanics."

"Anyway, Carlos sold me this stuff in the men's room. It's fresh off the plane from a mega lab in Mexico. This shit is special. Carlos even gave me his business card in case I need more."

He slid off the bed and lurched unsteadily to the bathroom, eventually returning with a cocktail straw and a razor blade.

"Do you always carry an extra blade and straw in your shaving kit?" she asked.

He waved the straw in front of her face. "This is my 'tooter.' It's our gateway to ecstasy," he explained, sitting naked and cross-legged on the bed. "Like the Boy Scouts, I'm always prepared. Nothing like topping off our evening with a little meth. Much better than coke."

She shook her head. "I'm just a country girl from backwoods Maine. I haven't even tried coke," she confessed, "although I did a little pot last year. Got it from a guy in my sociology class. He also bragged about meth, said I should try it, but I decided pot was heavy enough for me."

"Come on," he urged. "This little packet of pleasure is the perfect finish to a great evening. I guarantee you'll love it. It's an aphrodisiac, too. If you thought sex was good this afternoon, wait till you see what we can do after a little meth."

He crawled to the nightstand, opened the packet and used the razor blade to shape the little pile into two lines of white powder. Then he handed the tooter to her.

"You first," he invited.

She shook her head. "Show me how to do it."

He grinned. "You'll owe me big time for this." He bent over and snorted deeply. She followed his lead.

Chapter Sixteen

Sunday morning Judy drove Rick to the Palmetto Airport terminal, then returned the rental car to West Palm Beach International Airport and boarded a direct flight to Boston. With luck, she would be home by early evening.

Rick filed his flight plan and completed his preflight details in preparation for the long flight to Maine. Shortly after noon he taxied the Cessna to the east end of the runway, received takeoff clearance from the control tower and moments later was airborne.

Banking sharply, he set a course northeast for Charleston, South Carolina. Climbing through four thousand feet, he felt a subtle engine vibration through the control yoke. Adrenaline slightly elevated, he scanned the instruments. The oil pressure was dropping.

"Palmetto Tower, this is 5647 Hotel. I'm about fifteen miles north of the field. My engine oil pressure is dropping. Returning to the field."

"Cessna 647 Hotel. We copy. Understand you have an engine problem. Do you wish to declare an emergency at this time?"

"Negative. I believe I can make the field."

"You are cleared to land on runway 4R," the controller said calmly.

He landed without incident and slowly taxied back to the hangar, parking the plane at the spot he had recently vacated.

He returned to the office and requested assistance. Within minutes, the chief mechanic removed the cowling and examined the engine. The inside of the cowling was covered with oil. Rick watched anxiously over the mechanic's shoulder.

"It's the crankshaft seal," the mechanic concluded, wiping his hands on a greasy rag. "I'm afraid you're grounded until it's replaced. It'll take at least three days to get the parts and make the repairs. We've got to pull the prop to replace the seal. And the engine should be torn down and inspected because you were running on zero oil pressure. I recommend pulling the cylinders and the pistons, rings and valve train. They probably need to be overhauled or replaced. Check with the office for an estimate of the repair cost."

"What's your best guess?"

The mechanic shrugged. "At least $3,000, depending on how long it takes to get the job done. Have you got an account with us?"

"No, this is my first flight into this airport."

"Let me clue you. Company policy requires payment in full before we can release the plane."

"Damn. Does the company accept credit cards for repairs?" he asked as they walked to the office in the midday heat.

"Sure. A bank card or cash is okay, too."

"Good. I'll check back with you tomorrow. If you could expedite these repairs, I'd appreciate it."

"Can't promise anything, but I'll do my best. Call me late tomorrow."

Rick entered the terminal and pulled out his cellphone, preparing to call a car rental company, when he felt a tap on the shoulder.

"Well, how about that? Nice to see you again," Carlos Munoz greeted him warmly. Momentarily confused, Rick wondered where he'd met this short, swarthy-complexioned fellow before.

Then he smiled and extended his hand. "You're Carlos, right? We met in the bar at the Black Voodoo a couple nights ago."

"Right."

"What are you doing here?" he asked.

"I use several planes in my businesses. One is based here. I stopped by to check that it was ready to head out to New York City.

"What about you?" Carlos asked. "Do you have business here? And how's that good-looking broad you were with? Not your wife, I assume," he smirked.

"No, no. Just a friend.

"Actually," Rick related, "I was barely airborne on my way home to Maine when my plane developed engine trouble. Looks like I'm grounded for a couple days for repairs. And Judy has already left on a commercial flight."

"So, have you got transportation and a place to stay?" Carlos asked.

"No to your first question, yes to the second. I can stay at my parents' condo in West Palm. Would you mind giving me a lift to a car rental office?"

"No problem. My car is right outside."

Rick picked up his overnight bag and followed Munoz to a late model Mercedes parked in a handicap spot at the front entrance. Carlos expertly maneuvered the heavy sedan through the parking lot and sped toward the interstate.

"You know," Carlos glanced across the seat, "I have a home nearby. You can stay with me for a few days. My place is closer than West Palm, and I'm right on the ocean. I've got plenty of room. You won't need a rental car. I'll loan you one of my other cars while you're here."

Rick didn't hesitate. "Sounds terrific. Thanks." He heaved a sigh of relief. "As a matter of fact, it would save some cash, too. I'm a little short of the green stuff right now and engine repairs were not part of my budget."

"What do you do for a living?" Carlos asked, casually weaving through heavy traffic on the outskirts of Ft. Lauderdale.

"I'm a college professor," Rick responded a bit sheepishly. "Everybody knows that professors are just one step ahead of bankruptcy. I pick up some spare cash through consulting with natural gas utilities."

They turned off Ocean Drive and drew up to an imposing gate. Carlos touched his remote and the gate slowly slid back. He eased the Mercedes along a drive lined with palm trees toward a spectacularly modern glass and stucco house.

"Whatever you do for a living, it must pay well," Rick observed, unable to conceal his surprise at the luxurious property spread out before him.

"I'm just a typical Miami businessman. Reasonably successful, as you can see," Carlos laughed.

He parked the car and the two men entered the house through massive double doors that opened into an expansive sun-lit foyer. To the left was an enormous living room whose wall of glass overlooked a large infinity pool with the brilliant white sand beach and turquoise ocean in the distance. Facing the entrance a wide curving staircase led to the second floor.

"Make yourself comfortable," Munoz invited, leading him into the living room. "You'll find a spare bedroom if you turn left at the top of the stairs. It's the corner room at the end of the hall." He waved at the balcony overlooking the living room.

"There's a Porsche Cayenne in the garage. The keys are in the ignition. It's yours for the duration. Maria is the maid," he continued. "She can get you some lunch. And there are extra swim trunks in the guest room. Consider mi casa su casa.

"I've got some business to attend to. I'll be back late this afternoon. Maybe you'd like me to show you around the area tonight."

"Great," Rick breathed, sinking onto a white leather sofa. "I'll just hang out here this afternoon." He gazed toward the pool and the ocean beyond. "Thanks, I really appreciate your hospitality."

Chapter Seventeen

Three days later Rick set the Cessna's nose on the runway's centerline, released the brakes and eased the throttle forward. The plane rose smartly into the early morning haze. He banked to the north once again, confident that the newly repaired engine would carry him safely to Charleston and ultimately home to Maine.

He scanned the instrument panel, eased back on the control column and climbed to his five thousand foot cruising altitude. Settling into a state of relaxed concentration he mulled over the happenings of the last few days. Clearly, Carlos Munoz, was a hugely successful businessman despite the apparent absence of a college education.

When he wasn't making the rounds of the local discos, his heavily guarded and secluded oceanfront home was a party scene driven by a floating crowd of successful young professionals. Drugs and alcohol fueled the festivities while scantily clad women from a local escort service gathered around the pool. The parties apparently ran from sundown until dawn, whether the host was present or not. Whatever his business, and Rick had some suspicions about that, his host's south Florida lifestyle was fascinating. He had stumbled into a world he vaguely knew existed, one that was light years away from the university and home in Maine.

Thanks to a $3,000 loan from Carlos, Rick paid cash for his plane repairs. Now all he had to do was figure out how to repay his new best friend. Hours later, after a brief refueling stop in Charleston and a second one outside Baltimore, he set a course for New Jersey and the airport near Princeton.

He landed late that afternoon, phoned his father and suggested a meeting in the airport coffee shop. An hour later Hiram Stewart, retired president of Stewart Securities, formally shook hands with his only son.

They seated themselves at a table in a quiet corner of the nearly deserted shop.

"Thanks for coming on short notice, Dad. I'm on my way back from Florida. I had business in Atlanta and then followed up a consulting lead in West Palm Beach. By the way, I stayed in your condo last weekend. Hope you don't mind."

"Delighted you could use it, son" his father responded amiably. "How are Sue and my two grandchildren?"

"Fine. Enjoying the summer.

"I've been gone more than a week. I was delayed a few days with an engine problem, and the repairs tapped out my credit cards. I hate to ask a favor, but I could use a small loan to tide me over until I get paid for the consulting job. This is just a temporary cash flow problem."

Hiram Stewart looked pained. "How much do you need?"

"The repairs were $5,000. I can repay you by the end of the September. The consulting job in Atlanta is lucrative and the opportunity in Florida looks promising. If both assignments continue after the summer, I'll probably buy a larger plane."

"The loan isn't a problem. However, why you insist on flying your own plane is a mystery to me. Commercial airlines fly to Atlanta and West Palm Beach, you know."

"Yeah, but connections from Seal Point are lousy," Rick complained. "The plane gives me flexibility and I can maintain my technical proficiency. You know that flying has been my passion since prep school."

"Yes. I sometimes regret financing those flying lessons years ago. You were really bitten by the bug," his father's smile took the edge off his words. Hiram Stewart pulled out his checkbook and began to write.

"Thanks, Dad. I really appreciate this," Rick glanced at the amount before he folded the check and tucked it in his wallet. "Give Mom my love," he said cheerfully. "Sue and I will try to fly down for a visit soon."

"Right," his father said wryly, rising from the table.

Rick accompanied him to his car and promised to be in touch.

Minutes later he set a northeasterly course for Seal Point and settled back to enjoy the flight home. Asking for $5,000 was brilliant. It gave him an extra cash cushion that he and his father both knew would never be repaid. What the hell. The old man was loaded. Nothing wrong with taking a little advance on his inheritance. First thing tomorrow, he would send a $3,000 check to Carlos along with a note thanking him for his hospitality.

Chapter Eighteen

A national symposium on LNG safety issues in late August presented another opportunity to fly south, this time to Orlando for a three-day conference. Following the 9/11 terrorist attacks, protecting LNG terminals, nuclear power stations, chemical plants and oil refineries had become a national priority at Homeland Security.

Several years ago Stewart modified his research and consulting activities to focus on LNG terminal security. Recognizing the vulnerability of the enormous tankers and onshore LNG facilities, he quickly established a national reputation as a security expert, winning lucrative personal consulting contracts with the gas industry and Homeland Security. He also brought several million dollars of federal contracts to Reid University, generating funds for himself and for the university. He proved adept at leveraging his faculty position and impeccable academic credentials with well-honed presentation skills.

In Orlando his technical paper was well received by several hundred industry and government representatives. Rick spent two hectic but productive days networking with academic colleagues and government officials, building contacts with power brokers in a position to award lucrative consulting assignments.

As the conference wound down on Friday afternoon, he flew to Ft. Lauderdale, determined to solidify his relationship with Carlos Munoz. Shortly after landing, he took a cab directly to the beachfront mansion and joined his host on the terrace overlooking the pool.

"Cheers," Carlos greeted Rick, tipping a beer in his direction. "What brings you to Florida this time?"

Rick brought him up to date while they strolled beside the pool. A coterie of scantily clad women and men had already gathered, drinking, smoking and occasionally disappearing into the cabana.

"Get a load of that one," Carlos pointed out a blonde engaged in an amateur striptease show. With a final fling of her skimpy bikini top, she jumped into the pool, pursued by two fully clothed men.

"You can have her any time you want," he offered. "She gives great head. I know from experience."

"Thanks. Maybe later. Right now I could use a little of the white stuff. It's been a hectic week, and I'm ready to party."

"Let's go into my office. I've got some special shit for my best friends." They made their way through a mélange of bodies, some dancing to the heavy beat of a six-piece band, others engaged in heavy groping, oblivious to the action around them.

Carlos closed the heavy mahogany office door, flipped a switch, and bathed the room in soft light. He drew the drapes across the patio doors off the terrace. Approaching the bookcase wall, he pressed a hidden button and waited patiently as a section of the wall swung open, exposing a wall safe. Waving Rick to a soft leather chair, he opened the safe and pulled out a five-ounce bag of cocaine.

Casually tossing the bag in the air, he ambled across the room and sat down opposite his guest. "Any idea what this is worth?" he asked.

"Not a clue. Probably plenty, if it's as good as you claim."

Munoz opened the bag and carefully tapped a small amount of powder onto the glass coffee table. Using a credit card, he quickly shaped the powder into two lines. Munoz snorted deeply and then handed the tooter to his friend. Without a word, Rick leaned down and snorted. He slumped back in the soft leather chair and shuddered slightly, his heart racing as the drug slammed into his blood stream.

His eyes widened. "Wow, great stuff, Carlos. I needed that," Rick folded his arms across his chest, savoring the high. The two men were silent, intensely self-absorbed.

"You're leaving tomorrow, right?" Carlos asked, finally rousing himself.

"Yeah. But stuff like this makes me want to hang around another day."

"How would you like to take some with you—say the rest of this bag?" Through heavily lidded eyes, he watched Rick closely.

"Are you kidding? I can't afford that stuff. I'm a poor professor, remember?" Rick laughed, an hysterical edge creeping into his voice.

"Let me get to the point," Carlos said, suddenly all business. "I need a small favor. I've got to deliver two Nike sports bags of my best stuff to New York by Monday morning. Since you're flying north, how about dropping off the stuff in New Jersey on your way to Maine?"

Rick stared at him, stunned.

"You told me your folks live in New Jersey, right?" Carlos went on after a moment.

Rick nodded.

"My guy can meet you in northern Jersey. You deliver the stuff, and I'll take care of the details. No one would be the wiser, and it would only add an extra hour or so to your flight."

"You seem to have thought of everything," Rick said slowly.

"I'd pay for the service, of course," he continued. "Cash or coke, your choice. How does $100,000 cash sound to you?"

"Shit, Carlos. Is this some kind of joke? I take a couple of duffel bags to New Jersey and you pay me 100K?" He shook his head, incredulous, pacing nervously around the room.

"That's the deal, buddy. Practically no risk. Each bag weighs twenty-five kilos, 110 pounds total. That won't overload your plane. Consider it extra luggage." Carlos leaned over the glass coffee table and snorted a second line of white powder.

"My guy in New Jersey will pay you. If you want cash, I can arrange for hundreds or twenties, your choice. I'd even throw in a small amount of crystal meth as a bonus. Really special stuff," he waited patiently for Rick's response.

"Instead of cash, you can take your payment in coke," he offered after a moment. "A kilo is worth about $125,000 wholesale. Of course, you'd have to figure a way to distribute it. That might be a problem in a sleepy town like Seal Point, Maine or on campus at your university. I have a great distribution network in New York, but I'm not interested to distribute in Maine."

"So," Rick said, suddenly serious. "At least one of your businesses is drugs." He looked around the handsome mahogany-paneled study. "This house, the expensive art, the books, the yacht, your cigarette boat, those hot cars in your garage—God knows what else—bought with drug money."

Carlos nodded. "Exactly. My operations control everything from the source in Columbia and Mexico to the streets of New York. You might say my business is vertically integrated. But you don't need to know the details—at least not right now.

"Seriously," he continued, "drug distribution at this level is one of the safest and most stable businesses around."

"How can you say that?" Rick challenged.

"Easy. Less than three percent of the drugs brought into the country are ever confiscated. That's a fact even the government acknowledges. In my experience, the likelihood you'll be detected is way below three percent. There's virtually no risk, especially if you stay away from the retail end of the business."

"You may be right. I read somewhere that most drug busts are at the street level."

"True," Carlos agreed. "I figure the risk of detection at the wholesale level is probably less than one percent. For a math whiz like you, those odds should look pretty good. You can basically forget about being picked up. And you've got other insurance."

"What's that?" Rick asked.

"You don't fit any DEA or Homeland Security profile. A college professor who is a pilot and consults around the country is the last person they would suspect. And you've got a wealthy Princeton family background. My Hispanic looks and accent make me a target.

"Any way you cut it," said Carlos, the inadvertent pun going unnoticed by both men, "the risk of detection is almost zero."

He launched into his closing argument. "I bet you don't earn $100,000 a year as a professor. Here's your chance to pick up some untaxed cash. After only a couple of trips working for me you could buy a bigger plane—maybe that twin-Beech you've talked about. Or, I might offer you a good deal on one of my used planes."

Rick stared at the open bag of white powder. He considered the opulent surroundings financed with drug profits by a college dropout only a few years older than he. Carlos had guessed correctly. His annual university salary, while more than $100,000 a year, wasn't enough to maintain his lifestyle. And despite his most aggressive efforts, consulting activities generated only another $25,000. In forty-eight hours he could make 100K, tax-free. The decision was a no-brainer.

He reached across the table and shook Carlos' hand.

"It's a deal."

"Welcome to the real world, Rick. You'll be amazed how easy this is going to be."

"Get me to the airport with my luggage and the bags. I'll leave early tomorrow."

"I'll drive you myself. And I'll throw in an extra bag of meth. We're beginning to penetrate the New York market with great Mexican crystal. Feel free to help yourself to a few ounces. Try it, you're gonna like it. Maybe you can sell some to the students on campus."

"Thanks. I'm not ready to sell shit on campus."

"How long does it take to get to New York in your plane?" Carlos asked.

"Two days following my usual routine. I'll make an overnight stop in North Carolina and get to New Jersey by the day after tomorrow. You'll need to arrange the pickup at an airport near Princeton. I'll stay overnight with my parents, then fly to Maine the next day."

"And you'll be a whole lot richer after this trip," Carlos put his arm around Rick's shoulder and they rejoined the party.

Chapter Nineteen

Just after dawn the next morning Rick gunned the engine and lifted off from Palmetto Regional Airport and headed east into the rising sun. Two duffel bags stuffed with fifty kilos of pure uncut cocaine were stowed in the luggage compartment behind the rear seats. A five-pound bag of crystal meth was stashed in a small, insulated thermos bag on the seat beside him.

Following Carlos's instructions, he earlier had filed a flight plan for Wilmington, North Carolina, a destination that would take him over water most of the way. Ten minutes later he executed a ninety degree turn, and set a northerly course. The weather was unusually clear; from seven thousand feet he visually tracked the distant coastline off his left wing. He relaxed, monitoring the radio traffic and keeping a watchful eye for other aircraft. The first leg of his trip was remarkably uneventful and hours later he landed in North Carolina, right on schedule.

"Sue, I'm outside Wilmington, North Carolina. I'll spend the night in New Jersey with Mother and Dad, so I won't be home until Tuesday," he said from a motel room near the airport.

"I expected you home tomorrow," his wife complained. "The kids are being totally obnoxious, and I haven't had a break for days. I hate being tied down like this while you roam around the country having a good time."

"They're your kids, Sue," he retorted. "You wanted them, not me. Deal with it. By the way, I landed a terrific consulting assignment in Florida; the trip wasn't a waste of time. I'll make some real money from this one, maybe even enough to buy a new plane," he gloated.

"How about spending some of that money on the kids and me—like taking us on a real vacation for a change?" she whined.

"Yeah, we can do that, too. Maybe spend next Christmas in Disney World."

"That's more like it," said Sue, placated.

"I'll be home late Tuesday afternoon. Will you pick me up?"

"Sorry, I'm busy. I have a tennis lesson that afternoon with Jim Corbett. I can leave your car at the airport parking lot. You'll have wheels, but don't expect me to be home when you get here," she warned. "I've got a babysitter for the kids and will have dinner at the club after my lesson. You'll have to manage dinner on your own."

"Who is Jim Corbett? The new club pro?"

"Yes, and he's helped my game a lot."

"I'll bet. First you bitch about me being away for a week. Now you can't find time in your busy schedule to pick me up."

He hung up.

He dug out his cellphone and speed-dialed Judy Perkins' home number. When the message center came on, he left a cryptic message inviting her to meet at their usual place around seven o'clock Tuesday evening. If Sue wasn't happy to see him, he knew someone who would be.

Consulting his phone contacts again, he punched Munoz's unlisted number in Ft. Lauderdale and left a message with Maria, the maid, reporting his current location and indicating a three o'clock arrival time at the airport in New Jersey.

Midafternoon the next day the Cessna was cruising off the coast of northern New Jersey. Rick slowly descended to five hundred feet, below the radar monitored by the metropolitan New York air traffic control sector. He blended into the clogged airspace, banked west and set a course for the airport near Princeton.

Minutes later he landed and taxied briskly to the familiar terminal where he had learned to fly many years before. He strolled through the terminal, nodded to the friendly counter girl and walked outside to the parking lot. Carlos told him to expect a dark blue van to pick up his cargo. He watched in the late afternoon heat and humidity as a van appeared on the access road in the distance, entered the nearly deserted parking lot and braked to a stop in front of the terminal. A swarthy, muscular man about Rick's age jumped from the driver's side.

"How's Simon?" asked the man, displaying tobacco-stained teeth.

"Fine. He sends his regards to Felix," Rick responded, feeling foolish as he completed the identification sequence Carlos instructed him to use.

"You got something for me?" the man asked brusquely.

"In the plane. Two duffle bags. Let's go."

They walked around the terminal building onto the tarmac. Rick opened the passenger side door, hauled out the two duffel bags and tossed them carelessly to the tarmac. He strolled around the rear of the plane to the pilot's side, unzipped his overnight bag and stuffed the thermos bag containing the crystal meth into the bottom of the bag.

The stranger effortlessly hoisted the duffel bags and carried them to the parking lot. Dropping the cargo in the rear of the van, Rick and the stranger left the airport and merged into dense afternoon commuter traffic.

The driver handed him a heavy briefcase, dropped him at the car rental office, and took off toward New York City. Rick signed for a one day rental car and drove to his parents' home.

Returning to the airport the following morning, no one noticed the briefcase he carried along with the overnight bag slung over his shoulder. He stowed the luggage securely behind the pilot's seat, taxied to the refueling area and took on a full tank of fuel. Minutes later, his preflight inspection complete, he taxied to the end of the runway and took off on the final leg to Seal Point Municipal Airport, landing as the late afternoon sun cast shadows across the tarmac.

He secured the plane in its usual spot and finished his customary post flight inspection. Retrieving his overnight bag and the briefcase from behind the pilot's seat, he noticed Rob Carpenter seated in the cockpit of his plane, absorbed in a preflight inspection. Rob looked his way, waved and resumed his work.

Rick went into the small men's room off the pilot's lounge and entered the single stall. Placing the briefcase across the toilet seat, he unsnapped the latch.

His eyes widened at the tightly packed contents. Three solid layers of bundled currency filled the case. He gingerly wedged out a banded bundle and ran his thumb along the edge. As promised, his cash payment of worn hundred-dollar bills was bundled in packs. Adrenaline racing, he hastily counted the bundles. If it wasn't exactly 100K, it was damn close. He closed the case and left the men's room. Overnight bag slung over his shoulder and briefcase in hand, he headed toward the parking lot.

"Hello Rick, how's your summer going?" Rob Carpenter came up behind him as he speed-dialed Judy Perkins' number.

"Great, thanks. My consulting business is finally paying off; I may be in the market for a larger plane sooner than I expected. I could use a twin engine plane—maybe a twin Beech like yours, or a larger Cessna—to get me around the country more efficiently."

"When you're ready to move ahead, I can put you in touch with several dealers in the Boston area who specialize in used aircraft. Do you already have your multi-engine rating?" Carpenter asked.

"Yes. I got both instrument and multi-engine ratings some years ago when I was finishing my doctorate at MIT. Flying kept me sane while I worked on my dissertation. Whenever the stress got too heavy, I took off. I've kept up my proficiency ratings ever since."

"Give me a call when you're ready for a new plane."

"Thanks. I'll be back in touch in a couple months."

Rick watched Rob gun his Porsche through the gate and turn right toward Seal Point. Moments later, briefcase and overnight bag stashed in the locked trunk of his old Toyota, he headed south to Portland and a rendezvous with Judy Perkins.

*   *   *

He eased the beat-up Camry into his garage shortly after midnight, popped the trunk and set the cash-heavy briefcase on the concrete floor. A quick glance around the overflowing garage convinced him the case could easily be concealed amid the accumulated junk. Sue constantly bitched about the general clutter overwhelming the small two-car garage. On the other hand, she wouldn't dream of cleaning it. The garage was Rick's domain.

Crawling past the lawnmower and the kids' bikes, he wedged the briefcase behind the packed tent and sleeping bags in the far corner. The garage was safer than any bank, at least for now. Sue would never find the cache.

Housekeeping was never one of Sue's strengths. Indeed, he had begun to wonder exactly what her strengths were. Based on his two-month liaison with Judy Perkins, her sexual prowess was no match for Judy. Moreover, she was a lousy cook, and the kids spent more time with baby-sitters and in day care than they did with their mother.

He would deal with the money problem later. He chuckled aloud. What a problem. In the space of a few days he had flipped from concern about bank overdrafts to worrying about how to launder a pile of cash without attracting attention.

Rick was exhausted. Given the late hour, Sue was not likely to be in a mood for sex. Good thing. He wasn't up to the task, not after the last few hours with Judy.

He crossed the threshold into the kitchen and walked through the silent house. Entering the kids' bedrooms, he found them sound asleep. He smiled. His son and daughter were perfect kids only when asleep. Moments later, leaving a trail of clothing across the bedroom carpet, he slid between the sheets. Across the bed, Sue snored softly. He sank into a deep, dreamless sleep.

Chapter Twenty

Spring 2009. "What have you got for me?" Chief Craig Edwards asked.

Pete Byrnes handed over his thick file on the Lombardo investigation.

"Give me ten minutes to review this. Relax, get a cup of coffee," he suggested, "and please bring me back a cup—black, no sugar."

Edwards moved to the conference table in his cramped office and began to read. The information was startling, even to the seasoned security chief, a veteran of five years' service at the university following early retirement from the FBI.

Pete returned with two coffees and settled into a chair beside his boss.

"No wonder you took so long to complete this investigation. I was beginning to think you were dragging your feet," the security chief remarked.

"This investigation was more complex than I expected," Pete admitted. "The details are behind the first page summary. You may want to forward the report to others on the campus—maybe even to president Smythe. It's arranged so you can eliminate details as you see fit.

"As you directed," he continued, "I contacted campus security on two other campuses. I also dug up some interesting information in the computer records at the New Jersey district court near the Lombardo family home. Then I had to tie the details together."

"This is outstanding work, Pete. You've identified several problems; Lombardo's disruptive behavior in professor Prescott's class may be the least of them."

Byrnes reached into his briefcase and pulled out a duplicate report and handed it to Edwards. "These are the only two copies. I prepared the report on my laptop, printed the copies on my home printer, and saved it to a memory stick that I keep at home. I haven't discussed the contents with anyone."

"Let me assess every point with you before passing it along to dean Howard and the president," Edwards said.

An hour later they leaned back and regarded each other soberly.

"How do you want to proceed?" Pete asked finally.

"This is your investigation. Give me your recommendations."

"Okay. First, I believe Lombardo's past history should not be disclosed to professor Prescott. There's no need to frighten her. He's still in her class. I hope that situation will change very shortly.

"By the way, I'm keeping an eye on her when she's on campus. I drop by her office from time to time, and occasionally hang around outside her classroom. Just casual."

"Good, let's not upset her yet. An administrative action is required to remove him from her class, which may take some time."

Pete turned to the next issue. "I'm also keeping an eye on Lombardo. As my report indicates, the drug dealing he apparently carried on at two schools never led to any charges. I contacted the head of campus security at the Oregon school, who told me that no charges were filed and referred me to the campus detective for details.

"The detective was convinced that Lombardo was dealing controlled substances on campus, including cocaine and crystal meth. He told me his boss brought the matter to the president's attention. The president decided not to press charges. The school got rid of the problem by allowing Lombardo to leave.

"I got a similar story when I checked with campus security at the New Jersey community college that he attended. The detective was convinced Lombardo was dealing marijuana and cocaine, but found no specific evidence of crystal meth. Again, top administrators at the school refused to press charges. In fact, he was allowed to finish his program and get an Associate's Degree right before he transferred here. His family apparently wields some influence in New Jersey.

"In my opinion, family influence was a factor in both schools' failing to file formal charges. Typical resolution, don't you think, chief?"

"Yes. Unfortunately, schools don't press charges because they don't want negative publicity. Why draw attention to drug problems on their campus and upset parents? They take the easy way out.

"I hope that won't happen here," he went on. "If we can build a solid drug dealing case against Lombardo, I'll recommend arresting him and taking the case to district court. Whether the president will back me up is another question.

"Right now, though, we only have this guy's past history and your suspicions. Have you got anything more solid?"

"No," Pete shook his head. "On a separate matter, chief, I also have an ongoing watch on professor Rick Stewart, the environmental sciences guy who is publicly supporting the LNG terminal project."

"Why is that relevant to this investigation?" Edwards frowned.

"Lombardo is enrolled in an environmental sciences course that Stewart teaches. I've observed them together in various locations around campus—in the weight room at the Athletics Center and eating lunch in the Student Center. I saw him leaving Stewart's office in late afternoon about a week ago. They obviously know each other, although Lombardo has been on campus only a couple months."

"What have you learned about Stewart?"

"Not a lot," Pete admitted. "He goes to Georgia and Florida at least once a month, visits Atlanta, and then goes on to the Fort Lauderdale and Miami areas. He apparently consults with two natural gas companies. That ties in with his work with Randjumpp and the proposed LNG terminal here in Maine. I was only able to verify his consulting with the Atlanta firm, which appears to be a legitimate assignment.

"The most interesting news is that Stewart recently bought an expensive twin engine Beech aircraft. It's not a new plane; however, even used twin Beechcraft go for major dollars. He may be using his consulting fees to finance it, although they'd have to be pretty hefty fees.

"By a stroke of luck, I learned that he often stays in the Miami area with a suspected Columbian drug dealer. That doesn't prove he's transporting drugs into this area, but it's something to think about."

"You haven't put together a solid evidence trail between Stewart and drugs at this point?" the campus security chief asked.

"No."

"Keep working it.

"Getting back to my recommendations," Pete said, "I want to continue to watch Lombardo closely, looking for possible drug links between Stewart and him."

"How do you want to deal with the threat against professor Prescott?"

"That should be straightforward. Have the administration remove Lombardo from her class and order him not to approach her either on or off the campus. I recommend a court restraining order to take care of that. It's detailed in the report."

"Has he threatened faculty at the other schools he attended?"

"Honestly, chief, I don't know. Detectives at the other campuses have no knowledge of threats against any professors. Of course, that doesn't mean it hasn't happened."

Edwards continued examining the report. "You indicate that the district court in New Jersey issued multiple restraining orders against Lombardo. How many orders were issued? I need specifics."

"Four orders were issued in the last two years, each requiring Lombardo to stay away from female acquaintances. And the women who sought restraining orders against him were at least thirty years old.

"He may have problems with older women," he speculated. "Unfortunately, professor Prescott fits the profile. She's around forty."

"Why aren't those details in this report?" Edwards frowned.

"I didn't think you would want that data in an official report to the dean and the president. It's difficult to keep anything confidential on this campus, as you know. I thought the less said about Lombardo in writing, the better."

Chief Edwards glanced out the window at the clusters of students crossing the campus, heading to lunch in the Student Center. He shrugged finally. "You may be right."

Pete continued, "I suggest we use the detailed information only if Abby Prescott's dean and the president won't agree to remove Lombardo from her class. Call it backup ammunition."

"All right. Anything else I should know that's not in your report?"

"Yes. When I first interviewed Abby Prescott, she had trouble describing precisely the behavior that was so disruptive. She did say that some of the students complained to her privately about his behavior in class. They're angry, and they may feel a bit intimidated by him at the same time. One student moved to another seat to get away from him. The problem with removing Lombardo is that the charges are so vague."

"Those are pretty slim complaints, Pete."

"Still, there's something about Lombardo's behavior—an attitude that irritates students and has upset the professor."

"We don't dismiss students from the university because they've got a bad attitude," Edwards said drily.

"Well, he did make that cryptic remark in her office," Pete reminded him.

"But you said Prescott wasn't terribly upset by it."

"She is not aware of the restraining orders against Lombardo. I think this guy could be a serious threat."

Edwards leaned back in his chair and was silent for several moments.

"Here's what I'll do," he said finally. "I'll ask dean Howard to issue an administrative removal order based on the information about Lombardo's behavior on other campuses. Removing him from Prescott's class should be enough restraint for now; let him continue to attend his other classes."

Although not completely satisfied, Pete decided not to press the matter.

"I'll speak to Cory Howard right away," the chief promised.

"Meantime, continue to keep an eye on Lombardo around campus. Make sure he doesn't approach Prescott. And also quietly watch Rick Stewart. See if there is more than a friendly student-faculty relationship with Lombardo."

Edwards sighed. "If you dig up credible evidence linking them, I'll have a fight on my hands. Stewart is a tenured professor and Lombardo has a powerful father. I'm not sure the president would agree to press charges and alienate a wealthy contributor. The publicity could be brutal."

Pete nodded.

"The dean may be a hard sell because it's unusual to have a student administratively removed for disruptive behavior. It hasn't been done since I came here five years ago. And the dean refused to remove him when professor Prescott initially requested it. He wanted an investigation. Well, I think we've got enough ammunition to remove him from her class now." Edwards closed the file.

"Good work. Keep it up."

Chapter Twenty-One

Dean Cory Howard, his brown bag lunch open on his desk, scowled at the campus security chief seated across his desk.

"I can't remove a student from a class simply because a professor doesn't want to deal with him! How do you define disruptive behavior? Is there more to this matter than you're telling me?" he asked suspiciously.

"Yes. This is between us," Edwards warned. "John Lombardo had several restraining orders issued against him in New Jersey."

"What was the problem?" The dean stared at the campus security chief.

"Stalking. This guy may have a serious problem with women—older women he had personal relationships with. He also had problems at another college, although he was allowed to leave voluntarily. It's not unusual for schools to ease students out to avoid unfavorable publicity, you know."

"Be more specific, Craig," the dean ordered.

"My investigating officer contacted campus security at a school Lombardo attended in Oregon. There may have been drug problems. The sources wouldn't be specific. We just have to read between the lines.

"Lombardo has been a problem in Abby Prescott's class since he arrived in January. I'm only asking you to administratively remove him from her class."

"What about his behavior in other classes?" Howard asked.

"The problem apparently is unique to Prescott's class. Pete Byrnes talked to his other professors. They're not complaining about his behavior. The instructors in his other courses are male, however, which may be significant."

The dean reached for a memo pad and began to write. "You owe me for this, Craig. I've never taken this action before. You'd better have substantial evidence to back up this order if Lombardo appeals it. He has the right to appeal the decision, you know."

"No," Edwards shook his head. "I thought your word was law in the School of Business."

"It's not that simple. A student can appeal almost any administrative decision. If Lombardo appeals, I'll have to form a committee and go through an extensive process to protect his rights."

"But you have to do that only if he appeals the decision. I think he will go quietly."

"Don't count on it," the dean retorted. "This could get messy, especially if I have to bring other students into the situation."

"We can both hope that won't be necessary."

"I'll get a memorandum out later today for delivery to Lombardo and professor Prescott, with a copy to the president. After all, this student is the son of our chairman of the board of trustees."

"I know."

* * *

"John Lombardo will be out of your class tomorrow." Pete delivered the news late in the afternoon as a March nor'easter pummeled the campus.

"You just made my day." Abby's face lit up. "Cory Howard wrote the memo?"

"Yes. Chief Edwards said it took some heavy persuading, but he finally agreed to remove Lombardo from your class. He can attend his other classes, but he won't bother you or your students from now on. Chances are he'll just disappear, although he will still be here on campus," Pete cautioned.

"Thank you for dealing with this. Now I can get that class back on track and enjoy the rest of the semester." Abby leaned back in her office chair, relieved that her ordeal was over.

"The dean's memo was sent this morning by Federal Express to Lombardo's address in Portland. He'll get the message tomorrow. I expect him to be angry, but he won't bother you again. Your copy of the memo should be in your office mailbox.

"I'll stop by your classroom tomorrow morning to make sure he doesn't show up."

"That's not necessary, Pete. I can handle things from now on."

Abby dialed Jen's office. "Good news. Cory Howard just removed Lombardo from my class."

"Outstanding. You must be relieved."

"Right. Meet me at Starbucks to celebrate."

* * *

When Abby entered her class the next day, John Lombardo was seated in his usual place, a smirk on his face. She walked back to his seat.

"I'd like to see you in my office right now," she said.

"I don't think so, professor."

"You are no longer enrolled in this class," she said quietly, below the hubbub of students entering the room.

"Come with me now."

"Really?" Lombardo sneered. Several students paused to watch the exchange. "You're a little behind the times. You complained to the dean, and I got a stupid memo yesterday. Last night president Smythe got a phone call from my father. He agreed that I should continue with this class. Didn't you get the news?"

"No."

"Check your mailbox. The memo is signed by the president, not some lowly dean. Maybe we should call this whole episode 'memogate'," he snickered.

"Come with me to the dean's office. We'll deal with this right now," Abby said.

Lombardo slowly unfolded his legs and sauntered after her, delighted that the rest of the class watched the exchange.

Pete Byrnes intercepted them in the hall. "Good morning, professor. Isn't your class about to begin?"

"Yes. There's been a slight delay. Mr. Lombardo here informs me that a memo reinstating him in my class is in my office mailbox. Care to join us while I check my mail?"

"Who is this guy? This is a private matter between me and the professor." Lombardo glared at Pete.

"I'm detective Byrnes of campus security," he responded calmly. "I'll just walk along with you to the dean's office. Let's see if we can settle this peacefully. I understand you were administratively removed from the professor's class yesterday."

"How do you know that? What has campus security got to do with this problem? As of this morning, I'm back in her class for the rest of the semester. Professor Prescott can't throw me out of her class just because she doesn't like my style."

"What style is that, Mr. Lombardo?" Pete asked.

"Maybe she's feeling insecure because I know more about the subject than she," he sneered.

"I'm asking you again, why is campus security involved in an academic issue between the professor and me?" he asked belligerently.

Pete didn't respond. They walked silently down the hall, turned a corner and entered the School of Business offices. Abby found a single white business envelope in her mailbox. She opened and read the brief message.

She handed the letter to Pete. "He's correct. This memo directs me to readmit him to my class. It's signed by president Smythe and dean Howard."

Pete read it silently.

Abby turned to Lombardo. "I have no choice but to readmit you to class. Let me be perfectly clear. Do not try to disrupt the class or intimidate me. Change your behavior now or I'll have you removed. That's a promise. And Mr. Byrnes is my witness."

"You can't have me removed, professor," Lombardo sneered. He pointed to the memo. "This letter clearly states that I'm in your class for the rest of the semester."

"We'll see."

Abby turned to Pete. "We are going back to class. Would you please schedule a meeting with dean Howard, chief Edwards, president Smythe and both of us as soon as possible."

"Hey, what about me? I should be in that meeting, too," Lombardo protested.

"Not this meeting," Abby retorted.

"Let's try for three o'clock this afternoon, Pete, after my last class."

"I'll take care of it. And then I'll join you in class."

Abby's problem student displayed exemplary behavior during the next seventy-five minutes in her class. Pete Byrnes, quietly seated in the last row, monitored the proceedings.

*   *   *

"Bad news," Pete reported when he met Abby after class. "The president is off campus until next Thursday. That's the first day I could book a meeting for all of us. Meantime, Lombardo will be in your class.

"Until then, I'll attend your class and sit in the back of the room. I've already cleared this with my boss," he assured her.

"Really, that isn't necessary. Lombardo wasn't at all disruptive today. I think my warning changed his behavior."

"I doubt it," Pete said. "My presence in your classroom will keep him under control. And I'll pick up some pointers on organizational behavior," he smiled.

Chapter Twenty-Two

A week later, Abby, Cory Howard, Craig Edwards and Pete Byrnes were ushered into president Roger Smythe's office. Seating themselves on the leather sofa and chairs grouped near the tall windows overlooking Founders Court, they waited for the president to begin.

"Professor Prescott, I understand you want to discuss my decision to reinstate John Lombardo, one of your students, into your class," he began formally.

"Yes, that's correct," she said, outwardly calm. She was ready, having prepared and rehearsed her presentation before the meeting.

"After I called attention to this student's disruptive behavior in my class, detective Byrnes and chief Edwards conducted an independent investigation, which I understand was at your request."

The president nodded agreement.

"Based on their investigation, they recommended that Mr. Lombardo should be removed from my class. Early last week dean Howard issued the necessary administrative removal memorandum and the student was notified. As I understand it, that evening you discussed the matter with Lombardo's father, after which you directed the dean to rescind the removal order," she went on calmly.

"Because we couldn't arrange this meeting for more than a week, Lombardo continues to sit in my class."

"And how would you describe his behavior this past week?" Smythe asked attentively.

"His behavior is fine, presumably because detective Byrnes is sitting in the room observing him."

"Let's back up for a moment, professor. Exactly what is so disturbing about this student's behavior?"

Abby paused, her pulse quickening, tension rising. "Let me explain in detail. From the moment he entered my class late in January, he has tried to dominate the discussion. He constantly interrupts me, challenging me on the content of my lectures."

"I assume you welcome students challenging you in class," Smythe interjected, suppressing a smile.

"When appropriate, of course," she responded evenly. "Although I've never taught in a high school, Lombardo displays the sort of immature 'acting out' that troubled teenagers sometimes engage in. Of course, this student is 25 years old.

"His behavior has alienated the rest of the class. He rudely interrupts students trying to join the discussion. And he ignores my attempts to control him. The class has become chaotic."

Abby reached into her brief case, retrieved a two-page handwritten petition and handed it to the president. "This is a copy of a petition signed by fifteen students asking me to remove Lombardo from the class."

The president glanced at the paper. "Did you invite your students to circulate this petition?"

"Of course not!" she retorted, her voice rising.

Cory Howard stepped in to defend her. "Abby has a superb teaching record. Since joining the faculty six years ago, she has consistently received outstanding student evaluations. She is admired and respected by students and faculty alike. Last spring she was voted the outstanding business school professor by the faculty. I wish more of my faculty were as effective in the classroom."

"I see. That is very high praise, indeed," the president smiled, suddenly charming.

"Apparently, this student has been an unusual challenge for you. I assume you know his father is our chairman of the board of trustees and a major benefactor as well. Your problem presents a delicate situation for the university. It is essential that this issue not damage our relationship with the family."

He paused, his fingers steepled under his chin. "Professor Prescott, I want you to continue teaching John Lombardo for the remainder of the semester. I understand this will be difficult. However, accommodating him is in the best interest of the university."

Abby was silent for several moments. "It's the end of March. You want me to allow him in class for the next two months?" she asked incredulously.

"Yes," the president said firmly.

She stared out the windows overlooking Founders Court, oblivious to the students rushing to late afternoon classes.

"If his father is that important to the university, I don't have much choice, do I?" Abby said, resigned to the inevitable. "Lombardo's presence has destroyed the learning environment for my students and me," she said bitterly.

"His presence isn't the only problem, however."

"What do you mean?" the president frowned.

"His current grade, based on his performance so far this semester, is an F," she explained. "He failed two mid-term objective examinations; given his disruptive behavior, his class participation grade would also be an F. Even if he remains in the class, it's highly unlikely he will pass the course."

"Perhaps his behavior will improve. You say he hasn't been disruptive during the past week," Smythe reminded her.

"That's probably because he knows I'm sitting in the back row watching him," Pete interjected, speaking for the first time.

The president turned to him. "Would you be willing to continue to monitor that class?"

Pete glanced toward his boss. "Consider that your assignment," the security chief said.

"Fine, I'll sit in the class two mornings a week for the next eight weeks."

The president turned to Abby. "I appreciate your cooperation in this very sensitive matter. Thank you."

"You understand that Lombardo is in danger of failing the course?" Abby reiterated.

"Of course, you are completely responsible for evaluating his performance. I'm confident you will issue an appropriate grade," he rose, signaling the end of the meeting.

Taking Abby by the elbow, the president led the group to his office door. "By the way, aren't you coming up for a tenure decision later this spring?" he asked.

"That's correct, Roger," the dean cut in. "She has already received a unanimous recommendation from her department and the School of Business Personnel Committee. I intend to enthusiastically recommend her for tenure and promotion. Abby has an outstanding research record, her teaching is exemplary and she also does more than her share of faculty committee work. She is the business school's strongest candidate for tenure and promotion this year."

Smythe smiled warmly. "That's a very strong endorsement. I'm sure you will handle this matter with your student appropriately."

Bile rose in Abby's throat. She understood exactly the president's meaning. If John Lombardo remained in her class, if she ignored his academic performance and behavior and issued him a passing grade, the president had just virtually assured her promotion and a tenured position at Reid University. She glanced at Pete, not surprised to see him turn away in disgust.

"Well, now," the president said, breaking the awkward silence, "we've accomplished a great deal this afternoon." He opened the office door and shook hands with each of the participants.

Pete Byrnes lingered in the doorway. "May I speak with you for a moment privately, sir?"

"Of course. Chief Edwards, will you join us?"

The men retreated behind the closed door.

"What else is on your mind, Mr. Byrnes?" the president asked.

"On your orders, I was assigned to investigate professor Prescott's problem with Lombardo. The investigation required three weeks of legwork on and off campus. I submitted my report to the chief and we discussed it in detail last week."

"I haven't shared that report with you, Roger," Craig Edwards interrupted, flashing Pete a warning look. Pete ignored him.

"Based on my investigation, I recommended removing Lombardo. When dean Howard agreed, he was aware of several serious issues in my report."

The president frowned. "I see. You prepared a confidential report on Lombardo that has not been forwarded to me."

"Yes," Pete acknowledged.

"Go ahead, summarize the report," Edwards directed resignedly.

Minutes later, the president angrily slapped his hands on the desk.

"This situation is much more serious than I've been led to believe. My decision has been based on incomplete information.

"Withholding your report, for whatever reason, places me in an untenable position with the chairman of the board. I cannot reverse my decision and remove the student from that class without revealing the information in your report."

"President Smythe, some of my information is not evidence that would hold up in court," Pete said. "It may be a coincidence that John Lombardo and one of our faculty members know each other and both are persons of interest in a drug investigation. If we had adequate proof of drug dealings, of course charges would be brought. For now, I have suspicions and need to continue my investigation."

"I see," the president said more calmly. "Name the faculty member you suspect," he directed.

"Sir, that would be premature and could damage his reputation unnecessarily."

Smythe was silent for a moment. "I'll accept that for now, Byrnes," he said reluctantly. "Have you got an action plan?"

"Yes. I'll keep an eye on professor Prescott, both on and off campus. If I'm openly monitoring Lombardo in her class, he may behave until the end of the semester, when she will be finished with him.

"I'm very concerned about the threat Lombardo made in her office. Maybe it was nothing more than idle talk. However, given his record of multiple restraining orders in New Jersey, we can't ignore the possibility of violence."

"Is there some other explanation for his behavior? Is he personally involved with her?" the president asked. "After all, she is rather attractive and unmarried."

Pete smiled. "I'm certain he has no personal relationship with Abby Prescott. I questioned her directly, and she frankly admitted she couldn't stand him.

"She believes Lombardo may have a problem dealing with women in authority," he went on. "His other professors are male and they haven't experienced similar problems.

"She is genuinely desperate to have him removed from her class. Her relationship with him is intensely adversarial now. Although she agreed to allow him to continue in her class, surely you noticed how upset she was. She is well aware that a lot is at stake for the university and for her professionally."

"Do you believe she is in any sort of physical danger?"

Pete was silent for a moment. "I don't know," he said finally.

"Basically I'm relying on past experience in situations like this. Occasionally, a female student will file charges of sexual harassment against a male student. Usually, it boils down to disagreements between two young people who are ending a relationship. Restraining orders in those cases are rarely necessary.

"The situation is different with the professor," Pete said, "because it involves a faculty-student relationship. I doubt that she is in any physical danger, but I can't be certain. It's a judgment call."

"What about the possible drug link between a faculty member and Lombardo? How do you intend to proceed?" the president asked.

"That investigation could take a month or two. Then again, I may get a break next week," he shrugged.

Smythe turned to Craig Edwards. "Do you endorse this action plan?"

"Yes. Pete will work exclusively on these issues. Other officers can cover his routine duties."

"That settles it, then. Keep me informed of any new developments."

* * *

Abby and the dean crossed Founders Court to the School of Business. "Cory, thank you for supporting my promotion and tenure application," she said quietly.

"You've earned it, Abby. Frankly, I was stunned when Roger linked your problems with Lombardo to your promotion."

"Apparently, it's politics as usual," Abby responded, angry and disheartened.

"One thing we learned today. Despite his lack of academic qualifications, John Lombardo was admitted to the university because he is the son of our chairman of the board," said the dean.

"I'm sorry that you've got to deal with him for the next two months. If he fails your course, I promise to support your evaluation. Perhaps this young man will flunk out and fade away."

"Not likely," Abby said resignedly.

Chapter Twenty-Three

Seated in Jen's office an hour later, Abby recounted the details of the meeting.

"Can you believe this? Roger Smythe essentially promised me tenure and promotion if I allow Lombardo to continue in my class and issue an 'appropriate' grade! We both know what that means. I'm expected to pass him regardless of his academic performance," she concluded bitterly.

Jen shook her head, disgusted. "It sounds like the president all but offered you a bribe. Granted, he's very manipulative, but this goes way beyond manipulation. And what a bribe he's offering—tenure and promotion! Are you sure you didn't misunderstand him?"

"Positive. Everyone in that room understood exactly what he meant."

"Abby, you're highly qualified for tenure and promotion without doing the president any favors. Keep in mind, though, Roger completely controls the promotion process."

"I dread the next two months. I hate walking into that class. My heart begins to race, my hands are clammy and I'm emotionally drained by the end of every class. I've never experienced anything like this before. I guess it's a classic fight or flight response."

"You can deal with it," Jen said sympathetically, concerned that her friend was near the breaking point. "With Pete Byrnes sitting in the back of the room you can concentrate on teaching. Ignore Lombardo. Don't let him psych you out."

"I'm more comfortable with Pete in the classroom, that's certain," Abby smiled for the first time. "The students are curious about him. Yesterday, a few came to my office and asked about the stranger in our class."

"What did you tell them?"

"I said he was auditing the course in preparation for a graduate program in human resource management. They seemed satisfied.

"I'm puzzled that my problems with Lombardo apparently haven't arisen in his other classes," she went on. "Maybe he just hates female professors."

"That's possible," Jen agreed. "I'm not a psychologist, but his behavior is really bizarre and he seems obsessed with you.

"By the way, you know the rest of the faculty support you."

"Yes, and I appreciate that. But I'm the one out front dealing with this nut case. Lombardo will be the death of me yet," Abby said gloomily.

Chapter Twenty-Four

Spring arrived late in April. Flowering shrubs displayed brilliant colors and onshore breezes and seventy degree temperatures lured students to the grassy expanses of Founders Court. A brilliant mid-day sun and azure sky transformed the Atlantic into a blinding sheet of sparkling diamonds.

The Student Center overflowed with boisterous students soaking up the warm sun on the wide terrace above the cliffs overlooking the sea. Jen and Abby, sandwiches and bottled water in hand, waited patiently until two students vacated an outside table.

"What is the academic status of your problem student now? Is Lombardo going to pass your course?" Jen asked, settling into her chair.

"He's currently failing with very little time to turn things around. All that is left are the final objective examination and a ten-page research paper that is due the last day of classes. If he does well on both, he conceivably could pass the course with a D."

"Is that likely?"

Abby shrugged. "Not based on his past performance. Don't misunderstand, Jen, I hope he passes the course. I don't look forward to issuing a failing grade and having to justify it to Cory Howard or president Smythe."

"Is he behaving himself in class?"

"Yes. I've had surprisingly few problems since Pete began monitoring the class. Lombardo sulks, but at least he's quiet. That's fine with me. The class has slowly come alive. The other students simply ignore him. I'm actually enjoying the class again."

"Bring me up to date on your tenure and promotion application. What's happening there?" Jen asked.

"It's slowly moving through the process. The dean gave me a copy of his recommendation, which was very positive. The recommendations from the various committees and supporting documentation were sent to the president's office last week. There won't be a decision until early June. The board of trustees deals with those decisions during graduation weekend. My future at Reid University currently is in Roger Smythe's hands."

"In my twenty years on this campus, the trustees have never rejected anyone the president recommended," Jen told her.

"I really want to build my career here. The faculty is first rate, the campus is beautiful, and the students, except for Lombardo, are a joy to teach. I'd love to settle down here for the rest of my life," Abby confessed.

"I'm confident you will be approved," Jen reassured her. "After your promotion is announced, I'll give you a party to celebrate. We'll invite your friends, the faculty—even Roger Smythe and his wife.

"Speaking of friends, Rob and I saw you and Pete walking along the waterfront in Portland last Saturday night. You seemed totally absorbed in each other. Want to tell me about it?" Jen invited.

Abby smiled noncommittally. "It's not serious, at least not yet. We both enjoy art films and good food. Although it may seem out of character for a security guy, he's a very good cook. We've had dinner at his apartment a couple of times. I haven't invited him to my house yet, although he stopped by a few times on weekends, checking to see that I'm okay."

"What do you know about him?"

"Not a lot. He's from Boston and has an undergraduate degree in criminal justice from Northeastern University. He joined the Massachusetts National Guard in college, and served fifteen months in Iraq after he graduated. He was wounded by shrapnel when an IED hit his Hummer. He's currently unattached, although he apparently had a serious relationship that ended a year ago."

"Is he damaged goods—psychologically, I mean?"

"Let's not go there," Abby warned. "Pete has been very supportive during the past couple months, and I feel more secure knowing he's nearby. Of course, that's his assignment."

Jen regarded her friend quizzically.

"I don't know where this might lead," Abby confessed after a pause. "For now, it's enough to have someone around who is relaxing and enjoys the same things I do. He may walk away in June when Lombardo is out of my class."

"I doubt that, Abby. This sounds serious. You've been holding out on me!" Jen teased. "At least now you have someone to share good times with, even if it doesn't lead to anything serious. Forget your problem student. Kick back now and then."

"We're going sailing this weekend, if the weather holds. Pete has a twenty-seven foot Hunter that he wants to show off," Abby confided.

"Sounds like fun."

They vacated the table, deposited their trash in containers and walked back to their offices.

Chapter Twenty-Five

They left Seal Point harbor Sunday morning under cloudless skies. Jeans, heavy sweaters and windbreakers protected them from a brisk, six-knot breeze. Pete Byrnes, relaxed and in his element, adroitly maneuvered his Hunter 27 among the dozen or so craft headed out to sea.

"What a beautiful day for sailing," Abby exclaimed.

"I've been waiting for a day like this for the past six months. The Folly went into winter storage late last October. It's great to be on the water again," Pete said.

"Where are we headed?"

"Down east for a couple hours with the wind, then we'll find a protected cove near shore and eat lunch. We'll start back around three o'clock, which should give us plenty of time to reach Seal Point before dark."

Abby settled back on the rear cushion, bundled up against the cool April wind, sunglasses shading her eyes from the brilliant sun. She watched Pete handle the boat with the ease of an expert sailor. A sailor since childhood along coastal Connecticut, she relaxed.

"Let me know if you want help with the sails."

"Relax, Abby. You're my guest, along for the ride. I know the past month has been difficult for you. Let's not discuss work, just enjoy the day."

"That's a deal," she smiled, facing the brilliant sun in the eastern sky. Two hours later, she went forward and set the anchor in a protected cove thirty yards from shore.

"Would you hand up the picnic hamper from below? And don't forget the wine in the fridge," Pete asked.

Abby climbed down the ladder into the narrow cabin, passed the large hamper to Pete, opened the compact refrigerator and selected a bottle of California sauvignon blanc. She rummaged through a drawer beside the sink, found a corkscrew and passed the wine to Pete through the open hatch. Reaching for two plastic wineglasses, she clambered topside.

"What's for lunch,?" she asked.

"Nothing fancy. Chicken sandwiches, macaroni salad, fruit, and some oatmeal raisin cookies I baked last night. And I didn't forget the paper napkins," he grinned.

"What a feast! I can't believe I found a sailor who cooks! I'm starved. Let's eat."

Using the picnic hamper as a table, she arranged the food and utensils, while Pete opened the bottle and poured the wine.

"Sailing brings out the appetite in everyone," he observed. "It's the combination of ocean air, sun, and water."

They touched glasses and settled back to eat.

"I haven't asked whether you're on duty today or if you're my new best buddy," Abby remarked.

"Today is definitely personal time," he said decisively, reaching for more salad. "And I thought I was more than your buddy."

"You are more than a buddy," Abby affirmed softly. "We've been together so often, I'm not sure where your official duties end and our personal time begins."

"I've spent more time with you in the last six weeks than with my poker buddies on the security force. And your company is a lot more interesting," he smiled.

"However, Abby Prescott, you're a professor and I'm only a campus security guy. Some faculty and staff probably would frown on our little outing today," he said more seriously.

"Pete, don't belittle the importance of your work on campus," Abby chided him. "You and the others in security are essential to creating a safe environment for students and faculty. And your job doesn't go away at five o'clock every evening. I admire the professional way you go about your job." Her smile lightened her serious words.

"Until the problem with Lombardo came up, I never thought much about campus security," she mused. "I can't thank you enough for your support these last six weeks," she said. "You're my protector, the guy covering my back. I wouldn't have survived without you." She regarded him pensively over her wineglass, her sunglasses nestled in her thick dark hair."

"Thank you, madam, for those kind words," Pete said, embarrassed. "We aim to please."

"By the way, I don't care what others think of my personal relationships. I date whomever I want. Actually, this may not be a real date. Maybe I'm just being safely stowed away from campus for a few hours."

"I consider it a real date," Pete responded evenly. "After all, I made the lunch, it's my boat, and you're all alone with me."

They laughed together, relaxed and comfortable.

"You know, Abby, you haven't told me much about yourself or your life before Reid University. I admit I checked out your bio on the School of Business web site."

"Aha, you've been spying on me!"

"Not exactly," he protested. "It's a public web site available at the click of a mouse. Besides, I wanted to know more about you."

"What did you learn?"

"Let's see," he said, "you grew up in Greenwich, Connecticut and graduated from Bowdoin College with an degree in American Lit before you went to Harvard. You picked up an MBA degree from Harvard Business School, then went to work with one of those big consulting firms, probably earning major bucks."

"I'll give you an A so far," Abby said. "But that doesn't say much about who I really am."

"Okay, tell me more," he invited. "Why did you leave what must have been a lucrative consulting career to come to coastal Maine?"

She was silent for a moment, her gaze fixed on a lone seagull soaring near the rocky shore. "The answer to that is easy," she said softly. "I left consulting because I was burned out from the constant travel and the seventy hour work weeks. I didn't have a life outside of work. Unfortunately, I thought I could manage both a demanding career and a marriage."

Pete was silent, startled by her frankness. He reached for the wine and refilled her glass.

"The five years I spent in consulting were not all bad," she went on. "I learned a lot about how companies are organized and managed. As a consultant in human resource management, I led teams that designed benefits programs for Fortune 500 companies. I dealt with issues like health care benefits and stock options programs.

"That experience has been invaluable in my teaching. I bring examples of issues into the classroom that make the subject come alive for my students, at least I hope so."

"You mentioned marriage. If it's not too personal, what is that about?" Pete asked quietly.

"It's not personal anymore. My marriage ended a long time ago. We simply drifted apart, had different careers, different interests. He was a research scientist working in a government laboratory outside Washington. I worked out of the Washington office of my firm, but I was seldom in the office. I would fly out on assignment to a client early Monday morning and return home late Friday or early Saturday. Then I had to decompress from work. By Sunday night, I'd wound down just in time for the cycle to begin again.

"Given my obsession with work, it's not surprising that my ex finally found someone else. Chris and I were married only three years. Thank God, we didn't have children, although I love kids. We had a fairly amicable divorce and went our separate ways.

"In retrospect, I realize that my life during those years was much too hectic. Frankly, between work and the divorce, I nearly had a nervous breakdown."

Pete pulled her close. She settled into his arms, faced away from him, gazed across the water, her head resting against his down vest.

"One positive outcome of those years is that I earned a very good salary which I didn't have time to spend," she continued. "I invested my money aggressively—I'm a risk taker in the stock market. Of course, the internet bubble helped—and with impeccable timing, I cashed out before the bubble burst," she said with a touch of pride. "I'm probably one of the few people who actually made tons of money during the bubble and managed to hold onto most of it. Now I can afford to teach here on an assistant professor's salary."

She was silent for a while, her thoughts far away. Pete waited patiently.

"Changing careers probably saved my life," she admitted. "I went back to Harvard for a few years while I worked on my doctorate, and taught part time. I discovered that I really enjoyed being in the classroom. The intellectual stimulation from the academic portion of the program at Harvard was comparable to my consulting assignments, but without the insane pressure. I took a couple of years to research and write my dissertation. They were good years, time that allowed me to heal emotionally.

"I already had plenty of money, but I continued investing, this time more conservatively, while I worked on my dissertation. Now I have financial reserves that will carry me the rest of my life, despite the current turmoil in the market. Living in Seal Point, Maine isn't expensive compared to Boston or Washington. I can afford to teach and still enjoy a lifestyle that's beyond the reach of most faculty."

"Now I understand how you can afford a beautiful house overlooking the ocean. Your home in Seal Point must be worth big bucks," Pete said.

"Yes," she admitted. "It's in a million dollar location and the contemporary design is unusual—not at all like a traditional Maine house. And I actually love the solitude."

"Your property is beautiful, but isolated. That's why I keep an eye on you out there by the ocean. I'll continue to do that until Lombardo is out of your class."

"I can't wait for the end of the semester," Abby confessed.

Pete decided to change the subject. "You know, I could use some investing advice with my pension money, or what's left of it after the financial crisis."

"I'm available," she offered. "And my fees will be quite reasonable." She turned her head and looked into his dark eyes, and then settled back against his shoulder.

"Now that I've given you a capsule version of my life, what about you? Tell me about yourself and your family. I know you grew up in Boston and graduated from Northeastern University, then you began working at Reid until your National Guard unit was called up and you went to Iraq."

"Those are the essentials," Pete said. "As for my family, my parents died years ago. I have two brothers and a sister. My brothers are all more successful than I. We don't get together very often."

"Pete, I'm beginning to sense you seriously undervalue your work in campus security," she said softly.

"Let's be honest. The campus is loaded with people with doctorates, most of whom consider campus security a necessary evil. You're an exception. You deal with staff people professionally. Many faculty believe the staff exists to serve them."

"That's not true," Abby protested. "It doesn't reflect the attitudes of many faculty. In consulting, I learned that if you want to know what's really going on in a company, you gain the confidence of the midlevel staff. The executives tell you only what they want you to know. They're often more interested in protecting their positions than in dealing with problems. It's much more political in the business world than on this campus, at least that's my observation.

"Now let's get back to your family and what life was like growing up in Boston."

"There's not much to tell, actually," Pete said. "We lived in a triple-decker in a typical Irish neighborhood in South Boston. My dad died when I was ten. He was a steel worker; a crane killed him in an industrial accident. Mom got a little money in a legal settlement but the lawyers took most of that. She landed a job as a waitress in one of the Harvard Square restaurants in Cambridge, riding the subway to and from work. She had a heart attack and died while I was in college.

"I went to high school at Boston College High School, did okay academically, played football and got a partial scholarship to Northeastern. Between a work-study program at NU and the scholarship, I earned my degree in Criminal Justice.

"My older brother, Ned, also went to BC High School. He's the brains in the family. He landed an academic scholarship to Princeton; now he's an investment banker in New York. I rarely see him. He's way out of my league."

He was silent for a few moments. Abby waited patiently for him to continue.

"My younger brother, Jack, never went to college," he resumed. "He joined the air force right out of high school and made a career of it. He's a Master Sergeant now, with a wife and three kids. Jack was stationed in Kuwait during the Iraq war and we managed a couple of visits while I was in Iraq. We keep in touch occasionally by email; right now he's stationed in Germany. I haven't seen him in more than five years.

"My sister, Mary, got married right out of high school and moved to South Carolina to her husband's home town. I don't even have her address any more.

"You see, Abby, I'm a loner," he confessed. "I just do my job, play poker with my buddies, go hiking occasionally and spend as much time as I can on this boat. Being on the water is therapy, my way of dealing with the stress of my job."

The two were silent, enjoying the solitude broken only by the cries of seagulls overhead. He glanced at the sun descending slowly toward the western shore.

"We probably should head back. I want to dock before sunset."

Together, they stowed the empty wine bottles and trash in the picnic hamper and climbed down to the cabin below.

"Excuse the close quarters down here," Pete said apologetically. "Two can live aboard quite comfortably, but only if they're very good friends," he said, his hands on Abby's waist, squeezing past her.

Abby touched his cheek and kissed him lightly. He drew back, a question in his eyes.

Cupping his face in her hands, she drew him closer. Her next kiss was an invitation he didn't ignore.

Chapter Twenty-Six

They furled the sails and motored slowly into Seal Point harbor at dusk. Pete maneuvered into his slip and together they secured the boat. Pete retrieved the picnic hamper and with a final look around, locked the cabin door.

Minutes later he pulled into Abby's driveway and stopped in front of the garage.

"Would you like to come in?" she invited.

"Sure."

She unlocked the side door leading into the kitchen and flipped on the lights. "There's not much food in the fridge. We can order up a pizza from Romeo's and I've got plenty of wine," she said, pointing to the built-in wine cooler. "It won't compare to the feast you prepared for lunch, of course."

"Sounds good to me."

Pete glanced around the kitchen. "You don't have an alarm system in this house?" he asked.

"No. The house was built without one. And I don't need an elaborate alarm system. I'm a mile out of Seal Point Center at the end of the road. There's nothing but rocky cliffs and the Atlantic between here and Europe. I'm perfectly safe here."

He processed the information silently.

"Let me phone in a pizza order." She reached for the phone. "We can have a glass of wine while we're waiting for the pizza guy, and I'll show you the rest of the house."

Pete gazed around the sleek kitchen, admiring the granite countertops and high-end appliances. He would love to cook in this kitchen. A picture window in the breakfast nook faced west toward a dense stand of balsam fir trees marking the end of the property. On the horizon, brilliant splashes of mauve colored the cumulus clouds, signaling the end of a day he would long remember.

"How old is this house, Abby?"

"Twelve years. I bought it six years ago from a couple who retired to Florida. I made some changes, enlarged and modernized the kitchen, and added the breakfast nook.

"Come into the living room," she invited, leading him out of the kitchen and into the large living room. A glass dining table and four chairs occupied one end of the room. "Too bad it's nearly dark. The view is spectacular. Of course, if you hang around long enough, the moon will rise right there," she said, pointing out the wall of glass to the ocean beyond. "I love watching the moon rise out of the sea.

"On the other side of the house, I converted one bedroom into a study, tore out an entire wall, built in some bookcases and installed sliding glass doors connecting the deck off the living room. I can enjoy the ocean view while I work. Beyond the study is the master suite, and a separate guest room—plenty of space for me.

"I love the contemporary design and beamed ceilings—even in the master bedroom. Perhaps I'm compensating for all those years living in cramped apartments in Boston and Washington."

"This place is spectacular," Pete remarked, impressed. "From the outside, your house blends into the landscape so well that most people would have no idea how beautiful it is. My little apartment in Portland is a slum compared to this."

"But the dinner you prepared last week was a gourmet feast," Abby reminded him. "I can barely boil water. It's not a lot of fun cooking for myself. Maybe you'll come over some night and prepare another gourmet meal, this time in my kitchen."

"That's a deal. How about next weekend?" He suggested, eyes sparkling.

"Fine. Come out in the afternoon and spend the evening. You prepare a shopping list and I'll get the groceries. You'll be in charge of cooking," she warned.

"Are you serious?"

"Of course. Now, there's a Pinot Noir in the wine rack. How about popping the cork?"

*   *   *

Seated on the Oriental rug in front of the fireplace, they finished the pizza and emptied the second bottle of wine. Pete made a halfhearted move to leave. "It's getting late and I have the early shift tomorrow. Up at five, work out for an hour in the Athletic Center, then go on duty at seven o'clock. Of course, I'll be sitting in your Tuesday class as usual."

"Pete, you never explained how you spend your time at the university when you're not hanging out in my class. What is your normal day like?" Abby asked, curious.

He settled back against the beige leather sofa. "My job is pretty intense right now. I'm leading a three-person team working a possibly serious drug investigation. Of course, we are no different than other university campuses. Students do drugs and alcohol. The challenge is to keep it under control.

"Alcohol abuse is far more serious than drugs," he said. "Too many students take Thursday night off and get wasted on alcohol. In fact, Thursday night binge drinking is popular on campuses across the country."

"So that's why Friday classes are lightly attended," Abby laughed. "Students are sleeping off hangovers. I'm glad my classes meet on Tuesdays and Thursdays."

"We don't see much coke, heroin or meth here, at least not so far," he continued. "A fair number of students use pot, which we consider a minor violation as long as the student is not into dealing. When we identify students dealing pot, we haul them in, read them the riot act and threaten to turn them over to the Portland police. Usually, a good scare is enough."

Pete stifled a yawn, gathered up the glasses and headed for the kitchen. He reached for his down vest and Abby walked him to the kitchen door. "I'll look forward to spending an afternoon and evening out here next Saturday, if you are serious about letting me play in your gourmet kitchen."

"It's a date. You'd better leave before I bribe you to stay longer. Tomorrow is an early day for you." There was unspoken promise in their goodnight kiss. She watched him back down the driveway and turn toward the center of town.

Neither noticed a darkened car parked off the road at the edge of the cliffs fifty yards away.

* * *

"How was your weekend, Abby?"
"Fantastic. Pete and I went sailing on Sunday."

"Nice," Jen Carpenter nodded approvingly. "Come clean. Do I detect more than a casual friendship developing here?"

"Maybe." Abby shrugged noncommittally.

"When we got back to the dock around sundown, I invited him to the house for pizza. We spent the evening together."

"I hope this leads to something good for both of you," Jen said warmly. "Since Pete began monitoring your class, you're much more relaxed, more like your old self. And he seems like a nice guy. He's really good looking and obviously is taking good care of you."

"Easy, Jen. I've just had a couple of casual dates with him," Abby laughed. "I'll admit we learned a lot about each other on Sunday. I gave him an abbreviated version of my life story, including my divorce. It didn't seem to scare him off. If anything, he relaxed a bit more with me. I do believe he's a little intimidated by my position on campus."

"A little romance in your life may be just what the doctor ordered. In another month the president will recommend you for tenure and promotion, you'll have a permanent position at the university, and you'll be rid of your problem student. Things are looking up."

"I'm glad you're so confident about my promotion. But my problem with Lombardo could get messy. He's probably going to fail my course," she confided.

"Stop obsessing," Jen advised. "In a few weeks he'll get the grade he deserves, and be out of your life."

Chapter Twenty-Seven

"Pete! I need you! Lombardo just learned he failed my course. He's crazy—out of control. He screamed and cursed me over the phone. He's on his way to my office right now! I'm afraid to be alone with him."

"Calm down, Abby," he said firmly. "You can deal with him. I can't get back to campus right now; I'm on the outskirts of Portland." Cellphone in his left hand, he floored the unmarked patrol car and headed for an exit half a mile away.

"Ask Cory Howard to sit in on the meeting," he suggested. "Lombardo won't act up with the dean present."

Abby interrupted, "I already phoned the dean's office. Cory's out of town," she said, panic rising.

"Then get Jen to sit in on the meeting. Lombardo can't be too threatening if you're not alone," he spoke reassuringly.

"That should work," she agreed after a pause, beginning to calm. "She was in her office a few minutes ago."

"I'll be back around five o'clock. I'll come to your office. Let's have dinner together, my treat."

"Thanks."

Abby hung up, dashed down the hall, and entered Jen's office without knocking. Seated at her computer, she was absorbed in transmitting final grades to the Registrar's office.

"Jen, can you take a break and sit in my office for the next hour or so? Lombardo just learned that he failed my course," she explained. "He phoned me, completely out of control, ranting and raving about his grade, screaming that he was coming to my office right now. I don't want to be alone with him." She paced the floor nervously.

"Of course. Relax, Abby." Jen closed her laptop and reached for her coat. "If he shows up, I'll insist on staying while you review his grade. Don't let him intimidate you."

Jen locked her office door and they walked down the hall to Abby's office.

Moments later Lombardo barged into the office.

"I need to speak to you about my grade," he said, breathing heavily.

"I'm just making tea for professor Carpenter and myself. Would you like to join us?" Abby calmly turned her back and reached for another cup.

"No," he snarled.

"I don't think we've met," Jen interrupted.

"I need to speak to my professor alone," he glared, ignoring Jen's outstretched hand.

"Then you can wait outside until we finish our tea," she said mildly.

"I'm not leaving this office until she changes my grade to a B," he retorted, his voice rising.

Jen casually placed herself between Abby and the angry student. "Why don't you just take a seat?" she said. "I'm sure professor Prescott will be glad to explain your grade."

"I'll stand," he scowled.

"Relax," Abby pointed to the chair beside her desk, "and I'll explain why you earned an F in Organization Behavior. Unless you can offer compelling reasons to change your grade, it will remain an F." She projected a calm exterior she didn't feel.

Lombardo sat, folded his arms and crossed his legs. "You made a mistake," he said belligerently.

"No, John. Your failing grade accurately reflects your performance in this course."

"Prove it."

"First, you failed both midterm examinations," she began, "and last week you failed the final examination. Your average in those three examinations was fifty-three percent. As you know, a passing grade in this course is sixty percent."

"Well, I almost passed the exams," he retorted.

"What about the research paper I submitted? It's supposed to be worth fifteen percent of the final grade and I know it was a great paper. I should have at least a B in this course," he shouted, growing more agitated.

"Yes, the paper you submitted actually was rather well done," Abby said mildly. "However, you didn't write that research paper. The paper was purchased from a term paper source on the internet. You plagiarized a project worth fifteen percent of your grade. Therefore, you received a zero for the paper."

"You're wrong, professor." He jumped up and leaned over the desk. "I didn't copy that paper off the internet."

"Yes, you did. I found precisely that paper reproduced verbatim on a well-known web site that sells research papers to college students for a fee. You paid $100 for the paper, and I can prove every statement I've just made.

"Plagiarism is a very serious form of cheating," she went on. "If proven, it is grounds for dismissal from the university. I haven't filed charges against you with the appropriate university committee. Instead, I assigned a grade of F in the course. I suggest you retake the course this summer. Given your actions here today, however, I'm tempted to rescind my decision and bring this entire sordid matter to the attention of dean Howard, the head of the School of Business."

"Fuck you," he screamed, towering over Abby. "I want a B! This isn't over. My father will hear about this."

"That last remark is very immature, John. Take responsibility for your actions; let this be a lesson and learn from it. You're getting off lightly with an F."

Abby looked up at Lombardo, hands folded, outwardly calm, her heart racing.

"Go to summer school, take the course with another instructor. You can use a course replacement option to insert a better grade, that is, assuming you pass the course."

"You *will* change this grade to a B, or else," Lombardo screamed, spit escaping his lips.

"Or else what, John? Are you threatening me?" For the first time, Abby lost her poise.

Jen sat silently observing the exchange. Now she'd heard enough. She rose and opened the office door. "Mr. Lombardo, this discussion is over. Leave now," she ordered, her hand on the doorknob.

"I'm not going anywhere until she changes my grade." he shrieked, striding angrily toward Jen, who didn't budge.

"Young man, you've got ten seconds to leave this office before I phone campus security," she said icily.

Without another word, he stalked out the door. "Fuck! You bitches haven't seen the last of me!"

Jen closed the office door in his face and checked the lock.

"Whew. Are you okay?" she turned to Abby.

"I think so," she said shakily. "Now you see what I've been dealing with for the past four months."

"That student clearly has some anger management problems," Jen spoke calmly, trying to smile. "It's over, Abby. You won't have to deal with him again."

"I hope so, Jen," she shuddered. "I'm not changing his grade, no matter what strings he pulls with the administration or how influential his father is. Cory Howard promised to back me on this one."

"He will. It doesn't take much academic courage to back a professor who issues an F to a student who not only fails his examinations, but also plagiarizes an important research paper and disrupts a class. Lombardo can't successfully appeal that grade to the dean or anyone else."

*   *   *

"What happened?" Pete Byrnes strode into the office as the two women prepared to leave.

"Abby handled Lombardo very well, Pete. She can go over the details," Jen said over her shoulder, leaving the office and closing the door. Abby settled back and relatively calmly related every detail of the confrontation.

"Damn, I'm really sorry I wasn't here, Abby. I would have made short work of his bullying."

"That's okay. Jen was great, probably stronger than the dean would have been. She basically kicked him out of my office.

"I'm afraid Lombardo might follow up on his threat, Pete. He said I haven't seen the last of him, whatever that means."

"He won't bother you again. Let's have dinner; then I'll follow you home and check out the area," he said, "although he probably doesn't know where you live. We can eat out, or I can cook and then spend the evening with you, if you don't have other plans."

"I have a little more grading to do, but it can wait," said Abby, brightening at the prospect of an evening with him. "Let's pick up some groceries on the way home, you cook and we'll watch the moonrise together."

"That's the best offer I've had since our pizza and wine last month."

They left the building, walked across Founders Court to the parking garage. Taking separate cars, they stopped at Seal Point's well-stocked grocery store and then continued to Abby's Ocean Lane home. Pete parked his SUV in her driveway and scanned the area around her property. Fifty yards beyond her house, the paved road dead-ended at the cliffs. The area was deserted. The dense woods marking the western boundary of her land also appeared deserted in the gathering dusk. He would find an excuse to explore those woods on another visit.

Pete grilled the steaks while Abby prepared salad and asparagus. An hour later, seated at the dining table in the alcove off the living room, they finished their espresso under the soft glow of candlelight.

"Feel better, now?" he asked.

"Much better. Of course, wine always relaxes me," she said, carrying dishes to the kitchen and loading the dishwasher. She dimmed the lights and returned to the living room. Standing beside him near the sliding glass doors, they watched a full moon rise on the eastern horizon.

Pete took Abby into his arms and kissed her gently. He leaned back, searching her face in the dim light. She put her arms around his waist. "I know it's not the weekend and you have to get up early for work. Still, would you like to stay the night?" she whispered.

"I thought you'd never ask." They headed for the bedroom.

* * *

Absorbed in each other, they failed to notice the lone figure at the edge of the woods, watching until the lights in the bedroom were extinguished. An hour later, Lombardo boldly circled the rear of the house, checking for evidence of an alarm system, and quietly walking onto the deck, noting the design and lock system on the sliding glass doors stretching across the thirty-foot living room. Then he made his way through the thick forest near the house to his BMW parked beside an access road a mile away. Less than an hour later he drove into the underground garage beneath his condo overlooking Portland harbor.

Chapter Twenty-Eight

"The dean will see you now." Cory Howard's administrative assistant smiled and opened the door to his office.

"How are you?" he greeted Abby cordially, leading her to a chair beside his desk.

"Fine," she said coolly.

She seated herself and opened the slim folio she had brought.

"First, let me say I regret being out of town last week when you had a rather difficult encounter with your problem student."

"Difficult encounter is an understatement," Abby said calmly. "It was an ugly confrontation. Fortunately, Jen Carpenter sat in on the meeting, witnessed the entire episode and finally ordered Lombardo out of my office. He left only after she threatened to have him forcibly removed by campus security. I believe she sent you a memo summarizing the incident."

"This was a most unfortunate incident. Jen indicated that you continue to feel somewhat threatened by this young man."

"Yes."

"Now that the semester has ended, I'm confident you won't be dealing with him again," the dean assured her.

"I certainly hope not," she said. "Cory, I believe he has serious anger management problems. He's mentally on the edge."

"I understand," Howard said sympathetically. "I presume his outburst occurred because he was disappointed in his failing grade."

"Exactly. When student grades were posted on the university computer system, he went ballistic, demanding that I change his grade to a B."

"Please continue. I'd like to hear your assessment of the entire episode."

"During our confrontation, I calmly summarized his performance over the entire semester. He failed every evaluation measure in the course—exams, research paper and class participation. Further, he plagiarized his research paper. I probably should have filed charges of academic dishonesty and recommended his dismissal from the university."

"Tell me more about his term paper. How did you discover he plagiarized it?"

"The paper was very well written and documented with detailed footnotes and a bibliography. I was suspicious because Lombardo's writing skills were mediocre at best in the examinations I administered in class.

"So I Googled a few key phrases on the internet. Sure enough, my search went directly to a web site specializing in term papers. Students who don't feel like doing the research and writing a paper can go online and buy one. Lombardo's paper was a verbatim copy of one that was selling for $100. There's no question that he plagiarized."

"You know, Abby, our academic standards provide severe sanctions for plagiarism. A failing grade is probably a minimal penalty under the circumstances. I support your decision. Lombardo obviously didn't earn a passing grade."

Abby was relieved. Despite Jen's assurances that the dean would support her, she was not convinced he would defend her if the matter reached the president's office.

"Cory, after I stood firm on his grade, Lombardo simply wouldn't accept my decision."

"Exactly how did he threaten you? Do you remember his exact words?"

"Yes. I won't forget his words, especially since he also made a threatening remark to me during the semester."

"I recall your earlier concern," the dean said.

"His exact words this time were 'you'll change this grade to a B, professor, or else.' He used a very threatening tone. The 'or else' comment prompted me to ask if he were threatening me. Then Jen interrupted and ordered him out of the office."

"As you relate it to me now, Abby, it doesn't seem terribly threatening," Howard said.

"Perhaps you're right. But during the confrontation, his aggressiveness made me very uncomfortable. John Lombardo has a ferocious temper. He is tall and strong and he can seem very threatening. Maybe he's on drugs. Whatever. I'm convinced he needs counseling of one form or another."

"Let's not attribute his behavior to drug use," the dean chided. "You have no evidence to support that."

"Be realistic, Cory," she retorted, "students everywhere use recreational drugs. This university is no exception."

The dean was silent for a moment. "Abby, this matter has reached the president," he revealed finally. "Lombardo's father contacted Roger Smythe last evening. I've been directed to discuss this issue with you."

"Oh, great," Abby shook her head. "Do you think this problem will affect the president's decision on my tenure and promotion?"

"No. When I explain the entire episode as you've related it to me, I'm sure he'll support you fully."

"When will I be notified of the tenure decision?" she asked.

"The trustees meet next weekend just before graduation exercises. They will vote on all tenure and promotion recommendations; the decisions will be made public the following week. It won't be long now, Abby. I'm looking forward to your contributions as a faculty member for many years to come." The dean offered his most engaging and confident smile.

"Thank you. I appreciate your support."

*   *   *

"How did your meeting with Cory Howard go?" Jen inquired late that afternoon.

"Surprisingly well. I was prepared for a struggle. When I explained my reasons for issuing the failing grade, he agreed that Lombardo deserved to fail the course. That should be the end of it."

"Excellent. Now, did he offer any information about the status of your tenure and promotion application?"

"The board of trustees is scheduled to act on my application at their meeting during commencement weekend. He seems very confident the trustees will approve it."

"More good news. Congratulations, it won't be long now," Jen said, "and I've promised a faculty party for you after the decision is announced."

"That would be fun. I'll be ready to celebrate."

"Have you plans for the summer? I hope you're taking a break. It's been a tough semester."

"Yes. Pete and I are tentatively planning a three week hiking and camping trip to Colorado in July. We're going camping and hiking near Mount Katahdin in June, a warm-up for the Rockies. We enjoy hiking almost as much as sailing."

"Sounds good. It's beginning to look like you and Pete are a couple." Jen observed, inviting a response.

"We've been seeing each other several times a week, either at his place or mine, but don't make too much of that," Abby warned. "I don't know where this relationship is headed. For now, I'm enjoying the ride."

Chapter Twenty-Nine

"You're telling me that Abby Prescott refused to change Lombardo's grade to a B?" The president didn't bother to conceal his anger.

"That's correct, and I agree with her," the dean said firmly. "Her decision was based on an objective evaluation of his performance," he continued, summarizing the reasons for the failing grade, including Lombardo's latest crude attempt to bully her.

"Granted, the incident in her office last week was unfortunate. Nevertheless, she's got to change that grade," the president insisted.

"Roger, the grade should stand," Cory protested. "It's academically dishonest to issue anything but an F in this case."

"You don't understand what's at stake here."

"Apparently not," the dean sat back, stunned by the president's reaction.

"What I'm about to tell you is confidential. It cannot leave this office."

"Fine." Never part of the president's inner circle, the business school dean was surprised and curious.

"At commencement ceremonies two weeks from now the university will award an honorary doctorate to Robert Lombardo, this student's father. And at the Commencement Dinner the evening before, the Lombardo Family Foundation will present the largest gift in the university's history."

"Now, I'm beginning to understand," Cory said. "How much are they pledging?"

"A total of $90 million over the next five years, enough to immediately build and equip our new Environmental Sciences building and endow two academic chairs, one in Marine Biology, the other in Environmental Studies."

"Wow! Congratulations." Cory reached across the desk to shake the president's hand.

"Thank you. Now you understand why John Lombardo's grade must be changed. Otherwise, the funds may not be forthcoming."

"Really?" The dean was incredulous.

The president leaned forward. "Bob Lombardo called me yesterday about his son's academic performance, and specifically about this failing grade. I checked the grade on the computer and if this F is not changed to at least a C, and preferably a B, Lombardo will be on academic probation next fall. He earned a D in American Lit, a B in Environmental Studies and this F in Organization Behavior. His grade point average for his first semester is below a 2.0."

"That's a very weak academic record for his first semester on campus," the dean observed.

"I agree. His father is not at all pleased with the situation. He bluntly directed me to change the failing grade or delete it from his record completely."

"Roger, you know that grade changes must be initiated by the faculty member and Abby Prescott won't change that grade. Also, grades are never deleted from a student's record at Reid." Cory suddenly realized where the conversation was heading.

"These are extraordinary circumstances," the president retorted. "We have a $90 million pledge in hand that will change the future of this university. I cannot jeopardize this gift because a junior faculty member refuses to change a grade."

"Sorry, Roger, I can't go back to Abby again. That grade is fair and justified. It should stand."

"You don't need to go back to her."

"Why not?" Cory asked.

The president leaned forward. "You're the dean. You can change that grade from an F to a B directly. You know the computer access codes. Just do it. Prescott probably won't bother to review her grade records again. And the university will have a $90 million gift."

The dean took a deep breath. "If I understand you correctly, you're ordering me to override Lombardo's grade without Abby's knowledge or approval."

"That is putting it rather crudely," the president chided. "However, it's the bottom line." He leaned back. "I don't enjoy bending academic standards, but in this case it is absolutely necessary."

"The standards are being violated, not bent," the dean retorted, "and the entire School of Business faculty will be furious if this becomes public. Of course, I could tell Abby that you ordered me to do it."

The president eyed him coldly. "The university issues thousands of grades every semester. This is one trivial grade. Focus on the prize, Cory.

A single grade change is a small price to pay for a $90 million gift. With these funds we can build a national, even an international, reputation in Environmental Sciences."

"Let me think it over for twenty-four hours, Roger."

"No, do it now. Bob Lombardo is waiting for my call."

Cory was silent for several moments. "If I change the academic records, is Abby Prescott assured of getting tenure and promotion to associate professor?" he said finally.

"Absolutely," the president smiled, "and I'll throw in a ten percent salary increase as a bonus."

"All right. I'll change the damned grade when I get back to my office. But there's a finite risk that Abby will recheck her grade records," he warned. "And there will be hell to pay with my faculty if they learn that I changed a grade."

"It's a small risk with a very big payoff," Smythe assured him.

* * *

Back in his office minutes later, Cory opened his laptop computer, accessed the Registrar's site and inserted a series of codes. He searched several screens until he found Abby's grade report, filed a week earlier. He deleted the F next to John Lombardo's name and student identification number and inserted a B. Exiting the site, he pulled up his word processing program, wrote a memo to himself, printed it, and saved the file to his thumb drive. Then he deleted the memo from his laptop. He stored the tiny thumb drive in his briefcase. It would be his insurance policy in the event the grade change became public and created a problem with his faculty. The memo would be safely filed in his private records at home.

* * *

The president telephoned Lombardo Metalworks International in Manhattan and was connected with Robert Lombardo's administrative assistant, who immediately put him through to the president.

"Bob, the grade change you requested for your son was executed this afternoon. John is now in good academic standing at the university. We look forward to his return to classes next fall."

"Excellent, Roger. John's a good kid, but his lack of interest in academic studies has been a disappointment to his mother and me. He's just a bit immature.

"I'm looking forward to commencement," he continued. "I'll bring along a check for the first $10 million installment from my foundation."

"Wonderful. We will announce your extraordinarily generous gift at Commencement Dinner the evening before graduation exercises.

"I'll make certain that television and print reporters are on hand for the announcement and to interview you as well. The presentation of your honorary PhD will be the highlight of the commencement exercises Sunday afternoon."

"Isabella and I are looking forward to it. Please fax the schedule of events and program details to my office."

Chapter Thirty

The president glanced around the university dining hall. Several hundred guests, seated around candlelit tables for ten, were finishing the traditional Commencement Dinner on the evening before graduation. Strategically placed ferns, soft lighting and the music of a string quartet transformed the hall into a lovely banquet setting. Outside, a huge tent dominated Founders Court, site of the graduation ceremonies scheduled for the next morning.

Roger Smythe reached for his notes tucked in the inside pocket of his dinner jacket and strolled to the podium, nodding to the distinguished guests seated at the head table, smiling in anticipation. On his right were the senior senator and governor of the state of Maine and their spouses. To his left, seated next to the podium, sat Robert Lombardo, chairman of the university's board of trustees, and his wife, Isabella. Other members of the board of trustees rounded out the head table.

He turned to the audience, poised and self-assured, every inch the successful college president. In a few moments, the president was certain that his announcement would electrify his audience.

"Good evening, ladies and gentlemen. I am very pleased to welcome all of you to the Reid University campus. We are delighted you could join us for this prelude to our graduation ceremonies tomorrow."

"He sounds a bit pretentious, don't you think?" whispered Abby, seated next to Jen at a table in the rear of the hall.

"He's got his public face on for the television cameras," Jen murmured. They watched several cameras pan across the audience and then back to the head table and the president.

"Earlier this afternoon," the president continued, "the board of trustees completed its business and approved the list of graduates who will receive degrees during commencement exercises. I invite everyone to attend the ceremonies tomorrow at eleven o'clock and share one of the most important days in the lives of our students, their families and friends. Personally, the graduation exercises each June are the public highlight of my role as president of the university.

"And now I have an historic announcement to make." He glanced around the room, pausing for effect.

The president began to read from his notes. "It is my privilege to announce the largest gift ever pledged to Reid University. The Lombardo Family Foundation has just donated $90 million dollars to the university, and they have presented the first installment of this five year pledge." He turned and gestured to Robert and Isabella Lombardo to rise. From behind the dais, two students carrying a huge facsimile of a $90 million check, walked to the front of the head table and faced the audience.

Abby was stunned. The family of her problem student had just made the largest single gift in the university's sixty year history.

The room erupted in wild applause as the guests spontaneously rose to their feet. Television cameras recorded close-ups of the donors, the check and others at the head table. Jen and Rob stood beside Abby and Pete, joining the applause, astonished at the size of the donation.

Robert and Isabella Lombardo acknowledged the ovation. After a suitable interval the president regained control and the audience settled back into their seats.

"Would you like to know how this wonderful gift will be used to benefit our campus?" the president asked rhetorically amid more applause and enthusiastic shouts.

"An estimated $70 million of the proceeds is dedicated to constructing and equipping the new Lombardo Environmental Sciences Center. The remaining $20 million dollars will be placed in the Endowment Fund. Income from these funds will finance two endowed academic chairs, one in Marine Biology and one in Environmental Studies." The president led the applause, turning to recognize Robert and Isabella Lombardo once again.

"With this extraordinary gift, the university takes a giant step toward achieving its strategic vision," he resumed. "We now have the resources to develop the finest Environmental Science and Marine Biology programs in the country. Our institutional history will mark this turning point in our progress toward recognition as a world-class university. We owe an enormous debt of gratitude to Bob and Isabella Lombardo for their generosity."

He turned to the couple. "On behalf of the entire university community, I thank you."

More enthusiastic applause and a few whistles reverberated through the hall. Digital cameras flashed and reporters scrawled hurried notes as television cameras recorded the scene for the eleven o'clock news.

"Now, it is my pleasure to introduce our chairman of the board of trustees and university benefactor, Robert Lombardo."

Bob Lombardo stood at his chair. Smiling and acknowledging the applause from throughout the hall, he leaned over and kissed his wife. He waved to friends seated at tables in the audience and walked to the podium.

"Thank you, Roger, for those kind words," he began.

"During the past three years, I have served as chairman of the university's board of trustees. It's been an interesting experience. There are some similarities and quite a few differences between managing a large family business and offering guidance to the administrators of this university. As chairman, I've spent countless days here on campus and working in my study in New Jersey learning about the academic programs, reviewing budgets, assessing fundraising efforts and making recommendations for improving administrative operations.

"Last year, when Isabella and I reached our sixtieth birthdays, we decided to begin the process of distributing the wealth we have accumulated over the past forty years. We established and funded the Lombardo Family Foundation and set about planning how our good fortune might be used for the greater good. I can think of no finer purpose than to support higher education at Reid University.

"As globalization moves into the next phase, competition from Asia and other developing parts of the world will become even more intense. Our country will be challenged in ways we cannot imagine. In order to maintain our place among the leading nations of the world, we must provide the most challenging and innovative education for the scientists and engineers of tomorrow. The goal must be to move forward without damaging our environment or depleting the earth's scarce resources as we deal with the problems of global warming, population growth, fossil fuel shortages and myriad other challenges still unknown.

"If, as many of us believe, life on this planet evolved from the sea, we must continue to preserve the oceans, safeguarding their bounty for future generations. That is why Isabella and I have made this gift to build and equip a state of the art facility for the study of environmental and marine sciences. The scientists who staff this facility will not be limited in their research. The impact of global warming on our oceans, together with basic research in environmental science and marine biology will be intensively investigated.

"For example, I've been assured that researchers here at the university will search for medicines extracted from the plant, animal and mineral life found in our oceans. They will study ways to assure the lasting preservation of all forms of marine life.

"Our objective in endowing two professorships is to assist the university to attract and retain world class researchers and teachers. The researchers selected for the endowed chairs will possess international reputations in their disciplines. They will lead our research efforts and have at their disposal the most advanced tools with which to investigate a wide range of topics.

"Equally important, they will teach and mentor our students. Our expectation is that this gift will enable the university to attract a diverse, highly qualified group of students from around the globe. These future graduates will become the leaders of tomorrow in environmental and marine sciences in this country and throughout the world.

"Isabella and I will be actively engaged in developing the Environmental Sciences Center and selecting the endowed professorships. Then it will be the task of the administration and faculty to move toward our common vision as the preeminent global university in the ongoing effort to save our oceans and precious environment. Thank you."

He folded his notes and returned to his seat amid extended applause.

Abby leaned over to Jen. "Now I understand why Cory Howard wanted me to change Lombardo's grade. Daddy Lombardo doubtless intervened with the president when he learned that John had failed my course."

"You're probably right," Jen conceded. "This is a huge gift, and the president must have worked every angle in order to land it. To his credit, though, Cory backed you; and the university is getting the gift."

"I'm going to recheck Lombardo's records on the computer, just to be sure that grade is still an F."

"Give it a rest, Abby. You're sounding paranoid," Jen laughed. "Forget about Lombardo. Enjoy the moment. By the way, has the board of trustees approved your tenure and promotion application?"

Abby shook her head. "I don't know. I'll be notified by letter early next week."

"Call me with the news." Jen ordered. "Then I can plan your party."

"Absolutely. You'll know right after I tell Pete."

Chapter Thirty-One

Abby dashed down the hall to Jen's office, letter in hand.

"It's official. I'm now a tenured associate professor in the School of Business!" Abby greeted her friend.

The two women hugged gleefully.

"There's more news, Jen. According to the letter, I'm getting a ten percent salary increase, effective July 1. I'll be earning over $150,000 for the academic year. This raise almost gets me back to the salary I earned years ago in management consulting. That's progress."

"Whoa," Jen exclaimed. "When I earned tenure and promotion to associate professor twenty years ago my salary went to $50,000, which I thought was incredibly generous. Salaries are finally reflecting the university's commitment to attracting outstanding faculty."

"Does Pete know?"

"Yes. He's treating me to lunch to celebrate. He promised to take me to a fabulous new spot on the Portland waterfront. Want to come along?"

"Thanks for the invitation. I think you should share lunch with Pete alone. Three's a crowd."

Hearing voices from Jen's office, Pete strolled into the room, arms outstretched. He enveloped Abby in a bear hug and kissed her with a passion that surprised and delighted Jen.

"That's a fine way to congratulate our newest tenured associate professor," said Jen. "I hope Abby has exclusive rights to that treatment."

"Absolutely. Has she told you the news? We're officially a couple now."

"No," Jen smiled. "I'm not exactly sure what that term means these days, although I suspected your relationship had changed recently. Which do you prefer, partner or significant other?"

"Either term will do. You might as well know the rest of the news." He glanced toward Abby, who smiled and nodded. "I'm giving up my apartment in Portland and moving into Abby's house by the ocean."

"Outstanding," Jen beamed. "That's a serious step. And her house is only a mile from mine. We're practically neighbors." She turned to Abby. "Remember I promised you a party to celebrate your promotion?"

"Yes, and I intend to hold you to it."

Jen consulted her Blackberry. "How about two weeks from Saturday? We can have a barbeque on the terrace. If the weather is clear we'll see a full moonrise over the ocean. I'll invite the School of Business faculty and spouses, plus Roger Smythe and his wife and Pete's friends in campus security." Jen was already in planning mode. "I'll need a guest list from each of you, and then I'll manage the details. We'll celebrate your promotion, the end of the academic year, and the beginning of summer."

* * *

The party was well underway as the sun set in a blaze of red over the balsam firs behind Jen and Rob's property. Guests stood on the terrace, drinks in hand, watching Rob fire up the gas grill for steaks and chicken. A huge lobster pot boiled over a roaring fire in the brick fireplace. In the kitchen, Jen set out salads, prepared corn for roasting in burlap over the open fire, and made sure that everyone had fresh drinks and canapés.

She walked outside to the terrace, wineglass in hand.

"Everyone, please gather around while we toast our newest tenured associate professor."

Abby moved beside Jen.

"Roger, would you do the honors?"

Concealed in the thick stand of balsam firs a hundred yards away, John Lombardo surveyed the party. He watched Abby and the others listen to the words of the president, glasses raised, toasting their newest colleague.

He reached deep into the pocket of his windbreaker and fingered his .38 automatic, obsessively clicking the safety off and on, his face a mask of loathing.

The mellow sounds of recorded jazz drifted toward the woods. He waited and watched as the guests ate and drank, their voices floating on the warm evening breeze. An hour later the guests and the stalker observed a spectacular moonrise over the ocean.

At eleven o'clock, the party winding down, he retraced his steps to his car, hidden a mile away. Headlights off, he wheeled the BMW around and drove slowly along the dirt road leading to Seal Point Center. Skirting the darkened town commons with its antique gazebo, he turned left onto Route 1 and headed south toward Portland.

He parked in the underground garage, rode the elevator to the tenth floor and entered his condo overlooking the harbor. Showering quickly, he opened his medicine cabinet, reached for his supply of crystal meth, crushed an eight ball and snorted. Half an hour later, he entered The Goose, a gay disco on a back street near the harbor.

Chapter Thirty-Two

"Whoa, that was some tough hike," Abby gasped. Hands on hips, her heart pounding, she gave Pete a fist bump and then pulled her sweat-soaked tee shirt away from her shoulders. High on endorphins after the challenging five hour climb, they gazed triumphantly at the panoramic view from the summit of Mount Katahdin.

She spread her arms and embraced the chill wind swirling across the peak, savoring the spectacular views of balsam firs and hardwoods stretching to the horizon under a cloudless cobalt sky. Braced against the wind on the boulder-strewn summit, she glanced down the narrow, serrated-edged trail they had just traversed. She judged the return hike might be even more demanding than the ascent.

Minutes later, buffeted by a rising wind on the peak, they retraced their steps down the trail and stashed their backpacks on a narrow ledge between two boulders.

"We need to rehydrate," Pete said, digging out a fresh bottle of energy drink from his pack. He unscrewed the cap, took a long draught, and passed the plastic bottle to Abby.

Clouds of swarming black flies ferociously attacked them in the relative calm of their protected shelter, buzzing their faces, biting sweaty arms and legs, raising ugly red welts and drawing blood. They swatted futilely at the pesky insects.

"Damn black flies are eating us alive." Abby spit a fly from her mouth and grabbed the Deet from her pack. She frantically lathered her arms, legs, face and neck, and handed the can to Pete.

"This little trek is just a warm-up for Colorado," he remarked, spreading the bug juice over his exposed arms and legs. "The fourteen thousand foot peaks in the San Juans and east of Vail will be a hell of a lot more challenging. Five years ago I climbed a few 14,000-footers in the Gore Range near the Continental Divide. At least out there we'll be way above tree line, very exposed, but away from the rattlers and these damn flies."

"We're ready," Abby said confidently. "I intend to notch a half-dozen peaks. Think you can keep up with me?" she challenged.

"No problem," he laughed. "But steep trails won't be the only challenge. I know from experience the altitude can be a serious complication. We'll need to take a few days to acclimate to the elevations."

Sheltered from the wind on the narrow ledge, they rummaged through their backpacks for the lunch they'd prepared just after dawn. Seated side by side, backs against the rocks, they devoured ham and cheese sandwiches, granola trail mix and fortified themselves with two more bottles of Gatorade. Abby leaned back, legs sprawled in front of her, resting against the granite boulder, drinking in the scene.

"I climbed Katahdin with my father as a teenager," she revealed, munching on an apple, "but I don't remember the climb being this difficult. That was literally a peak life experience of my teenage years."

"You probably took the Hunt Trail, which is part of the Appalachian Trail that runs all the way south to Georgia," Pete told her. "We hiked the Knife Edge Loop Trail today. It's much more challenging—good preparation for the terrain and difficulty we'll face in Colorado.

"We probably should head down to camp soon," he suggested an hour later. He leaned over and kissed her lightly.

Abby groaned and crawled to her feet. Her calf muscles had stiffened in the cool mountain air and her hiking boots chafed. She glanced at her watch. "I suppose you're right. If we don't start soon, it'll be dark before we get back."

* * *

Exhausted, the endorphin high that had sustained them long gone, they reached their secluded campsite as the sun hung low on the western horizon. They tossed aside their backpacks and rested on the bench beside the camp table. Pete pulled the tabs of two cans of Michelob from the camp cooler and handed one to Abby.

"What's for dinner?" he asked, stowing the empty cans in a plastic trash bag.

"I'll make the salad if you grill the burgers and toast the buns," Abby offered.

"That's a deal. What else?"

"For your pre-dinner appetizer, we have crackers and cheddar cheese. And the bottle of merlot we hauled up here will be a perfect accompaniment to our burgers. For dessert, I suggest apples baked in foil. Or do you have something else in mind?" she asked.

Pete cocked his head.

"Okay, so it's not exactly gourmet fare," Abby laughed. "Look at it this way. There's nothing but birds and wild animals within five miles of here. We're camped beside this lovely lake and the view of Katahdin is awesome. What more do you want in the middle of the wilderness?"

"Forget the baked apples. That's not the dessert I had in mind," his eyes gleamed in the light of the open wood campfire.

Abby nodded. "We're not on a schedule. We can eat at midnight."

They raced to the two-person domed tent pitched beside the lake, frantically disrobed and crawled into the double sleeping bag. Unshaven, Pete's three-day growth scraped her throat and breasts. Abby gently drew his face to her own and kissed him, demanding relief, yet wanting the moment to last forever. The fire cast a mellow glow on the canvas tent as they made love in the stillness of early evening.

Later, snug and warm in the sleeping bag, they relived the day's hike. "Katahdin is a real challenge, not a trivial walk in the park. The Colorado hikes we're planning probably won't be any more challenging than today's climb," Pete assured her. "Of course, the elevation changes will be much more demanding."

Abby unzipped the bag and sat up, massaging her sore calf muscles, examining several raw blisters on each heel.

"Let me take care of those blisters," Pete said. He opened the first aid kit, took out a tube of antiseptic cream and bandages and dressed the blisters.

"Unfortunately, the black flies did some damage, too. They are the nastiest little buggers God ever made." Abby scratched several welts on her arm. "Our bug juice was practically worthless," she groused.

"Would you like a massage?"

"That would be wonderful. Thought you'd never ask," she sighed and rolled onto her stomach.

Pete reached for a tube of Arnica; with long smooth strokes, he stretched and massaged her calf muscles.

"You know, if we'd waited a few more weeks to avoid the black flies, we'd have to contend with swarms of kids camping with their parents," he said.

"I prefer the privacy, thank you."

Massage completed, she groped for her sandals. Squirming awkwardly in the cramped space she slipped into the thong and tee shirt she'd hastily discarded an hour earlier. Wriggling into a fresh pair of jeans, she stooped, unzipped the netting across the tent flap and prepared to crawl out.

"I'm starved. Must be the hike and the cool mountain air," she said over her shoulder.

"No, Abby. Sex makes you hungry." He laughed and slapped her butt.

It was nearly midnight when they banked the fire and settled down for the night. Bodies spooned, they drifted off to the mournful cry of a solitary loon somewhere across the lake.

* * *

They slept soundly, awakening well past dawn to the unremitting beat of rain on the tent. Donning ponchos, they hastily packed their gear, supplies and trash. They rolled up the sleeping bag and tent and slogged through a steady downpour to Pete's Toyota.

An hour and a half later they reached the lone vehicle parked in the dirt lot next to a gravel road leading out of the park. Pete opened the power rear door and stowed their gear. Sheltered by the raised rear door, they hastily prepared a cold lunch of sandwiches, fruit and trail mix. Tossing their wet ponchos onto the back seats, they climbed into the front. Pete started the vehicle, set the heater controls to high and in a few minutes, they were comfortably warm and dry.

"We lucked out yesterday," Abby remarked. "We'd never have made it up Katahdin today."

"Right. Except for today's rain, we've been very lucky. I think we're ready for the Rockies. By the way, have you booked the campgrounds out there?"

"Yes. Three confirmations came by email before we left."

Abby shivered. "I hope Colorado is a lot warmer in August, than Maine in June."

The rain deepened and gloom shrouded densely forested Baxter State Park as they backed out of the parking lot and headed for Millinocket. From there, a four-hour drive would take them to the coast and home. Abby, her down vest balled into a pillow, curled up against the window and slept soundly until they reached Augusta.

Chapter Thirty-Three

John Lombardo, his hand shielding the Maglite's intense beam, bushwhacked through the dense stand of balsams along the west end of Abby's property. Minutes later he reached the open meadow bordering the marsh behind the house.

The shuffle of his heavy boots punctuated the silence as he tramped across the tall grass, heavy with dew. In the distance the solitary bark of a dog shattered the early morning silence.

His heavy backpack was stuffed with burglar tools, his digital camera and a dry pair of Nikes. Based on his earlier surveillance, he was confident his intrusion would go undetected. Now, long past midnight, he prepared to enter Abby's home.

Three days ago, concealed in the shelter of the woods, he watched Abby and Pete load the SUV with camping gear and food supplies and drive away. He trailed their vehicle north to Augusta and watched the SUV turn toward Millinocket and Baxter State Park. Lombardo turned around, confident that his quarry would not return for several days.

Now, he crossed the back yard to the garage and the side entrance off the kitchen. Dropping his backpack on the granite entry, he pulled off his wet boots and donned dry Nikes. He dug out his lock-picking tools, slipped on a pair of latex gloves, and set about unlocking the door. A soft click, a turned knob and seconds later he entered the darkened kitchen.

Maglite in hand, he prepared to photograph the layout and contents of each room. He shot photos of the kitchen's upscale appliances and granite center island and then entered the living room with its wall of sliding glass doors and six-foot panes of glass above the doors.

Taking his time, Lombardo inspected the locks on the sliding doors, finding one slider unlocked. Very careless, Abby, he thought. He laughed aloud at the absence of an alarm system in the spacious home. Entry would be a cinch when he was ready to execute his plan. He photographed the upscale furnishings—the leather sofa, the glass dining table, and what he thought must be expensive art work.

He moved into the bedrooms and study, inspecting, photographing and mentally mapping the layout of each room. In the bathroom, he checked the cabinet for drugs. Noting several packs of unopened birth control pills, he concluded Abby apparently wasn't planning to make Pete Byrnes a daddy any time soon.

Retracing his steps to the kitchen, he opened the door leading to the two-car garage. Her late model Lexus was parked near the far wall. Storage boxes neatly lined the front and two bicycles hung from hooks in the ceiling. Walking through the kitchen a final time, he exited the house by the side door.

Seated on the damp granite stoop, he pulled off his gloves and stowed his Nikes in the backpack. He laced his heavy boots and tramped around the house to the front deck overlooking the ocean. He took several exterior flash shots, oblivious to the brilliant swath of Milky Way marching across the moonless sky. Then he retraced his steps across the back meadow, skirted the marsh and slipped into the woods.

Fifteen minutes later Lombardo unlocked his BMW parked at the edge of a deserted gravel road. Headlights off, he slowly drove into town, passing through the slumbering village. He switched on his lights just before reaching the Route 1 intersection and merged into early morning traffic heading south toward Portland.

It had been a good night's work.

Chapter Thirty-Four

Pete eased the Toyota into Abby's garage in late afternoon amid a heavy downpour. He unloaded the SUV and dumped their gear on the master bedroom floor, then wandered through the house unobtrusively checking the doors and windows.

He returned to Abby, surrounded by piles of soiled and wet clothing. "One of the sliders to the deck is unlocked," he reported. "Didn't you check the doors before we left?"

"Of course I did," Abby said shortly. "I'm sure the sliders were locked when we left."

"Well, at least one was unlocked," he insisted. "I really think you should install an alarm system before we leave for Colorado."

Abby looked at him. "What brought this on? I've lived in this house for six years without an alarm system. I don't want ugly detectors all over the place."

"External detectors are unobtrusive; you wouldn't notice them. You've got to admit, there's some valuable things a burglar might like to get his hands on," Pete persisted.

"What's so valuable?" she asked absently, sorting wet and dry clothing into two piles.

"For starters, your art work and jewelry. Your paintings obviously are expensive, and that glass bowl in the corner must be worth a small fortune." He pointed to the exquisite Chihuly bowl, a collector's item and Abby's most valuable piece of art.

Irritated, she didn't respond, fighting a splitting headache.

"Is this stuff insured?"

"Yes," she retorted shortly.

"I don't mean to hassle you, but I worry about this place and about you. In my professional opinion, you're a prime candidate for a robbery."

"I'm not worried and it's my house, remember?" she replied, unable to conceal mounting anger.

Abby sighed. She gazed at him through tangled hair. "Are we having our first argument?"

"I hope not."

"Pete, as long as you're living here, I don't need an alarm system. You're my protector," she smiled complacently.

"Is that all I'm good for? To be your protector?"

"Whoa. Time out." Abby climbed over the piles of clothing in the afternoon gloom. Cradling his face with her hands, she kissed him deeply. Collapsing together onto the bed, their lovemaking consumed them, their disagreement and Abby's headache forgotten in the midst of passion.

* * *

"Well, that was some time out," Pete whispered, kissing her breasts, their naked bodies gleaming with sweat.

Legs entwined, she molded her lithe body to his muscular torso.

"Pete, can we talk seriously for a minute?"

"Sure. What's on your mind," he asked softly, his hand gently caressing her thigh.

"Please don't distract me," she pleaded. "You were serious about my needing an alarm system. Now it's my turn."

"You call this a distraction? Okay, I'll stop." He rolled away from her, their bodies no longer touching.

Raised on one elbow, she stared into his eyes. "You're not just my protector," she began. "I hope you know that. Granted, we met only five months ago when I needed protection. But the episode with Lombardo ended in June. Surely you realize how much I care for you."

"But you've never said the L-word," he said softly.

Abby was momentarily unsure of his meaning. Then it dawned on her.

"And you haven't said you love me, either," she whispered.

"I moved in with you. I share this bed with you. Isn't that enough proof that I love you?"

"It would be nice to hear you say it now and then."

"Okay. I love you," he said, a grin tugging at the corners of his mouth.

"Be serious, Pete, please. You've never talked about your past relationships, although I was very open about my marriage and divorce."

"My few past relationships aren't important now," he said abruptly.

"Fine, I don't need to know," she said, sorry she had brought it up. "Perhaps we should discuss where this relationship might be heading."

"All right, let's discuss."

"I'll be completely honest," she began. "I really love being with you. And from my perspective at least, we're great in bed together. But that doesn't mean this relationship will last. I've been burned once. I don't intend to make the same mistake again."

"Why worry about whether our relationship will last? Let the future take care of itself. One lesson I learned in Iraq is not to plan too far ahead."

Abby's finger lightly traced the deep scar that extended from his temple into his dark hair, effectively covering most of the ugly wound.

Pete brushed her hand away.

"You never told me how you got that scar. Did that happen in Iraq?" she asked gently.

"Yes," he replied after a long silence. "Let's just say it's my Iraq souvenir. On the way to Baghdad International one afternoon to pick up a Washington VIP, our Hummer hit an IED. Every day the mirror reminds me how incredibly lucky I was to get out of that hell hole relatively intact. And that's all I'm going to say about that." He glanced away, reliving the day in Iraq when a shrapnel fragment nearly killed him, the only MP who survived the blast.

"There's something else we probably should get out in the open," he said after a moment.

"Fine. What's bothering you?" she asked, hoping that some unspoken issues they had ignored for months would finally be addressed.

"I know we don't have a lot in common," he began. "Face it, we come from different worlds. I'm just a campus cop. You're a professor with a doctorate from Harvard. I've got a degree in criminal justice. And look at our backgrounds. You grew up rich in Connecticut. I grew up poor in South Boston."

"But our worlds have intersected now," Abby interrupted him. "Granted, our backgrounds are different, but that has not inhibited our relationship, at least not from my viewpoint. We share more common interests than many couples—besides great sex, of course." Lying naked beside him, she counted on her fingers. "Let's see, we both love to sail and hike, and you're the expert in both areas. I'm teaching you about jazz and classical music, my contribution to your informal education. You've got me working out—even jogging to stay fit. I think we're building a fair number of mutual interests together.

"Now, let me ask you a serious question, and promise you won't get defensive with me."

"How can I be defensive lying in bed with you?" he asked. "You've got me in a compromising position."

"Pete," she looked beyond him, struggled to find the right words. "Do the differences in our careers and backgrounds make you feel just a little inferior?"

He drew back. "Well, I hadn't thought about it exactly that way," he said after a moment. My salary is probably half as much as yours. I've been contributing to the house expenses since I moved in, but it's busting my budget. I still owe thousands on the boat and the SUV. Financially, I'll never keep up with you.

"Maybe your background and money are a little intimidating," he admitted finally .

"Now let me be frank," Abby said. "I really don't care about your financial status or your background. I care about your strength of character, your values, how kind you were when I was having problems with Lombardo, and yes, how you treat me in bed."

Pete laughed. "You've taught me a few things in bed, too, professor. I don't want to know where you learned some of those moves."

"Ready for another lesson?" she invited.

"You're on." He reached across her body and turned off the bedside lamp.

Half an hour later Abby stretched and hopped out of bed. Donning a clean thong, jeans and a sweatshirt, she retrieved her bra from the floor and tossed it on the pile of dirty clothes.

"I need to start the washing, and there's nothing in the house to eat. If I make a list, will you drive into town and pick up some groceries?"

"Your wish is my command," he saluted smartly. "How about steaks, salad makings, corn, and sourdough bread?"

"Perfect."

He padded across the room to the walk-in closet, opened a drawer, pulled out a clean pair of shorts and tee shirt and headed for the bathroom.

Standing under the steaming shower, he realized that Abby had not said she loved him, neither today nor in the past.

Chapter Thirty-Five

Late the following morning, Abby rushed down the hall to Jen's office.

"I don't believe this!"

"Don't believe what?"

"Check this grade report I just printed off the Academic Information System." Abby thrust a sheet in front of Jen.

Jen examined the paper. "This is John Lombardo's grade report from last spring semester." She looked up. "Why are you showing me this? I thought we were finished discussing that guy's grade problems."

"I finally got around to rechecking Lombardo's grade report on the computer," Abby related. "Take a look at the grade for M301, my Organization Behavior course." She pointed to the details. "His grade is now a B, not the F that I recorded a month ago. How the hell can a grade be changed without my knowledge and agreement? Has this creep hacked our Academic Information System and changed his grade?"

"Take it easy, Abby. There's got to be an explanation." Jen noted that the student's grade point average was a respectable 2.7 of a possible 4.0.

"I decided to check the grades in Lombardo's other classes to see whether he was dismissed from the university for failing to meet our academic standards. If I hadn't looked one more time, I'd never have known my grade was changed. Now it's on his permanent academic record."

"There's probably a rational explanation for this, although right now I can't imagine what it would be," Jen said, puzzled.

"This is outrageous," Abby fumed. "I never agreed to change that grade from an F to a B. And remember, Cory Howard backed me on the failing grade. Will this battle with Lombardo ever be over?"

"Slow down, don't jump to conclusions," Jen cautioned.

"Aren't all faculty computer passwords confidential? Who else could possibly know my password? Maybe some computer science student hacked the university's computer systems," Abby speculated, "in which case, all students' grades will need to be audited for errors."

"I doubt that a hacker got past the system firewall," said Jen calmly. "There must be some other explanation."

Abby shook her head. "No one can change a student's grades without faculty authorization. Obviously, Lombardo's grade has been doctored. I intend to get to the bottom of this."

"Actually," Jen said quietly, "I believe the dean can access all student records on the university's computer system."

"Really? I didn't know that. But Cory supported me when I explained why Lombardo earned an F. Would he arbitrarily change a grade without consulting me?"

"I suppose it's possible, but not likely. Sit down, Abby. Relax." Jen motioned her friend to a chair. "Let's review the timeline. You spoke to Cory before the board voted on your tenure and promotion. And during graduation weekend the board of trustees approved your promotion and gave you a ten percent salary increase."

"Right."

"Then the night before commencement the university announced the $90 million gift from the Lombardo Family Foundation."

"Do you think Lombardo's family is involved in this? Could this grade change is related to that gift?" Abby was incredulous.

Jen shrugged. "It's a stretch, I know. But not impossible. We don't know much about Robert Lombardo and his family except that he's obviously wealthy, the most generous benefactor in the university's history."

"I can't believe the trustee chairman would be directly involved in this." Abby dismissed the possibility. "Lombardo got the failing grade he deserved. I'm changing the record back to an F right now. He will get a warning letter telling him that he's on academic probation next week. I'll watch the computer and see whether the grade gets changed back to a B again. Two can play the cat and mouse game."

"Maybe you're overreacting, Abby."

"What do you suggest?" she asked angrily.

Jen thought for a moment. "Why not speak to the dean first? Tell him you found this grade change and you're puzzled. Pretend you don't understand how this could happen. See if he has an explanation. Maybe he'll admit that he changed the grade. Or reveal who might have changed it."

"That may work," Abby conceded more calmly. "Cory dislikes confrontation; I need to be careful not to accuse him outright."

"Actually, do you really want to make a major issue of this?" Jen asked.

"Don't tell me you think I should let the matter die," Abby said, disappointed.

"It's your decision," Jen said patiently. "Lombardo really lost control during that confrontation in your office. I was there, remember? Perhaps anger management is not his only problem. It's possible he was high on drugs that day."

"Do you think so, Jen?"

"People snorting meth often exhibit paranoid—even violent behavior. Lombardo was extremely aggressive in your office two months ago and that wasn't the first time."

"Now, I don't know what to do," Abby fumed. "If he has a drug problem, he needs counseling. This grade issue would make matters more complicated."

"You've got the entire summer to deal with this. Wait. Cool off a bit," Jen advised.

"I'll talk to Pete, see what he thinks," Abby said decisively. "He's working on a campus drug case right now, although he won't discuss the details with me."

Chapter Thirty-Six

Under cloudless skies and a moderate northwest wind, they left Seal Point harbor and headed southeast under a following breeze. They anchored two hours later in a tiny inlet, furled the sails and settled down to lunch near the stern.

"Pete, what do you know about drugs on campus?" Abby asked, handing him a sandwich and a Sam Adams Lager.

"Why do you ask?" he countered.

"Just curious. You're working a campus drug case; Jen suggested recently that Lombardo's behavior might be related to drug use, perhaps meth amphetamines or cocaine. She thinks it could explain his aggressive outbursts."

Pete was noncommittal. "She may be right, although I have no evidence that he's a heavy user. Drugs like cocaine or crack, speed, and designer crystal meth or ice as it's called on the street, if taken frequently, push some people into paranoid behavior. Frequent users of crystal meth can become violent when they're high. Crack cocaine and crystal meth are highly addictive and very dangerous."

"What about marijuana?"

"Most of us in law enforcement consider weed relatively harmless. Long term use apparently can produce a decline in short term memory. For the most part, recreational use is not a big deal."

"Is drug use a serious problem on campus?"

"A certain level of use goes on in the residence halls," he admitted. "The few times we've busted students on campus usually involved marijuana, not the more addictive drugs.

"Every campus has it share of drug users, Abby. It's a fact of life, and Reid University is not immune. If students use marijuana occasionally to mellow out, we'll usually look the other way. But we are constantly on the lookout for evidence of hard drugs in the residence halls.

"We differentiate between dealing and using drugs. Dealing on campus is a very serious matter. We crack down hard on dealers, no pun intended," he smiled. "If we identify anyone dealing drugs, we arrest them and haul them into court. Of course, students can drive to Portland and buy drugs fairly easily."

"It sounds like drug use on campus is relatively benign," Abby said.

"Alcohol abuse actually is a more serious problem," Pete continued. "Too many students drive to Portland every Thursday night and get wasted on booze in the bars and clubs, then drive back to campus seriously impaired.

"Underage drinking starts in high school, of course. We worry about alcohol abuse, but there isn't much we can do to combat it. We run alcohol awareness programs every semester, focusing especially on freshmen, spelling out the campus rules, warning against abuse."

Abby snuggled in his arms, facing the distant shore, resting her head on his shoulder.

"Right now I'm leading an assessment of the use of hard drugs, like cocaine, heroin and crystal meth on campus," Pete volunteered.

"Have you found evidence of an increase in those drugs?"

"Maybe."

"Can you tell me about it?"

He reached into the cooler for another beer and pulled her back into his arms.

"I can give you a few general details, but please, Abby, this is very confidential."

"Of course."

"It's possible that a faculty member is involved in delivering cocaine, either to the New York area or to Portland," Pete went on. "There's no specific evidence that he's dealing on campus, but we're reasonably sure he is transporting significant quantities of coke. A major distribution network may be developing here in northern New England. We're working with Homeland Security, and state and local law enforcement in Massachusetts, New Hampshire and Maine. We're just a small cog in the investigation."

"Who is the faculty member?"

"I can't give you his name. I've already violated regulations."

"Don't be ridiculous. Tell me. I can keep a secret."

"He's in Environmental Sciences, not the School of Business," he admitted.

"My God, I bet it's Rick Stewart," Abby exclaimed.

Pete was silent.

"There's a lot of speculation among the faculty about the source of Stewart's money," she mused. "It doesn't take a genius to realize that his salary alone can't support his lifestyle. He uses a private plane in his consulting assignments, often brags about his lucrative clients in Georgia and Florida. And he recently traded a small Cessna for a used twin-engine Beech that probably cost hundreds of thousands of dollars."

"Abby, you seem to know a lot about Rick Stewart. What do you know about his flying habits?" Pete asked.

"Jen Carpenter's husband, Rob, is a pilot and has his own plane. He knows Rick, often runs into him at the airport. I think he helped Rick buy his latest plane.

"Rick and I also work together on a citizen's committee supporting the proposed offshore LNG terminal north of Bar Harbor. Rick leads the public relations committee advocating for the natural gas companies. Some of us consider him a shill for the industry.

"It all adds up, Pete," she said, excited. "Rick Stewart is the target you're investigating, isn't he?"

He shook his head. "Please don't ask me to confirm that."

"Your secret is safe. Now tell me more," Abby demanded.

"Stewart makes frequent trips to Florida and Georgia—sometimes one a week. During the spring semester he missed a number of classes. His department chair and the dean in the School of Environmental Sciences are concerned about that. Apparently, he just cut the classes. Of course, his students didn't complain about a few extra days off," Pete said.

"I know Rick is married and has a couple kids," Abby said.

"Yes. He also is friendly with a female student who flies south with him from time to time."

"That's news," Abby exclaimed. "The university has an unwritten but well understood rule strongly discouraging faculty and students from engaging in personal relationships. I'm sorry to hear that Rick may be playing around with a student. Who is she?"

"She's divorced, goes to school part time, works in a branch bank just off campus. In fact, she was in your class last semester along with your problem student. It's probably just a coincidence, but she and Lombardo both were enrolled in Stewart's introductory environmental issues class."

Abby was silent, digesting the information. "Rick's wife brags to friends about his family's wealth. To be fair, that could explain the source of their funds. Do you suppose his wife is involved with drugs, too?" she asked.

"I doubt it. She and the kids don't fly with Stewart. The trips south seem to be reserved for the girlfriend."

"If this investigation leads to a major drug bust involving a faculty member, the university could be hit with some bad publicity," Abby said.

"Right. Chief Edwards and the president are working up a strategy to deal with possible fallout if a faculty member is accused of dealing."

"Do you think Stewart is distributing cocaine or heroin on campus?"

Pete shook his head. "We haven't found any evidence of that. Of course, summer is relatively quiet at the university; I don't expect serious problems until September at the earliest. Everyone in campus security has been directed to stay alert for signs of change in the usual routine."

Abby gathered the empty beer bottles and remains of their lunch and went below. She stowed the trash and handed Pete another beer.

"Now let me quiz you for a moment," he said.

"Shoot," Abby said, settling back on bench.

"Why did Jen suggest that Lombardo might be using meth or crack cocaine?"

"I'm not sure," Abby admitted after a pause. "She seems knowledgeable about the local drug scene, maybe because Rob is a criminal defense attorney.

"She speculated that Lombardo may be a crackhead only recently."

"It's possible," Pete said, "but you don't need to worry about that anymore. He won't be bothering you again."

"Don't be too sure. I checked his grade report last week to see if he had flunked out of school."

Pete glanced at Abby, annoyed. "Why don't you just forget about him?"

She ignored his question. "Guess what? The failing grade that I recorded at the end of the semester has been replaced with a B—without my knowledge or permission."

"How is that possible?" Pete seemed genuinely surprised. "I thought computer firewalls prevented anyone hacking into the university's systems."

"You tell me," she retorted, cranking up the anchor and helping unfurl the sails. "There are only two possibilities."

"And they are?"

"Someone may have hacked the academic computer system, in which case the grades for every student in the university would be suspect."

"That's a long shot," he said. "What else?"

"Someone using my unique password changed Lombardo's failing grade to a B. All the other students' grades were correct."

"Abby, have you shared your password with anyone?"

"Of course not! However, Jen believes the deans can access faculty files, including grade reports. If she's correct, Cory Howard could have changed Lombardo's grade without my knowledge."

"I really doubt that Howard would change a grade. What do you intend to do?"

"I've scheduled a meeting with him to discuss the grade change. In other words, I'll play dumb and see how he reacts."

"When are you going to see him?"

"Probably next week, just before we leave for Colorado. He's on vacation until then."

Chapter Thirty-Seven

"Come in, Abby," the dean greeted her cordially. "How is your summer going? Have you firmed up any vacation plans?"

"Yes," she said, seating herself beside his desk. "Pete Byrnes and I are driving to southern Colorado to hike and camp in the San Juans for three weeks. Instead of our New England hills, we'll tackle some 14,000 footers."

"I didn't know you were a hiking enthusiast. Sounds like a nice change of scenery for both of you.

"Now," he leaned back, "what's on your mind this morning? My secretary didn't indicate the reason for our meeting."

Abby was silent for a moment, organizing her thoughts. "Do you recall the problems I had with a student in my Organization Behavior class last semester? His name is John Lombardo, the son of our chairman of the board of trustees."

"Yes, of course. Pete Byrnes sat in your class, and his presence helped you control Lombardo's behavior."

"Cory, I issued a failing grade to Lombardo in that course because he failed all of the objective exams and also plagiarized the major paper required in the course."

"Didn't we meet recently about this student's grade? I thought the issue was settled," the dean appeared puzzled.

"Yes, we did," Abby said evenly. "Last week I decided to review the rest of Lombardo's grades for the semester."

"Why are you interested in his other grades?" Cory asked.

"I wanted to see whether he failed any other courses."

"And did he?"

"What I found is puzzling and disturbing. Lombardo's grade in my course was changed from an F to a B. I rechecked my original computerized grade report for the entire class, all thirty students. His grade was the only one that was changed.

"How can a grade be changed when I supposedly have exclusive access my grade reports? It doesn't make sense."

Cory Howard frowned. He was silent for several moments, and then replied, "Because those access codes are not, in fact, completely confidential."

"Who else in the university can get into my grade reports?" Abby asked, feigning bewilderment.

"Several people, including me," he admitted. "The Information Technology Department maintains a closely guarded database of access codes assigned to every employee on the campus, including faculty members. It is a basic security measure the IT department needs in case a file is corrupted or hacked by a source outside the university."

"I can understand the need for a master list," Abby said slowly, "but surely no one in the IT department would change grades assigned by faculty. Maybe an outside hacker has gotten into my file. If that's the case, then all the grades in the university are at risk and we probably should notify IT to alert all faculty to review their grades for last semester."

"That won't be necessary, Abby," the dean said quietly. "I changed John Lombardo's grade in your course," he confessed.

"But why?" Abby asked, genuinely bewildered. "You agreed two months ago that the failing grade was appropriate."

"Abby, what I'm about to tell you must not leave this room," Cory said grimly.

"Fair enough. Now what's going on with Lombardo's grade?"

"The president directed me to change the grade. Under the circumstances, I had no choice. When you understand the reasons for his decision, I think you'll agree that it was necessary."

"Don't tell me this grade change is related to the $90 million gift from the Lombardo Family Foundation," Abby eyed him suspiciously.

"Exactly," he admitted. "Let me explain."

"I can't imagine why you would violate one of the university's most important academic policies," she retorted.

"Do not discuss what I'm about to tell you with anyone, including Jen Carpenter and Pete Byrnes," Howard warned.

Abby reluctantly nodded assent.

"Robert Lombardo telephoned the president a few days before graduation to discuss the $90 million pledge to the university. He brought up the subject of his son's failing grade in your course and appealed directly to the president to change the grade to a B in order for his son to remain here at the university."

"And the president agreed?" Abby asked, incredulous.

"Yes. I assume Lombardo applied some pressure about the gift. A quid pro quo, in other words."

"More like blackmail, in my opinion," Abby said bitterly.

"Roger called me to his office and ordered me to change Lombardo's grade without your knowledge," he said.

"So you were simply following the president's orders," she shook her head, disgusted.

"Yes."

"Let me get this straight, Cory. A $90 million gift to Reid University was contingent on a single grade change for the donor's son."

"I wouldn't put it that crudely, but that was the result."

"Abby," the dean continued, "consider the financial stakes. The university has received funds to build a new research center and support two endowed chairs for distinguished faculty. Weigh $90 million against a single violation of our academic standards—issuing a passing grade to a student who didn't earn it."

"And I was the sacrificial pawn in the process."

"But you also were a beneficiary of this admittedly sordid deal."

"How did I benefit? My grades were manipulated and you violated the academic standards of the School of Business."

"You received two direct benefits, Abby, although you were unaware of them until now."

"What are you talking about?"

"You were promoted and received tenure," the dean leaned forward, his hands flat on his desk. "As part of the arrangement, the president approved a ten percent increase in your salary. That salary increase is the largest raise any faculty member has received in the last five years."

"You're saying I didn't receive tenure and promotion based on the merits of my application and the support of my colleagues during the past six years?" Abby asked, stunned.

"Exactly. My strongest recommendation as dean and the support of your colleagues were meaningless. Roger Smythe controls this university and he would not recommend you unless that grade was changed."

"This is disgusting, Cory."

"I'm sorry. I've never changed a faculty member's grade before, and I regret it deeply. In this case, however, the global interests of the university took precedence over a single faculty member's decision on a student's academic work."

"Apparently, money talks at this university," Abby observed bitterly.

"Few universities can afford to turn away a $90 million gift," the dean reminded her.

"This insults every other student who legitimately earned a B in my class," Abby said.

She stood to leave. "I'm changing John Lombardo's grade back to an F, Cory. In fact, I may be doing him a favor. The failing grade can serve as a wakeup call. Besides, that grade won't end his academic career at the university. He has friends in high places."

"Abby, I forbid you to change that grade back to an F," the dean said, his voice rising.

"I refuse to become a knowing participant in this sorry episode." Abby teared up. "I intend to do the right thing, Cory."

"There is something else you need to know."

"You mean there's more you haven't told me?"

"Yes. The university has received only $10 million so far. The rest is pledged over the next five years, which apparently provides an important tax advantage to the Lombardo family.

"And let me be clear on a final point. The Lombardo Foundation can rescind the donation and demand that the university return the funds already received. We can't afford to offend the Lombardo family. Now you have the complete picture," Cory concluded.

Abby faced him. "Basically, this university has just been bought for $90 million. John Lombardo can flunk as many courses as he wants. The faculty will have to give him passing grades to avoid offending his daddy." She rose abruptly and headed for the dean's office door.

"What are you going to do?" the dean asked.

"You'll know soon enough," she replied over her shoulder.

She hurried across Founders Court to her office. Confidentiality be damned. She would consult with Jen and Pete. And unless they were more convincing than Cory, she would change the damn grade back to the F the student deserved and let the chips fall where they may.

Chapter Thirty-Eight

"What happened at your meeting with the dean?" Jen asked.

"You were right. Cory admitted that he changed Lombardo's grade," Abby said grimly. "That's not all. He swore me to secrecy about why he changed the grade. He specifically singled out you and Pete, and warned me not to discuss the conversation with either of you."

"Really?"

"He can't muzzle me," Abby said angrily. "I'll tell you and Pete the whole story, confidential conversations be damned."

Jen had never seen Abby so upset.

"Are you sure you want to violate the dean's confidence?"

"Of course I'm sure! Do you want to hear the story or not?"

Jen reached for her coffeepot, poured a cup for Abby, refreshed her own and settled back to listen.

*   *   *

"I walked out of Cory's office right after he ordered me not to change Lombardo's grade back to an F. He didn't exactly threaten me with reprisals; in fact, he seemed worried about controlling me," Abby concluded bitterly.

"Now you know how the administration really operates," Jen said soberly. "Don't be too hard on Cory. He was just following orders.

"I'm disappointed that he didn't resist, Abby, but I understand why. If he had refused to make the change, he could be eased out of his position as dean. He enjoys being dean, with all the prestige that goes with the title.

"The villain here is Roger Smythe. The possibility of losing a $90 million gift for the university is far more important than a single grade issue."

"You're probably right," Abby agreed glumly.

"The president has deniability because he didn't change the grade," Jen pointed out. "Cory will be left hanging in the wind if this incident becomes public.

"Thank God you got tenure last month. The university can't fire you for doing what any self-respecting faculty member would do when her grades are tampered with."

"I need your advice. What you would do?"

Jen was silent. "A lot of money is at stake, Abby. If you defy the president and change that grade, there will be retribution," she warned, shaking her head. "Roger Smythe doesn't forgive or forget faculty who oppose him, regardless of the circumstances," she said finally.

"What can Smythe do to me?" Abby asked.

"A lot. For example, you can forget about a promotion to full professor as long as he is president. He can make life uncomfortable for you in many other ways, too." Jen silently regarded her friend.

"Talk to Pete. See what he recommends," she urged.

*   *   *

"I think you should let this sleeping dog lie," Pete advised that evening.

"So, you agree with Jen," Abby said, disappointed.

"Time out," he said firmly. "You asked my opinion and I'm giving it to you. Sure, Lombardo's grade shouldn't have been changed. But the stakes are obviously high. Roger Smythe can't fire you, but he can ruin your opportunities for future promotion and salary increases.

"Have you forgotten that Lombardo threatened you last spring and caused you serious anxiety during the past six months? Why don't you just forget about him?"

"Pete, I think you just don't get it," Abby said testily. "Faculty members take academic integrity very seriously. Issuing a grade in a course is not a trivial, routine evaluation. It's what we're paid to do.

"Think about all the other students in my class who worked hard and earned their grades legitimately. How would they react knowing that I caved to pressure because Lombardo's father gave the school a lot of money?"

Pete looked at her across the candlelit dinner table, taken aback by her intensity. "Right. I don't understand why this grade change is such a big deal. I'm not an intellectual faculty member who can spend hours debating the value of a single grade in one course. If this student is as stupid as he seemed when I sat in your class, he'll flunk out next semester anyway. Why invite reprisals from the president over this?"

"I'll tell you why," she retorted. "It's damned dishonest. Besides, what's to stop him from pressuring other faculty who fail Lombardo in their courses?"

Pete was silent.

"I've seen enough dishonesty in my life," Abby went on heatedly. "When I worked as a consultant, I watched companies bend the rules—avoiding taxes through tax havens in the Cayman Islands and Bermuda, outsourcing decent manufacturing jobs to the Far East and Mexico, laying off thousands of American workers so corporations could shave a few bucks off their costs and increase their bottom line so top executives could pick up stock options worth millions.

"I kept my mouth shut and played the game, designing stock option plans that made top executives filthy rich while they sent jobs overseas to sweat shops. I finally resigned when they asked me to develop severance packages for workers being outsourced. I couldn't stomach minimizing their severance pay while executives were walking away with millions of dollars."

"Whew. I didn't realize you felt so strongly about this," Pete cocked his head. "If it's this important to you, get into the computer and change the damn grade back to an F. Consequences be damned."

"Do you really think I should?" Abby asked, suddenly uncertain.

"It's your decision, not mine. I respect your stand on principle, but I doubt that it's worth jeopardizing your career over this sleazebag's grade."

"I've got to live with myself, Pete," Abby said more calmly. "I can't compromise on this. Tomorrow I'll go to the office and make the change. We're leaving for Colorado the next day; if there's an uproar, the president will have a hard time finding me."

"Jen has your cell number and the itinerary. If there's a huge crisis, she can call you in Colorado. Let's go to bed," he suggested. "You've had a tough day."

"Is that an invitation?" Abby asked, her mood instantly brightening.

* * *

Pete couldn't sleep. The clock on the bedside table registered two a.m. as alarming scenarios cycled endlessly through his brain. Should he have told Abby, sleeping quietly beside him, the details of Lombardo's violent background? Should he have been more forceful in advising Abby not to change the grade?

Based on the court documents that he'd discovered, Abby might be in physical danger. And an obliging Manhattan police detective casually disclosed suspicions that John Lombardo's father had links to the mob.

Recently, Pete reported Lombardo's possible Mafia connections to Craig Edwards, who would doubtless report up to the president. He didn't envy his boss confronting Roger Smythe with suspicions that the university's new research center and endowed academic chairs might be funded by tainted money.

He sighed and turned over. With a little luck, Abby and he would be far away from Reid University when it all hit the fan.

* * *

"You can't be serious, Craig." The president regarded his campus security chief in disbelief.

"Dead serious, Roger. Pete Byrnes verified that John Lombardo has three restraining orders currently in effect in northern New Jersey. In each instance, the threatened females had broken off relationships with him.

"Byrnes was told confidentially that Lombardo assaulted one of the women. She eventually dropped the charges. His source believes the senior Lombardo paid her off. John was protected by his father's money.

"This is proof of Lombardo's violent past. He may be a psycho waiting to explode, posing a serious threat to Abby Prescott. I believe he should not be allowed on this campus."

"Not so fast, Craig," the president interrupted. "I understand that Byrnes and Prescott have developed a personal relationship. Perhaps his report is colored by his relationship with her."

"I disagree," the security chief didn't back down. "Pete Byrnes is my top officer on the force. After his trip to New York last week, he handed over a very carefully documented report of his findings. Do you want a copy?"

"Yes. Send it over today and mark it confidential. I don't want my assistant to read it."

"This is a complex problem," Smythe agreed finally. "Our chairman of the board of trustees and major benefactor expects his son to earn a degree in business. By the way, the son's failing grade was changed to a B in order to keep him in good academic standing."

"You must be joking," Craig said, incredulous. "After all the grief that student gave Abby Prescott, she changed his grade? I invested a lot of resources protecting her last semester, and now she gives the kid a passing grade. Some faculty have no principles at all."

The president didn't correct Edwards' misimpression. Nor did he mention Robert Lombardo's veiled threat to cut off funds unless his son's grade was changed.

"Send me a copy of the New York report and do not discuss this matter with Byrnes," the president directed. "We'll work out a strategy later."

"No problem. Pete is on vacation beginning today. He and the professor are climbing in the Colorado Rockies. They won't be back until early August."

Chapter Thirty-Nine

"Stop!" Abby gasped, bent over, hands clutching her knees, struggling to catch her breath. She shrugged out of her light daypack and collapsed against a boulder beside the steep trail. Pete hurriedly retraced his steps down the trail to her side.

"I shouldn't have eaten breakfast," she said weakly, her face pale, hands shaking. "I'm going to throw up." She bent over and reached for her water bottle.

"Don't drink water; that's the worst thing you can do," he said sharply, taking the plastic bottle and setting it on a rock nearby.

"You've got a touch of altitude sickness and you're hyperventilating," he explained matter-of-factly. Crouching beside her, he unzipped her daypack and emptied the brown paper bag with their lunch sandwiches.

"Cover your mouth with this bag," he directed. "Seal it completely around your lips. Then breathe slowly in and out into the bag. You need to adjust the balance of oxygen and carbon dioxide in your system. You'll feel better in a few minutes." He watched her follow instructions.

"We'll need another hour and a half to reach the peak, then we can rest and eat lunch before starting down."

Abby lowered the bag. "Please don't talk about eating lunch," she pleaded wanly.

"Keep breathing into the bag," he ordered. "You'll be fine."

Eyes wide, she held the bag firmly around her lips and breathed slowly in and out. Pete stood by, waiting, watching her closely.

He pointed up the trail to a tall cairn silhouetted against the distant horizon. "We're above thirteen thousand feet; the air is a hell of a lot thinner here than back on Mount Katahdin," he reminded her. "We have another thousand vertical feet to go. You can see the summit from here."

He turned and looked west, appraising a bank of towering cumulus clouds. Midafternoon thunderstorms in the Colorado mountains were a virtual certainty. They would need to be well below the summit before two o'clock.

"Pete, I can't go on."

"Sure you can," he said more confidently than he felt. "Before you know it, we'll be at the summit—it will be worth the pain—and you can log your first 14,000-footer."

Ten minutes later he pulled Abby to her feet. She adjusted her daypack over her shoulders and trudged up the trail, gamely struggling on, head down, willing herself to put one boot in front of the other, pausing to rest and catch her breath every twenty yards. Her lungs screamed at the oxygen deprivation, her heart pounded and every bone in her body ached. She was acutely aware of a raging headache developing behind her temples.

Silently, they labored toward the summit along the narrow, rock-strewn dirt trail marked by cairns at each switchback. They finally reached the fourteen thousand foot level marked by a crudely carved sign stuck in the rocks beside the trail. Abby, realizing that the peak was little more than three hundred vertical feet above them, felt a surge of confidence. Her steps quickened; it would not be long now.

Pete suddenly slowed his pace as the thin air exacted its toll on his body. Panting heavily, he stopped. "Keep going," he gasped, "don't wait for me, I'll be fine in a few minutes." Feeling stronger with each step, she hiked on ahead, reaching the summit ten minutes ahead of him.

Completely spent, they eased their backpacks to the ground and collapsed against the wall of the crude rock shelter at the 14,350 foot summit. Minutes later, refreshed, they surveyed spectacular vistas in every direction. To the east and north a series of majestic snowcapped peaks marked the Continental Divide. In a few days they would tackle several of those 14,000-foot peaks in the Front Range east of Vail.

Abby looked southwest, tracing the dry, clearly marked trail they had just climbed. More than five thousand vertical feet and four miles below, she spotted the tree line, a vast swath of green lodgepole pine. Surely the return hike would be easier. Granted, this was the most difficult climb she had ever attempted; the lack of oxygen and the elevation change had proved more challenging than the climb itself. Exhausted, she rested against her daypack, her weary body pumping residual endorphins, feeling simultaneously euphoric and exhilarated.

"Ready to start down?" Pete interrupted her reverie.

"We just got here," she protested. "I'm hungry." She reached into her pack and offered him a sandwich. He shook his head.

"What's the rush?"

"Check those clouds." He gestured southwest toward a towering line of dark and threatening cumulus. "There's lightning heading this way," he warned. "We're completely exposed here; a thunderstorm at this elevation can be deadly. We need to get down to the tree line for protection. Let's go."

He hoisted his heavy backpack onto his shoulders and started down the trail.

Abby took in the ominous front rumbling their way, gathering speed by the minute. A chill breeze swept the summit, raising goose bumps through her sweat soaked tee shirt. Lunch forgotten, she grabbed a power bar and jogged after him.

"Was that thunder I just heard?" Abby shouted at Pete, well below her on the steep trail.

"Yes," he stopped, waiting for her to catch up. He eyed the approaching storm. "It's probably still three miles away, but lightning is already near. We need to pick up the pace."

He jogged down the dusty boulder-strewn trail. Half running, Abby scrambled desperately to keep up. Suddenly the wind freshened, the noonday sun disappeared and an eerie twilight cloaked the mountain. The temperature dropped fifteen degrees as sheets of sleet and frigid rain attacked them. Jagged lightning crackled and flashed nearby, followed instantly by earthshaking thunder.

"Run, Abby!" Pete yelled. Slipping and sliding along the rain-slicked trail, they raced toward the distant tree line miles below.

Abby lost her footing and pitched forward, arms flung out in a futile effort to break her fall, her foot jammed between shifting rocks. A stab of piercing pain shot up her ankle and left leg.

"My ankle! Damn, I've broken my ankle!" she screamed. Pete ran back up the trail and knelt beside her. Sprawled on the muddy trail, she clutched her boot. Thunder drowned out her voice as waves of hail and rain pummeled them.

"We can't stop now," he screamed over the noise, his hair plastered against his forehead. You've got to put some weight on your foot."

"I can't!" she shrieked.

He hauled her to her feet, a dead weight in his arms.

They clung to each other, fighting to retain their balance as a flood of icy water raced down the trail, turning what had been a dry, rocky path minutes earlier into a slippery mass of mud.

Blinded by the storm's fury, Pete peered down the trail, his body partly shielding Abby against the wind. They huddled together, disoriented, isolated in a dense whiteout as the full fury of the maelstrom swirled around them. The relative safety of the tree line, invisible thousands of feet below, was an unreachable goal.

Fifty feet down the trail, a powerful bolt of lightning struck a huge boulder, cracking it in two. The ground hummed with electricity as earsplitting thunder rocked the trail. The hair on their heads stood straight out and the acrid odor of ozone surrounded them. A second flash of lightning and deafening thunder instantly followed the first horrifying bolt.

Abby screamed, consumed by the chaos.

"Keep moving! We've got to get lower on the mountain!" Pete screamed over the wind. Grabbing her around her waist, supporting most of her weight, they staggered down the treacherous trail.

As quickly as the storm engulfed them, the dangerous low pressure cell raced east toward the Continental Divide. Ten agonizing minutes later, the rain finally slowed to a harmless drizzle. Thirty minutes after it began, the crisis was over.

The sun returned, warming the air. Slowly, painfully they descended to the tree line far below. Safe at last, they slipped off their backpacks, ecstatic to be alive. Drenched to the skin, hair plastered against their faces, they laughed deliriously under brilliant sunlight and a cloudless blue sky.

Pete took Abby's face in his hands and kissed her deeply.

"I'm sorry. That storm came up so fast, I almost got both of us killed."

"It wasn't your fault. We'd have made it down a lot faster if I hadn't fallen," she said, giddy with relief. "I guess it just wasn't our time."

"Let's take a look at your ankle." Pete knelt beside her. "Be prepared, it will start to swell as soon as I take off your boot. I can tape it, but it's going to be very painful by the time we get back to the Toyota. We've still got at least three miles to go," he warned.

"Then don't unlace the boot now," Abby suggested. "Maybe it's not broken, only sprained," she said optimistically. Her hand braced against the boulder for support, she gingerly eased onto her left foot, grimacing in pain. "Let me try to walk to the car."

She waited while he attached her daypack to the top of his heavy backpack with a bungee cord and hoisted it onto his back.

"If we take things very slowly, maybe we can do this. Be careful, the trail is very slippery. We don't need another accident," Pete warned. Holding her firmly around the waist, they hobbled down the trail.

Two hours later, utterly exhausted, they reached the Toyota. Pete unlocked the SUV and lifted her onto the rear seat. He gently unlaced her left boot and inspected the damage. The swollen areas of her ankle and foot already were streaked with red and purple bruising. Abby moaned softly as he probed the swollen tissue.

"You may have some broken bones in your foot and ankle," he told her soberly.

She leaned forward to see for herself. "Ugh, no wonder the pain is killing me."

"You need x-rays and a diagnosis by an orthopedic specialist. We're heading to a hospital emergency room in Durango right now. I'm afraid this ends our hiking days in the Rockies this year."

"You think it's that bad?" she asked anxiously.

"Yes," he said, patting her gently, placing her leg along the seat and elevating her foot on her small daypack.

He tossed his gear in the back and climbed behind the wheel. He turned on the ignition, executed a three-point turn and maneuvered slowly along the rutted dirt track.

"Durango is at least an hour drive from here, Abby," he said over his shoulder. "Once we reach the highway, I can make pretty good time." He watched her in the rear view mirror. She was unresponsive, displaying early signs of shock.

"I'm really sorry," he said. "Depending on what the doctors find, we may want to head home as soon as possible."

Abby reached out and touched his shoulder. "Pete, don't blame yourself," she said weakly. "We climbed our first 14,000-footer and we're lucky nothing worse happened up on the mountain. I won't forget this day, for sure. That storm was a peak life experience—a negative one," she said.

"Bad pun, darling. At least you haven't lost your sense of humor."

Chapter Forty

"What the hell is going on up there?" Robert Lombardo shouted into his cellphone. "You assured me that my son's grade problem was settled weeks ago."

He deftly shifted lanes in the usual heavy commuter traffic along the New Jersey Turnpike, heading toward the Lincoln Tunnel and New York City.

"There was an unfortunate administrative mistake. I'm dealing with it now," Roger Smythe responded from Maine.

"Your son's professor recently changed the grade in question back to an F in the computer system. That triggered the probation letter John just received," he explained. "It's a bureaucratic snafu. Unfortunately, the professor is out of touch on vacation. When she returns, I will direct her to change the grade back to B." Smythe fiddled with John Lombardo's grade report on his desk, annoyed that once again he needed to deal with Abby Prescott's student problem. Nonetheless, his diplomatic personal touch was necessary to placate the university's most generous benefactor.

"John is mad as hell, and he has a very bad temper," Robert Lombardo related, somewhat mollified. "He's ready to kill the professor who issued that failing grade. And what's this probation thing all about?"

"Let me explain," said the president. "After the failing grade was placed in his record, John's semester average fell below our satisfactory academic standing. The letter warns him that he must improve his grades or be dismissed from the university. Tell your son to destroy the letter. I can straighten this out in a few days. I regret the problem."

"Take care of it now," the senior Lombardo ordered angrily. "I don't want my son upset. He's working directly for me in our New York office, and I need him fully engaged, not obsessing over some stupid grade."

Half an hour later father and son met in the senior Lombardo's Manhattan office.

"Dad, I'm heading up to Maine tonight. If I drive straight through and take care of business, I can be back the day after tomorrow."

"Hold on, son. I just talked to the president. He's dealing with the screwup. It will take a few days to get the mess straightened out because the faculty member is on vacation. Cool down, John. It's being taken care of. I need you here, not in Maine."

* * *

"Abby, where the heck are you?" Jen asked, seated on her terrace overlooking the ocean.

"We're on Interstate 76 somewhere northeast of Denver. I can still see the Rockies in the rear view mirror." With the Toyota's cruise control set at eighty-five miles an hour, they raced across the high plains of eastern Colorado under an endless blue sky.

"This is utterly desolate country," Abby related to her friend. "Nothing but a four lane divided highway, lots of eighteen wheelers and sagebrush." She glanced out the side window at a lone turkey vulture circling high above, searching for road kill.

"I've got your schedule right in front of me," Jen said. "You're supposed to be near Vail, not on the high plains."

"We're heading home early. I had a little mishap two days ago, broke my ankle and tore some ligaments. I've got a cast halfway to my knee," Abby explained. "I won't be hiking the rest of the summer. Guess we'll stick to sailing for the next few months."

"Abby, I'm really sorry to hear about your accident. I'm calling because there's news from campus and it's not good." Jen gazed absently at the waves crashing against the rocky shore, the aftermath of a major storm passing far out at sea.

"What's going on?"

"It's about your problem student, John Lombardo. Changing his grade back to an F created a minor firestorm. Things hit the fan when Lombardo was notified that he's on academic probation. Apparently, his father complained about the change to Roger Smythe, who phoned me this morning, asking whether I could contact you."

"You didn't give him my cell number, did you?" Abby asked, alarmed.

"Of course not. I pleaded ignorance, said you were out of touch somewhere in the Colorado Rockies. Abby, the connection is breaking up. I'm losing you. Call me right back. I'm at home."

Thirty seconds later, they reconnected.

"Thanks. I owe you, Jen. I'll deal with Lombardo's grade when we get home. We should be back Sunday afternoon at the latest."

"Tell me what happened on the mountain," Jen demanded.

"Actually, we were caught in a bad storm near the summit of our first 14,000 foot peak."

"Are you both okay?"

"We're fine," Abby assured her. "I learned the hard way how dangerous it is to be above tree line during a thunderstorm. Hiking in the Rockies at high altitude is a real challenge. Despite having a touch of altitude sickness during the ascent, we managed to make it to the summit," she related with a touch of pride.

"Starting down from the summit, however, we were caught in a horrendous thunderstorm. Lucky we weren't killed; lightning was all around us. I slipped on the muddy trail and took a bad fall. Pete was awesome, got both of us safely back to the Toyota. However, I'll be hobbling around in a cast for at least six weeks."

"Doesn't sound like the kind of adventure I'd enjoy," Jen said wryly. "Take care. Tell Pete not to drive more than twenty miles over the speed limit."

Abby laughed. "All I can do is ignore the speedometer. See you in a few days."

"What's Jen's problem?" Pete glanced across the console toward Abby, her seat belt loosely fastened across her waist, reclining in the front passenger seat, her injured foot propped on the dash.

"Jen doesn't have a problem. I do. There's an uproar about that grade change I made before we left Maine. Lombardo's father is raising hell on behalf of his son. The president phoned Jen when he couldn't contact me. She told him I was unreachable, climbing in the Rockies. At least I have a few days to figure out how to deal with this mess."

"You knew when you decided to make an issue of his grade that Lombardo won't take an F without a fight," he reminded her. "And if his father is involved, you can bet the president will insist on giving him a passing grade."

"Tough. He failed the course and I'm not changing the grade," Abby said stubbornly.

Pete took a deep breath. There was no good time to inform her about her student's background, but he decided that it had to be done. "Abby, I haven't told you the full story about Lombardo," he said quietly.

"What do you mean? That creep gave me nothing but grief during the entire semester. He deserved a failing grade. How many times have we been through this discussion? There's a principle involved here and I'm not backing down," she said hotly.

"I'm paid to assign grades. It's what I do. Roger Smythe can't force me to change that grade. And his father certainly won't influence me."

"I know, Abby. Take it easy. There's more to Lombardo than you know. Perhaps I should have told you earlier, but I didn't want to upset you."

"What's to tell, Pete? He's just another rich kid whose family gave the university a pile of money." She frowned. "Now they expect a quid pro quo, namely, a degree from the university, whether their son has earned it or not."

"You're probably right. But there's more to the story," he repeated.

"What more is there to tell?" she asked angrily.

"A lot." Pete switched on the emergency blinkers, slowed the SUV and pulled onto the breakdown lane. He turned to face her. "Lombardo has a criminal record," he said bluntly.

Abby stared at him, speechless.

"Are you serious?" she whispered finally. "You mean he's been in prison?"

"Yes."

"How long have you known this? And why are you telling me now?" she asked, stunned.

"I've known for a while. I didn't tell you because I didn't want to upset you. I wanted you to forget about him."

"Thanks for caring about my psyche," she said sarcastically. "Now I want the whole story, Pete."

"Remember, he only has a community college degree despite the fact that he's twenty-five years old?" he continued.

"I'm well aware of his age and his academic record," Abby said angrily. "What else do you know?"

"Lombardo spent time in prison in New Jersey."

"Get out! I don't believe you!"

"Let me explain."

"Go on," she said coldly.

"A few weeks after Lombardo threatened you the first time, I went to New York and New Jersey to check out the family background."

"But you were monitoring my class," Abby interrupted him. "How could you sneak off to New York without my noticing?"

Pete smiled. "We weren't dating then, remember? I was away two days on that first trip. I traveled to New York a second time in April while you were visiting your family in Connecticut."

Abby shook her head in disbelief. "And what did you learn about John Lombardo and his lovely family?"

"I checked local court records near the family home in New Jersey. Multiple restraining orders were issued against him; in fact, he has a thirteen-page rap sheet. The charges range from assault with a deadly weapon—a gun—to multiple drug distribution charges. The most serious charges involved cocaine. He was convicted in New Jersey and spent eighteen months in prison. It was so serious that his father's influence couldn't keep him out of jail."

"You knew about Lombardo's record when he was still in my class? You and your boss allowed a convicted felon to sit in my class, and you didn't tell me?" she yelled, her anger tinged with fear.

She moved away from him, awkwardly settling against the door.

"I'm sorry. I had no choice. Chief Edwards took my investigative results to the president. They ordered me not to inform you about his criminal background under any circumstances. They didn't want to frighten you. If it makes you feel any better, his other professors also were not informed."

"Great. None of us knew about his background," Abby said, reaching for a handkerchief, wiping away tears.

"You alone apparently were the focus of Lombardo's anger."

Pete sat back, pounded the steering wheel, frustrated. "I pleaded with the chief to let me tell you for your own protection."

Anger fading, Abby asked more calmly, "What else do you know about Lombardo? Don't hold anything back," she warned

He was silent for a moment. "What is unusual is that Lombardo's behavior in his other classes was fine. He only acted out in your class. He passed his courses taught by men, apparently with no problems. My conclusion is that he evidently hates women, especially women who exercise authority over him. Personally, I suspect he may be a sociopath, perhaps a psychopath."

Abby stared at him, waiting for more. "What else?"

He removed his sunglasses and rubbed his eyes. "I'm convinced Lombardo is a heavy drug user—crack cocaine, heroin, meth amphetamines—maybe all three. I can't prove it, at least not yet. Despite his prison record for dealing, I haven't found any evidence that he's distributing drugs now.

"Lombardo is under close surveillance when he's on campus. You're not in any danger now," he assured her. "He's working in his father's business for the summer. He left right after the semester ended. That's the whole story, or at least as much as I know myself.

"You can understand why the administration treated this student with kid gloves, Abby. The president was deep into negotiating that huge gift from the Lombardo Foundation; he didn't want to jeopardize the donation to the university."

Abby gazed unseeing at the eighteen-wheelers roaring by. "Pete, how could you not tell me? Did you think I couldn't handle it?" she asked.

"Believe me, I wanted to tell you. I had no voice in the matter. The president also notified your dean and ordered him not to inform you. Lombardo had to remain in your class. The decision was final."

"I can't believe this," she whispered, tears streaking her face. "I thought he was just another wise guy, a rich student who thought he could float through my class. Now I realize that he actually meant it when he said his new goal in life was to get me! I'm an even bigger target now." She broke down completely.

Pete reached for her.

She pushed him away.

"I'm sorry, Abby. I was following orders from my boss and the president," he said defensively.

"That's a lousy excuse, Pete. I thought we were dealing with my problem student together. You were holding back on me. You could have told me long ago. Your behavior is completely unacceptable."

She turned away, staring blindly out the window at the barren high plains landscape.

Pete silently eased the SUV into traffic heading east.

Chapter Forty-One

The late model BMW sped north through the early evening twilight. Friday traffic on I95 was heavy leaving New York, heading for Newport and Massachusetts coastal resorts on the final weekend in July.

Hours later, John Lombardo neared the New Hampshire tollbooths, pulled off the highway and entered the one story brick rest stop. He fed the lobby vending machine and carried the coffee back to his car. Reaching into the glove compartment, he pulled out a dime bag, fashioned a neat line of coke on the center console and snorted. He gasped as the purest crack hit his bloodstream.

Seat reclined, he savored the coke high, his iPod tuned to his favorite heavy metal band. Half an hour later he gunned the Bimmer and raced up the entry ramp onto the interstate; shortly after midnight he entered the parking garage beneath his Portland condo overlooking the harbor and pulled to a stop. A few minutes later he reached his top floor two bedroom unit, popped an Ambien and sprawled across his king bed fully clothed. He would sleep until Saturday evening, when under cover of darkness, he would take care of business.

*　　*　　*

Lombardo parked in Abby's fog shrouded driveway well after midnight. A cautious driveby an hour earlier assured him that the house by the ocean was deserted.

Seated in the darkened car, he snorted a line and savored the cocaine jolt. Then he took his Maglite from the glove box, popped the BMW's trunk lid and surveyed the contents. He stored his loaded gun in the wheel well; it wouldn't be needed tonight.

He pulled on a pair of hospital latex gloves, reached for his set of lock picking tools and walked to the side door. The tools made short work of the lock and he strolled into the deserted kitchen, flicked the light switch by the door and immediately touched the dimmer. Soft lights illuminated the center island and the rest of the kitchen. He left the kitchen door open, returned to the open trunk of the car and retrieved a nine-inch hunting knife, a sledgehammer and an axe from the trunk. And then he set to work.

His first target was the inviting glass top on the breakfast table. A single blow of the sledgehammer shattered the heavy glass. A sea of broken shards sprayed across the floor in the breakfast nook. He turned his attention to the high-end gas cook top and adjacent double oven. A few blows damaged the appliances beyond repair. Then he addressed the kitchen cabinets, gleefully smashing the glasses and dishes, avoiding flying debris and chopping the cupboard doors into fragments.

He strolled into the living room and calmly surveyed Abby's prized artwork. It required only a second to smash a beloved African soapstone sculpture, a prized acquisition from her days in management consulting. Taking the nine-inch hunting knife, he methodically slashed every painting in the room, then attacked the oversized leather sofa and chair, laughing hysterically as a blizzard of down feathers floated to the floor. One blow of the sledgehammer pulverized the glass doors of the gas fireplace. Three heavy blows were required to destroy the eight foot cherry dining table, leaving the legs staggering at crazy angles.

Lombardo walked into Abby's study and switched on the desk lamp. Ripping drawers from the file cabinet, he dumped the contents on the floor, tossing them across the carpet. The mess would take weeks to sort out. Several blows of the sledgehammer took care of the desktop computer monitor, the printer and the tower CPU under the desk.

He continued searching, frustrated that Abby's laptop apparently was missing. Then he realized that she probably had taken it on vacation in order to check email. He slashed her leather desk chair and hacked the expensive cherry desk to smithereens. He threw hundreds of books on the floor and destroyed the bookcases lining two walls with his sledgehammer.

Walking into the large master bedroom, he shredded the expensive king mattress, tossing fistfuls of feathers into the air and watching them slowly float to the carpet. A few blows converted the dressers into firewood. The walk-in closet, loaded with expensive suits and dresses, took five minutes to destroy. Abby would need a whole new wardrobe before the semester began in September.

He peeked into the guest bedroom and decided there was nothing worth destroying. It was the only room in the house he left untouched.

Sweating heavily, he entered the bathroom, doused water over his face and hair and casually toweled off. He inspected Abby's nearly empty medicine cabinet. He found no uppers, tranquilizers, or prescription drugs except a three month supply of birth control pills, which he dumped down the toilet. With a few swipes, he tossed the cabinet's remaining contents to the floor. His sledgehammer made short work of the commode, the sink and the glass shower stall. He opened the shower faucet and watched as a strong stream of water began to fill the shower.

Returning to the living room, he gazed at the full moon struggling through wispy fog. Turning away, he stepped over the debris, inspected the damage and grunted with satisfaction. He flipped the kitchen light switch and closed the door. The destruction of Abby's home had taken less than thirty minutes.

Lombardo threw his tools in the trunk, settled into the driver's seat and calmly backed down the driveway. Then he braked abruptly, returned to the kitchen door and picked the lock once more.

Re-entering the kitchen, he opened the interior door leading to the garage and switched on the light. Delighted to find Abby's Lexus parked along the far wall, he went back to his car and retrieved his hunting knife and axe. In moments, he ripped the Lexus's upholstery to shreds. He took a few heavy swipes across the driver's door, the hood and the roof with the axe. Satisfied with the damage, he left the house for the last time.

At the end of the driveway, he paused to view the darkened house as the full moon broke defiantly through the fog. When Abby and Pete returned from their vacation, he would be safely back in his parents' home in northern New Jersey, enjoying his usual Sunday afternoon golf date with his father.

Members of his father's private club would swear that Robert and John Lombardo, father and son, had spent a pleasant afternoon playing golf, miles from Abby Prescott's destroyed home in Seal Point, Maine. Lombardo only regretted that he wouldn't witness the bitch and her boyfriend's horror when they discovered the wreckage inside her home.

*　　*　　*

Pete pulled into the driveway late Sunday afternoon, touched the remote garage door opener and eased the Landcruiser into the garage. Abby glanced at her car, and then gasped in disbelief.

"Look at my car! It's been trashed!" she screamed. She hopped out of the SUV on one foot and opened the unlocked door to her Lexus. "Oh, no! The seats are slashed—the interior is ruined—somebody destroyed my car!"

Pete, stunned, surveyed the wreckage of the car's interior. A heavy object, possibly an axe or sledgehammer, had dented the hood, roof and the driver's door. He ran into the kitchen, Abby hobbling close behind.

They gazed in horror at the destruction. Stepping cautiously around the glass debris, they entered the wrecked living room. Pete flipped open his cellphone and punched 911. "My name is Peter Byrnes. I'm at a home on Ocean Lane in Seal Point. I want to report a break-in."

"Give me your name, exact address and cell number," the voice said calmly.

"Pete Byrnes at 123 Ocean Lane, cell number 430.569.1639," he responded, walking into the bedroom and study and finally glancing into the bathroom where water covered the tile floor.

"I'm contacting the police right now," said the voice at the other end. "Do you need medical attention?"

"No. The owner has just returned from vacation."

"A cruiser with two officers is on the way," the 911 voice responded. "Please stay on the phone until they arrive."

"Fine."

Speechless and in shock, Abby absently brushed away shards of glass and gingerly seated herself on the raised fireplace hearth. The enormity of the destruction had not yet registered.

Pete pulled her into his arms. "I know this is devastating," he whispered into her hair. "Thank God you are safe. No matter how serious the damage, your furnishings can be replaced. We'll get to the bottom of this break-in, I promise you."

His words failed to comfort her. She drew back and gazed into his eyes. "We both know who did this," she wept. "Lombardo did it and he would have killed me if I'd been home." She shuddered, her tear-streaked face a mask of terror and pain.

"Whoever did this doubtless knew the house was empty," Pete assured her, deliberately calm. "He wouldn't have invaded if we'd been home. You're safe now and I'll make sure you continue to be safe." He grimly looked over her head at the devastation surrounding them. She clung to him, her face buried in his shirt.

"Abby, we have things to do here," he said gently. "Try not to touch anything. The police will want to dust for prints." He seated her on the granite hearth.

"Please call Jen and ask her to come right away," he said, attempting to distract her, taking charge, outwardly businesslike, concealing the rage churning in his gut.

The piercing siren of a police cruiser finally was heard in the distance. "Sit right here while I go meet the police." He handed her his cell phone. Tearfully, Abby punched in the number of her best friend.

"Jen," she said softly.

"Abby, you're back! I've been expecting you all afternoon. How about coming here for dinner? You probably have an empty refrigerator." Jen's cheerful welcome brought her back to reality.

"I don't know how to tell you this," she whispered tearfully. "My house has been trashed—wrecked. We've had a home invasion while we were gone. My car has been trashed, too."

"No! Oh, my God, is Pete with you?"

"Yes. He's outside, talking to the police."

"Rob and I are on the way." Jen hung up and reached for her car keys.

Chapter Forty-Two

Two auxiliary officers on weekend duty detained Jen and Rob Carpenter outside Abby's home. Frustrating minutes later, Pete and Abby emerged and greeted them.

"I can't believe this," Jen hugged Abby.

"I'm having a hard time believing it myself," Abby admitted shakily. "You won't believe the destruction. All the treasures I've collected over the years—everything is lost. Pete thinks the intruder was either in a blind rage or on meth or coke."

Rob wrapped Abby in a bear hug, carefully avoiding the cast on her foot. He pulled back, smiled ruefully. "You had some vacation. A broken ankle and now you come home to this mess," he said sympathetically.

"I'll be fine, Rob," Abby said, pulling herself together.

"You're not allowed in the house or the garage," Pete told them. "The police have begun to examine the crime scene."

"Jen, take Abby back to our house," Rob suggested. "She and Pete can stay with us indefinitely, until they put this place back together."

"Of course, you and Pete must stay with us," Jen said warmly. "We have plenty of room and you'll have all the privacy you want. You can't live in this mess and we won't allow you to go to a hotel.

"Pete and Rob can deal with the police. I'll drive the SUV; we'll unload it at our house. And I'll help you settle into our guest suite."

Abby turned to Rob. "Will you act as my attorney in this mess?"

"Yes, of course. I can help you with police issues and insurance claims as well as legal advice."

Pete took Abby in his arms. "They're right. Go with Jen and get us settled. Rob and I need to be here while the police take photos and check for fingerprints. Let me grab my camera from the Toyota; I'll take some backup photos when the police finish their examination." He helped her navigate into the garage and lifted her into the passenger seat next to the damaged Lexus.

"I don't know how long the police will need today; perhaps a couple more hours," he said. "When they finish, I'll take photos and lock up and call you."

He handed the car keys to Jen and grabbed his digital camera from the glove box. The two men watched Jen back down the driveway, avoiding the squad cars parked haphazardly on the grass beside the driveway. She maneuvered through the gathering crowd of curious onlookers, attracted by the police sirens on an otherwise quiet Sunday afternoon. They disappeared down Ocean Lane, heading toward the center of town.

Pete and Rob were detained when they tried to enter the house.

"You can't come back in here until we finish checking for fingerprints and take photographs of the crime scene. Sorry, that's the law," a Seal Point police officer said.

They didn't argue.

"Where is the chief? Why isn't he here?" Pete asked.

"He's on the way," said the cop over his shoulder.

Roland Buchard, the Seal Point police chief, arrived on the scene minutes later. Ignoring Pete and Rob, he was escorted by an officer into the house, and then returned a few minutes later.

He greeted both men soberly. "I'd like to ask you a few questions," he turned to Pete.

"Of course."

The chief flipped open a pocket tablet. "Let me get some details out of the way first. What's your name and address?"

"My name is Pete Byrnes. I live here, but I'm not the owner of the house," he responded. "Professor Abby Prescott is the owner. She's in a state of shock at the devastation here; we persuaded her to go to Jen and Rob Carpenter's home," he nodded toward Rob.

"The Carpenters are friends. We'll be staying with them until we can get this house back in order," he explained.

"Would it be possible to delay questioning Abby until tomorrow?"

"Under the circumstances, we can take her statement later." Buchard made a note on his pad.

"If you're not the homeowner, what is your relationship to the professor?"

"We live here together."

"I see." Buchard smiled noncommittally.

He turned to Rob. "How are you?" He shook hands and warmly greeted the prominent Portland attorney. "What is your relationship to Mr. Byrnes and the professor?"

"Sorry to meet under these circumstances, chief. To answer your question, Abby Prescott and my wife, Jen, are colleagues at Reid University. Pete Byrnes is a detective on the campus security force. Incidentally, Abby and Pete returned this afternoon from two weeks vacation to find this incredible destruction in their home."

The police chief scribbled notes on his pad.

"You work under Craig Edwards at the university?" he asked Pete, his manner warming slightly.

"Yes."

"We haven't had a housebreak in Seal Point in at least ten years," the chief continued. "Based on my initial check of the house, this doesn't look like the work of local hooligans. More like a professional job by someone determined to destroy the property.

"Do you have any idea who might be responsible for this?" he asked, regarding Pete closely.

Pete shook his head. "I have absolutely no idea who did this. Before you arrived I called my boss and described the situation briefly. Craig Edwards will be in touch with you shortly. I believe he'd like to join this investigation because of our campus connection."

"No problem. I'll welcome any help he can offer." Buchard was silent for a moment, and then asked, "given your university connection, is it possible someone on campus was involved?"

Pete again shook his head. "No idea."

The chief of police jotted a note on his pad. "I'll look around more carefully, consult with my officers, see how the search for prints is coming along. Don't enter the house until I give permission. I'll be back with you shortly. Then you can leave."

"If you don't mind, we'll hang around until your crew has finished. I'd like to take some photos myself, then I'll lock up the house," Pete said.

The chief shrugged. "Suit yourself. This may take a couple hours," he warned, heading for the kitchen door.

"Let's talk, Rob. I need your advice," Pete said quietly. The two men walked around the house to the rocks overlooking the ocean, out of earshot of the police and curious onlookers.

"Why didn't you mention a possible connection to that student who gave Abby problems last semester?" Rob asked.

"Chief Edwards immediately suggested a possible link to John Lombardo. We agreed to keep him out of the picture with the local police until we hunt him down and question him."

"Be very careful," Rob warned. "You're emotionally involved in this; you need to establish parameters around your role in the investigation. If you question Lombardo, at least have Edwards or another officer present during any interview."

"I'll do that," he promised. "Right now, I think it's premature to point to Lombardo. He may be involved, but let's keep it to ourselves until I can check out his whereabouts during the past week."

"You think the break-in was recent?" Rob asked.

"I'd bet on it. For one thing, the water on the bathroom floor hasn't been standing for days. The break-in may have taken place as recently as last night."

"It's possible, I suppose," Rob mused. "You came home a few days early because of Abby's injury. You might have walked in on the intruder."

"Right. I did a quick check before the police arrived. Apparently nothing was stolen," Pete said. "Abby's jewelry, some of it very valuable even to an untrained eye, was strewn all over the master bedroom. Whoever did this didn't care about the valuables; they wanted to destroy everything in sight. They even smashed the medicine cabinet in the bathroom. If they were looking for drugs, they didn't find any because neither Abby nor I use drugs. Drugs were not the objective. Wanton destruction, not burglary, was the objective.

"Would you believe," he continued, "they destroyed the washer and dryer in the utility room? Who in their right mind gives a damn about a washer and dryer? I haven't seen such destruction since I left Baghdad five years ago. This could be the work of a psycho."

"Do you think more than one person was involved in this? A gang, perhaps?" Rob asked.

Pete shook his head. "I think it's the work of one person, perhaps someone high on drugs. Obviously, though, we can't rule anything out."

"I'm aware of Abby's problems with a student last semester," Rob remarked. "She phoned Abby at least once as you were driving back from Colorado. Apparently the president had a question about a grade."

"John Lombardo earned an F in Abby's class last semester," Pete explained. "He was furious with her and actually threatened her when she refused to change the grade. Jen witnessed the confrontation in Abby's office and finally ordered him out of the office. He refused until Jen threatened to call campus security. Apparently, it was an ugly scene. Abby was shaken."

"You seem convinced this student is involved in this break-in," Rob observed.

"I think there's more than a fifty-fifty chance Lombardo is involved," Pete replied.

"Does Abby share your suspicions?"

"Yes. When she saw the destruction, she immediately latched onto him as a suspect. Then she became hysterical, convinced that he really intends to harm her."

"Do you think she's in physical danger?" Rob asked, alarmed.

"It's possible," Pete admitted. "I'll make sure no one gets near her. Given Lombardo's anger over a stupid failing grade, it doesn't take a psychiatrist to question his mental health. I had my suspicions last spring, which I didn't discuss with Abby.

"Rob," he abruptly changed the subject, "since you've agreed to act as Abby's attorney, I need to brief you on some confidential information I developed on Lombardo."

"The attorney-client privilege has been in effect since Jen and I met you today," Rob assured him.

"This student is a bad dude," Pete said, staring out to sea as the setting sun turned the ocean to copper. "He has a prison record, served time for assault with a deadly weapon. Multiple restraining orders have been issued against him in New Jersey and New York. He's been involved with hard drugs. By the way, his family's foundation just gave the university a $90 million gift."

"So that's the connection. Now I remember the name," Rob nodded.

"I reluctantly told Abby about the prison record two days ago as we were driving home," Pete went on. "She was furious. We had a major argument."

"Why didn't you tell her before now?" Rob asked.

"Chief Edwards and president Smythe ordered me to keep Abby out of the loop. The president didn't want to jeopardize that huge gift from Lombardo's family," he said drily.

"To be fair, the chief and the president were honestly concerned not to upset her while Lombardo was in her class. Although she warned them in advance, they didn't expect him to fail the course.

"It took courage for her to issue that failing grade. She was torn. She wanted to be rid of him, and the F means he'd have to repeat the course. There is a chance he will be back in her class this fall," Pete said.

"Not surprisingly, Lombardo went ballistic when he learned he'd failed the class. He got his father involved, and the father pressured the president to have the grade changed. The president directed Cory Howard to change the grade. Cory actually went into the computer system and changed the grade to a B without consulting Abby.

"Shortly before we left for vacation, Abby reviewed her grades, found the grade had been changed to a B and she was furious. She asked my advice and I believe she also confided in Jen."

"What did you advise?"

"I told her to let the B stand and move on. Forget about Lombardo. When you consider the financial stakes involved for the university, the issue seems trivial."

"What did Jen advise?" Rob asked.

Pete shook his head. "I don't know. Just before we left, Abby confronted the dean about the grade. He finally admitted changing the grade and told her that only $10 million of the gift has been received so far. The rest of the funds are being spread over the next five years. The entire gift apparently was in jeopardy unless that damned grade was changed.

"Abby can be very stubborn when she believes a principle is involved," Pete remarked. "Lombardo clearly deserved to fail the course. Give her credit. She stood on principle. The day before we left for Colorado, she changed the grade back to an F. I'm speculating, of course, but Lombardo may have committed this break-in.

"Let's not speculate. We need facts," Rob said quietly.

"Right. I'll check out Lombardo's whereabouts tomorrow. Meantime, we need to distract Abby, keep her occupied with details."

Rob nodded in agreement. "I can't file insurance claims until she prepares a detailed inventory of the items destroyed. Jen can help her; that will keep both of them occupied for a few days. I'll arrange for a Portland firm to move this debris to the dump after the inventory is complete."

For the first time since he arrived, Rob smiled. "Women love to shop. Let's propose an excursion to Boston as soon as possible. That should divert Abby from obsessing about the possible perpetrator."

"Sounds like a plan," Pete said.

Chief Buchard rounded the corner of the house and joined them. "My men will finish up in another ten minutes," he reported. "I've sealed the site with crime tape to keep the curious away and assigned an officer to check the house every couple of hours, day and night, at least for now or until we make an arrest in this break-in.

"As for interviewing the professor, I'll give her a few days to settle down," he continued. "She can call me at the station when she's ready."

"Thank you, chief," Pete said. "She'll appreciate a delay."

"Can you to come down to the station tomorrow? Just call ahead to be sure an officer is on hand to take your prints. We can get the professor's prints later. Tomorrow I'll visit the university and talk to your boss. He may suggest others to question on campus.

"My guys lifted a number of prints off bottles in the refrigerator and some debris in the bathroom. We also lifted some hairs from the bathroom. Of course, they may belong to you or the professor.

"You can go into the house now, but be very careful. Don't disturb the scene," he concluded, crossing several items off his list.

The men escorted Buchard to his squad car parked in the driveway.

"I've never seen such destruction in a home invasion before," the chief remarked. "The vandal displayed an enormous amount of anger. Have you got any ideas about that, Mr. Byrnes?" He eyed Pete curiously.

"Not at this point."

Nodding briefly, Buchard backed out of the driveway and drove away, light bar flashing in the early evening dusk.

The two men re-entered the kitchen. "Pete, why didn't Abby have the house alarmed? It's a valuable property and isolated from other homes. Seems like a reasonable precaution," Rob asked.

"I suggested that several times; she absolutely refused to do it. She didn't want to spoil the interior with alarm devices. She felt very safe out here by the ocean, at least until today."

"There's nothing more we can do here. Let's lock up and go home," Rob suggested.

Pete shot some photos as they picked their way around the debris, extinguished lights and locked each door. Pulling out of the driveway, they waved to the lone patrolman seated in a squad car parked on the street.

Rob opened his cellphone. "Jen, what's for dinner?"

"You guys will have to share a large pizza and a Caesar salad. I'll phone Romeo's with the order right now."

"What about you and Abby?"

"We each had two martinis and some snacks. We're not hungry. An hour ago I persuaded Abby to go to bed. She's already sound asleep. It's been one hell of a day for her."

"That's an understatement," Rob said. "See you in about twenty minutes."

He turned to Pete. "Abby's asleep. Two of Jen's martinis did the trick. We get to eat pizza tonight."

Chapter Forty-Three

Abby greeted Seal Point's police chief at Jen Carpenter's front door.

"Thank you for agreeing to see me today, professor. I'm sure the break-in at your home has been traumatic for you."

"That's an understatement," Abby laughed grimly. Maneuvering on crutches, she awkwardly led the chief through the Carpenter home to the flagstone terrace facing the ocean.

"I feel personally violated, although we were miles away at the time," she said, settling on a chaise near Pete, who rose to greet the officer.

"Based on the level of destruction, I'm glad you were not home at the time," Buchard emphasized. "Whoever did this will be identified and charged," he assured her with more confidence than he felt.

"I understand you want to interview us together," Abby said.

"Yes. I hope you can help each other remember details or offer some rationale behind the crime."

"Please call me Abby," she invited. "I suspect we'll see a lot of each other before this investigation is over."

"No need for formalities at this point. I hope we can work as a team to get to the bottom of this," Pete said.

The chief seated himself at the patio table, rummaged through his briefcase and pulled out a notebook and pen. "Let me bring you up to date," he began. "I've already visited the university. Chief Edwards and I interviewed the business school dean and the president. They reported that you had some problems with a male student last semester. Can you tell me more about that, Abby?" he asked, watching her closely.

She glanced toward Pete, who nodded encouragingly. "Yes, I had behavior problems with a student in one of my classes," she admitted. "His name is John Lombardo and his father is chairman of the university's board of trustees. I suppose you want the ugly details."

"The more information you can provide, the better."

An hour later the officer leafed through his notes. "Abby, let me review just one point. This student initially threatened you in your office sometime last January, relatively early in the semester. Is that correct?"

"Yes."

"Do you recall his exact words?"

"I'll never forget them. His exact words were, 'my new goal in life is to get you.' I asked what he meant by his remark and he said 'you'll see soon enough.' Then he left my office, slamming the door behind him."

"How did you react to his threat?"

"Initially, I was a bit shaken, but I finally blew it off," Abby responded.

"I don't understand."

"At the time, I thought he was challenging my professional expertise, not my physical well being," she went on. "He had taken a somewhat similar course at a community college and considered himself an expert on the subject matter.

"I wasn't aware that he has a criminal record until Pete told me last week during our drive back from Colorado. I believe now that his comment had a completely different meaning."

"Did the dean or the president tell you I was ordered not to discuss Lombardo's record with Abby?" Pete interrupted.

"As a matter of fact, neither one mentioned it," Buchard said, a tiny smile on his lips as he jotted notes on his pad. Abby and Pete waited silently as a lone sailboat glided across the horizon.

"Abby, your former student is now a person of interest in this case. Based on your description of his behavior, he may have anger management problems. I won't speculate on the state of his mental health," the chief said.

"I plan to interview a few students from your class in the next few days. They doubtless have firsthand impressions of his behavior. Professor Carpenter is also on my list to interview. I believe she was present at your second, very unpleasant confrontation with Mr. Lombardo after he learned he'd failed your course."

"Fine. By the way, I believe Jen is working at the university today," Abby volunteered.

"I'll try to interview her this afternoon. I need her assessment of Lombardo's threat during that second confrontation in your office. Please don't communicate with her until after I speak with her."

"Of course."

"Thank you for your time today. This has been very informative. I'll keep in touch as the investigation progresses."

Buchard closed his note pad and stood to leave. "Your case is my number one priority," he assured her. "I assume you'll continue to stay with the Carpenters?"

"Yes. They've been very hospitable and supportive. Also, Rob has agreed to act as my attorney in this matter."

"Excellent. And Pete is a very competent protector. However, when you return home to clear out the debris, please have someone accompany you."

Abby reached for her crutches and rose awkwardly, balancing on one foot. She shook the chief's hand. "Thank you for all you and your men are doing."

"I'm sorry for your ordeal, Abby. Now relax and take care of that broken foot."

Pete accompanied the chief through the Carpenter home to the parked squad car. He leaned on the open door as Buchard settled into the driver's seat.

"Did Craig Edwards tell you that I've been officially assigned to provide protection for Abby?" he asked.

"Yes. That's a very good idea under the circumstances, at least until we get a break in this case."

"She'll be with me 24/7," he assured the officer. "We have a lot of cleaning and sorting to do. And Abby and Jen are planning a shopping trip to Boston to begin replacing the furniture and appliances. Rob and I will go along, just to keep the women from buying out the town," he laughed.

"I'm sure the professor is in good hands, Pete. But be careful. As I learn more about this Lombardo character, I'm becoming convinced he may be involved. He's my prime suspect now, although I wouldn't mention this to Abby. I'm sending one of my detectives to New Jersey to interview him tomorrow. He had better have an airtight alibi for this past weekend."

"I'd like to go along, chief."

Buchard shook his head. "You're too close to the situation to be objective. Besides, you need to stay with Abby."

"Frankly," Pete went on, "I've been dealing with Lombardo since January. I'm convinced he had a major part in the break-in. He may have hired someone to do it, but I'm betting he did it himself. I hope you find evidence to prove he was in the house."

"We're working that angle right now. Stick close to the professor. Don't let her out of your sight."

"Hey, this is the best assignment I've had in my life." Pete waved as Buchard slowly backed down the driveway.

Chapter Forty-Four

"Please hold the line for the president," Roger Smythe's administrative assistant said.

Cell phone in hand, Abby rested on a chaise on Jen's terrace, her foot elevated to ease the swelling. An overturned book lay across her chest and dark glasses shielded her eyes from the intense August sun. She gazed at the ocean, a sheet of sparkling diamonds extending to the horizon.

She turned to Pete, lying nearby. "The president wants to talk to me. Bet I know what's coming."

Pete advised, "Insist on a face to face meeting. Don't let him bully you into agreeing to change the damn grade over the phone."

Abby nodded.

"Hello, Roger."

"Abby, I'm so sorry to learn that your home was seriously vandalized. It must have been a terrible shock to return from vacation to find the destruction." The president sounded genuinely sympathetic.

"Thank you. You may not have heard that I had a hiking mishap in the Colorado Rockies. My foot is in a cast and I'm hobbling around on crutches. We drove home a few days early, only to walk in on a trashed home. I guess it just wasn't my week," she said.

"I hope your injury is healing properly?"

"Yes. The doctors in Colorado did a fine job. In a few weeks I'll get a boot cast and be more mobile."

"If I can help, Abby, let me know. I'll ask your dean to assign your classes to first floor classrooms."

"That shouldn't be necessary, Roger."

She rolled her eyes at Pete, waiting for the president to get to the point of his call.

"Abby, I'd like to discuss that grade change on your former student, John Lombardo."

"Yes, of course."

"I understand you reversed the B grade that had been recorded and replaced it with an F."

Pete smiled encouragingly, listening to one side of the conversation.

"He failed my course last spring," Abby said firmly, "and the grade I originally submitted was an F. Just before I went on vacation, I reviewed my grades on the university computer system to assure they'd been posted properly. The original failing grade that I assigned had disappeared into cyberspace and been replaced with a B. That obviously was an error. Of course, I changed his grade back to the original F. Then I left for vacation."

"I see," said the president, silent for a few moments. "Abby, can you meet me in my office during the next few days?" he asked. "I'd like to review this grade more fully. However, if getting around is difficult, I can visit you at Jen Carpenter's home."

"It would be easier if you came here. Of course, Pete Byrnes can drive me to campus. We can meet in your office, whichever you prefer.

"Frankly, Roger," she continued, "I don't understand why issuing an F to John Lombardo merits this sort of attention." She winked at Pete.

The president didn't respond.

"I'll drive over to Seal Point," he said finally. "Let me transfer you to my assistant to arrange a meeting."

Moments later she turned to Pete. "We're meeting here tomorrow afternoon at three o'clock."

"Great. Meet him on your turf."

"I may have a small strategic advantage," she observed. "I know he'll want me to change that grade back to a B. He doesn't want Lombardo on academic probation for the fall semester."

"Before tomorrow afternoon, you need to decide what you're going to do," Pete advised. "If Lombardo is linked to your house break-in, and I think he is, there's no telling how he'll react if that failing grade stays on his record."

"So you want me to give him a B he didn't earn," Abby said defensively.

Pete shook his head. "That's your decision. I'm not making any recommendations. You realize, of course, that Lombardo is not your average student. This guy is a very bad actor. He has a history of violent behavior and a prison record for drug dealing and assault. He's displayed serious anger management problems since he arrived on campus. Personally, I suspect he may be into heavy drugs—cocaine, perhaps crystal meth."

She reached for him and he took her in his arms.

"I can protect you, Abby. He won't get to you physically. However, think about how you felt when he was in your class last semester. You were completely stressed out."

"Yes," she shuddered.

"He nearly spoiled the entire semester for you, and he'll be back on campus next month. You can't avoid him entirely. Do you want to spend the next semester looking over your shoulder, afraid he'll confront you in the hall or the parking garage when you walk to your car?"

"I don't know. Maybe if I stand firm on the grade, he'll transfer to some other school," she suggested.

"You know that's wishful thinking, Abby. His father is chairman of the board of trustees and his family foundation just donated $90 million to the university. Lombardo is not going anywhere. He thinks Reid University owes him a degree."

"You're probably right," she said, her mood darkening.

"Pete, should I agree to change the grade to a B, or maybe a C?"

He shook his head. "I'm not advising you one way or another. I don't deal with academic issues, remember? I'm just a campus security guy."

"How far do you want to take this issue? If Lombardo really trashed your house because he didn't like his grade, is it worth another confrontation? If there's a next time, we might not be away on vacation."

He returned to his chaise. "You asked Jen's advice about that grade. What was her opinion?"

"She wouldn't give me a direct answer. My impression, though, is that she wants me to change the grade to a B."

"Just make a final decision before you meet with the president. You can't avoid it any longer," he said firmly.

"I'm not going to decide now," Abby said defensively. "I have until tomorrow afternoon. Lombardo deserved an F in my course. However, if he trashed my house, what will he do next? Kill me?"

"Don't go there, Abby," Pete warned. "Put that thought out of your mind."

"It's hard not to think about what he might do."

"We don't know who trashed your house," he reminded her. "When we find the criminal, the police and the courts will deal with it. You feel violated and depressed right now. I understand that." He pointed to the cast on her foot. "And your injury also affects your mood."

"Sorry. I'm not easy to live with right now."

Pete changed the subject. "Rob says the negotiations with the insurance company are coming along quickly. A whopping settlement check is almost in the mail. Think about the fun you'll have furnishing your house."

"I hope you'll help me," Abby said.

"Of course," he replied softly. "Rob is at work and Jen's at school. Think you can handle a little bedroom time? We can work around the cast if we're clever."

"I thought you'd never ask. Help me up," Abby ordered. "I'll race you to the bedroom."

"That's no contest. I'll carry you. We'll cross the finish line together."

Chapter Forty-Five

Pete greeted the president the next afternoon. "Abby is in the living room. We abandoned the terrace today," he remarked, stacking the president's umbrella near the door.

"How is she feeling?" the president asked quietly.

"Her spirits are improving, I'm happy to say. The home invasion was a real shock, and her broken foot added to the trauma."

"I wouldn't bother her now except that we need to deal with a grade situation for one of her students."

"Abby discussed that problem with me," Pete responded. "Are you aware that the chief of police here in Seal Point considers John Lombardo a person of interest in the case?"

"No," the president frowned. "That does complicate an already delicate situation, doesn't it?"

"You could say that. Chief Buchard and my boss are cooperating on the case. Buchard sent a detective down to New Jersey to check out Lombardo's whereabouts during the time we were in Colorado."

"Really?" the president raised an eyebrow. "I assume Craig Edwards will keep me informed as the investigation proceeds."

"Of course." Pete ushered the president into the living room where Abby, balancing on crutches, greeted him.

"Thank you for coming, Roger. I'm not allowed to drive until I get a soft boot cast on my foot. My lack of mobility is already wearing thin."

"Please sit down," Abby gestured to a wing chair near the fireplace. She awkwardly collapsed onto the sofa and propped her injured foot on a low stool.

"Would you like some coffee or tea?" Pete asked from the doorway.

"A cup of tea would be wonderful," Abby said. "Roger, coffee or tea?"

"Tea would be fine. Thank you."

Pete returned from the kitchen and arranged the tea and a plate of cookies on the coffee table. "I'll leave you to your meeting," he said.

"Abby, I'm sure the damage to your home must be devastating," the president began sympathetically. "I am truly sorry. Surely the police are working hard to identify the criminal responsible."

"Yes. Unfortunately, they haven't come up with many leads. They checked the house for fingerprints and came up empty except for mine and Pete's. This apparently was a very professional job. I'll be on edge until an arrest is made."

"I understand Pete is your bodyguard until this case is solved. You're in capable hands."

She smiled. "Yes, he takes his assignment quite seriously."

"Abby, I want to discuss John Lombardo's grade situation with you," the president said, finally turning to the subject of their meeting. "You need to understand the importance of his family's very generous gift for the future of Reid University."

"Roger, I'm well aware of the magnitude of that gift and its importance," she responded. "Would you please answer one question for me?"

"Of course."

"Has the Lombardo family threatened to rescind the gift unless he receives a passing grade in my class?"

The president was silent for a moment, his gaze averted, lips pursed. "The answer to your question is yes," he said reluctantly. "Please do not share what I'm about to tell you with anyone—not with Jen or Rob Carpenter, Pete Byrnes or your faculty colleagues."

Jen nodded agreement.

"I regret this situation more than I can possibly say," he went on. "Robert Lombardo telephoned while you were away and in unmistakable language threatened to rescind the remaining $80 million pledged by his foundation unless his son's grade is changed. He admitted that his son has had some problems growing up, but assured me that John is, in his words, 'a good person who needs guidance.'"

"So, the remaining gift is jeopardized unless I change this grade," Abby repeated quietly. "And I cannot overlook the possibility that Lombardo trashed my home or hired someone else to do it. I may be in some physical danger if I refuse to change the grade. Is that a fair assessment of the situation?"

"Perhaps."

"If I insist on principle to assign the grade this student deserved, the university will lose $80 million," she repeated again.

"Very likely," he agreed reluctantly.

Abby was silent, staring out the window as rain beat heavily against the glass. The grandfather clock struck the half hour in the silent room.

"I'll change the grade to a C, although he hasn't earned it," she said finally. "I checked his academic record on the computer this morning. The C will return him to good academic standing. He won't be on academic probation for the fall term."

The president was silent.

"One more question, Roger," she said after a pause.

"Go ahead."

"Who actually changed that grade from an F to a B on the computer system?" she asked, implying she didn't know the truth.

"Since we're being completely frank, I'll tell you exactly what happened.

"After my initial telephone conversation with Robert Lombardo about the grade, I discussed the matter with your dean. Cory Howard defended you vigorously. He noted the failed examinations and the plagiarism of a major paper. Lombardo clearly deserved the failing grade you assigned.

"Don't think less of Cory," the president continued. "I directed him to change the grade without your knowledge. The responsibility is mine."

"I see," Abby said softly, not acknowledging that Cory Howard already had admitted his action.

"Let me make one more observation, Roger."

"Of course."

"I'm absolutely certain that John Lombardo is not intellectually capable of earning passing grades at this university. When he enrolls in more challenging advanced courses, he will fail. Then another faculty member in the School of Business or elsewhere on campus will issue another failing grade. The problem won't end with this grade change," she warned. "And whoever dares to issue an F to this student in the future will be exposed to the same intimidation tactics that I have faced.

"You may as well simply sign a blank diploma," she said bitterly. "He can't earn a degree from this university honestly."

"I genuinely disagree with you," the president replied calmly. "Lombardo earned passing grades in his other courses last semester. In fact, he earned a B in an environmental sciences course. He failed only your course. With hard work, I'm confident he can complete our program satisfactorily."

"We'll just have to wait and see, won't we?" Abby said. "I believe he has a problem with female authority figures. Of course, if he managed to interact only with male professors, he just might squeak by."

"An interesting possibility," the president said heavily. He rose to leave. "Personally, this entire matter is extremely distasteful," he said again. "However, when I weigh the future benefits to the university against this single exception to our academic standards, the university's interests clearly must take precedence. The stakes are enormous."

"I'm well aware of that, Roger," Abby sighed. "I'll go online later this afternoon and change the grade to a C," she promised. "I hope this is the end of it. Somehow, I doubt it."

"Thank you for making this change. Please don't get up, Abby. I'll see my way out."

* * *

Pete returned, his cellphone in hand. "Chief Buchard needs to speak to you. His detective has information on Lombardo's whereabouts while we were on vacation."

"Great! Maybe he has good news," she said, taking the phone.

"Hello, chief."

"Professor, I have some bad news to report. My detective just phoned from New York to report that John Lombardo has an absolutely airtight alibi during the time you were away from home. Numerous witnesses outside his family also corroborated his whereabouts."

"No," Abby cried. "Your officer must be mistaken."

"There's no mistake. Lombardo could not have been directly involved in your house break. In fact, last Sunday afternoon he was playing golf with his father at their private club in New Jersey. And two bartenders and the club owner are certain he was in their New York city disco club until the wee hours last Friday night and Saturday morning when we believe your home was trashed. He could not have been in Seal Point last weekend."

"Chief, please tell Pete what you just told me."

He listened silently. "Thanks for the information, chief. When your detective returns from New York, I'd like to speak to him directly if you don't object."

"Not a problem," Buchard said.

Pete handed the phone back to Abby. "Chief, I can't believe Lombardo had nothing to do with the break-in. He's the logical suspect."

"I agree. He was our prime suspect and we'll continue to consider him a person of interest in our investigation. But he was not in Maine last weekend," he said firmly.

"Lombardo's father has provided alibis for the entire period you were on vacation," he continued. "He works in his father's company in New York and has been living with his parents in northern New Jersey since June."

"Did your detective speak to Lombardo directly?"

"No. His father refused to let my officer question him. Given the supporting corroboration from others, it wasn't necessary. Based on Lombardo's belligerent personality, I see no reason to pursue that avenue any further."

Abby sighed. "What's next in the investigation?"

"We're not exactly at a dead end, Abby. Although we identified only your and Pete's fingerprints in the house, we also lifted numerous hair samples for analysis. They may belong to both of you, or perhaps not. I need your samples for testing to see if we have any unidentified samples. The DNA analysis will take at least a couple weeks."

"Pete will bring our samples down to the station shortly."

"Thank you. We're not giving up on this case, Abby. However, knowing that your student was not involved is a major setback. Leads are slim at the moment. If a professional trashed your home, it will be very difficult to track him down. And linking a professional to your student is even more problematic."

"There's still the hair analysis," Abby tried to sound hopeful. "Perhaps that will produce a lead. If you find some hair samples that don't match our DNA, can't you access a database to check DNA samples of known criminals?"

"Yes, but don't pin your hopes on identifying the criminal through DNA technology," the chief warned. "DNA analysis can be useful as corroborating evidence. We would need more direct evidence to bring charges."

"Thank you so much for your work, chief."

"I'm sorry, Abby," Pete said. "This is discouraging. Still, we've been home only a week, and the police have a lot more investigative work ahead."

"Don't try to cheer me up," she said stubbornly. "I'm positive Lombardo is involved, but if he has such a strong alibi, it may be impossible to prove."

Smiling wanly, she pulled a strand of hair from her head and handed it to Pete. "There's a baggie in the kitchen. Please take my sample and one of your own down to the police station. I suppose the sooner we get the DNA results, the better. This may be our last hope for identifying who trashed my house and car."

Chapter Forty-Six

"Abby, I want you to agree to do something for me this afternoon. And please don't give me a hard time about this," Pete said after he returned from the police station.

"I never give you grief about anything," she smiled innocently. "What can I do for you?"

"Let me teach you to use a gun. Here's the plan," he continued before she could interrupt. "After a little instruction, we can go to a police pistol range in Portland and practice."

"What! Are you serious?" she said, instantly defensive. "You know how much I hate guns. When you moved in with me, you promised to leave your weapons at the security office on campus." She regarded him suspiciously. "Have you kept a gun here in Jen and Rob's house?"

He didn't answer.

"Isn't it enough that I finally agreed to install a security system in the house?" she asked.

"Please calm down," he said firmly.

"There's nothing more to discuss."

"Yes, there is," his voice rose. "You've got to realize that your life has changed. You need personal protection."

"That's what the security system is for," she retorted.

"The system will warn you of an intruder; it won't protect you personally if I'm not around."

"Are you planning to move out?" she asked, incredulous.

"No," he assured her. "I have a new assignment in campus security. I was hoping the police would make an arrest in your housebreak, but that may not happen anytime soon."

"What's your new assignment?" she asked. "Are you still going to be a detective?"

"Yes, of course," he responded. "Beginning in September, I'll be investigating possible drug distribution activities on campus. I'll be working several nights a week, and you'll be alone in the house."

"I see," she said, mollified. "Have you started the investigation?"

"Yes. I'm following the leads we have, tracking the source of the drugs. It may take a few months or even longer. Because drug deals often go down at night, you'll need protection when I can't be with you."

"I'm a big girl, Pete. I don't need to learn to use a gun," she insisted stubbornly. "Besides, whoever trashed my house wouldn't have the nerve to return. Thanks to the security system, I'll be fine."

"We don't know who we're dealing with, Abby. You need protection until we have an arrest. Learning to handle a gun is not a big deal, and you'll probably never have to use it. A few hours of instruction and then frequent practice on the range is all you'll need.

"Please do this for me," he pleaded. "I love you, Abby, and in my judgment, you need protection when I'm not with you."

She said softly, "I love you, too. And I respect your judgment and admire your professionalism. Let me think about it."

"Fine. Promise you'll give me an answer tomorrow," he said, convinced now that she would agree.

He took her in his arms and kissed her gently.

"Is that a promise of more to come?" she gazed into his eyes.

"Absolutely," he grinned. "Jen and Rob won't be back for hours." He lifted her from the sofa and carried her to the guest bedroom.

* * *

"Robert Lombardo is on line six," the president's administrative assistant announced.

Roger Smythe lifted the handset. "Hello, Robert. I want to report the outcome of my visit this afternoon with the professor who gave your son an F in that course last spring."

"Did you get the mess straightened out?" Lombardo asked coldly.

"Yes. She has agreed to change the grade to a C. She absolutely rejected my suggestion that she issue a B. However, John will be in good academic standing when he returns to the university next month."

"Good. Problem solved. John will just have to settle for a gentleman's C," Lombardo said more cordially. "Now we can move forward with plans for the new building. I expect to play a major role in its design since my money will build it."

"Absolutely. Your generosity is making possible an enormous step forward in meeting our long term vision for excellence," the president responded. "I'll be back in touch with you in September to begin the planning process." Smiling, he hung up the handset. Mission accomplished.

Chapter Forty-Seven

They stood side by side, separated by a low partition, in the indoor gun range. Holding the Ladysmith .38 revolver in the approved two-handed position, Abby aimed and squeezed the trigger repeatedly. She fired at the target, a paper image of a human head and torso hanging from wires thirty feet down the narrow firing range. She placed the empty gun on the shelf, removed the sound deadening ear protectors and pushed her safety goggles into her hair.

"Good job," Pete said, pulling the target back along the wires toward them, inspecting the results carefully. Two bullets pierced the target in the chest area, one tore a hole in the paper head, and two missed entirely.

"How much longer do I have to do this?"

"That's enough for today. Next week I'll teach you to use my 9mm service automatic. One lesson with it and then weekly practice should be adequate," he promised.

Despite initial resistance, Abby had proved to be a surprisingly apt pupil. For two hours a week over the past month, with Pete as her instructor, she rapidly gained confidence and proficiency in firearms safety and target shooting. Although she wouldn't admit it, Abby was secretly rather pleased with her progress. She found the experience interesting as long as she didn't dwell on the need for personal protection.

"Won't I need some sort of license or permit to keep a gun in my house?" she asked as Pete stowed Abby's revolver together with his own automatic in a carry bag along with the safety goggles and ear protectors.

"Yes. Chief Buchard can issue you a permit. You'll need to complete an application form and pay a $35 fee; the chief knows you are of good character and the reasons for needing personal protection. Getting a permit to carry a concealed weapon won't be a problem."

They left the firing range and passed through the deserted lounge. Abby had progressed to a soft boot cast on her foot and hobbled along with the aid of a cane. Pete inserted dollar bills in the vending machine near the door, punched two tabs and handed Abby a bottle of water, keeping a Coke for himself. Exiting the air-conditioned building, they were assaulted by a siege of late August humidity smothering the Portland area.

"You've made great progress, Abby. I'd give you an A so far. You're a natural shooter. You've got a steady hand, you've learned how to sight in the target and you squeeze the trigger nicely. Many people, and this is not gender specific, tend to pull the trigger, so the gun jerks and the bullet misses the target." He opened the SUV's passenger door and helped her into the vehicle, then climbed into the driver's seat and drove out of the parking lot.

"I consider that a high compliment coming from a pro like you," Abby said. "I was dreading these lessons. Now, I'm feeling much more comfortable around firearms. Just don't ask me to clean the guns, that's your job."

"Okay, I'll clean and oil our guns. But you have to agree to keep a loaded gun in the bedroom as long as whoever trashed your house is running around loose."

"If I must have a loaded gun in the house, it might as well be in the bedroom," she agreed. "I certainly don't want one lying around where friends might see it."

"Your new alarm system is a good warning device, but it probably would take ten minutes for police to reach the house in an emergency. Buchard knows about your training and he agrees that having weapons in the house is a reasonable precaution, at least until he makes an arrest."

"If he ever makes an arrest," Abby said glumly.

A month after the break-in, the couple finally moved back to Abby's house above the ocean. She loved her property with its panoramic ocean views and the sounds of surf pounding against the rocks below her windows. Fresh carpeting in the living room and the new furniture scheduled to arrive shortly helped ease her trauma.

"It feels good to get back into the house," Abby remarked. "The repairs are taking much longer than I expected. The rest of the furniture won't be delivered for another week. However, as long as we have a kitchen to cook in, and a new bed to sleep on, I can deal with it. At least we can eat at home now that the new appliances and granite are installed. I hated eating out all the time or imposing on Rob and Jen's hospitality."

"And I enjoy cooking in your kitchen," Pete responded, wheeling onto the interstate, heading north out of Portland.

"My study is still a mess," she remarked. "Sorting through all the papers on the floor and putting them back in folders is time consuming.

And thanks for setting up my new computer. Now I can prepare my lectures for the fall semester."

Pete settled back for the drive to Seal Point. Perhaps now was a good time to bring up an issue that had been on his mind for several weeks.

"Classes begin next week," he said, glancing across the seat toward Abby. "How do you feel about getting back into the classroom? John Lombardo will be on campus and you'll probably run into him from time to time. Are you ready to deal with that?"

"I can't wait for classes to begin," Abby said enthusiastically. "As for Lombardo, obviously I'm bound to run into him occasionally. I'll ignore him, look the other way. I can tolerate him as long as he's not in my classes," she said confidently. "Let's hope I never meet another student like him. Once in a career is enough. I checked his records on the academic computer system just last week. He's enrolled in four classes, two of them in the School of Business."

"You realize that this drug investigation will take me off campus from time to time," Pete reminded her, "and I'll need to work several nights a week."

Abby laughed. "Now you sound like a little old lady. Don't forget I lived alone in my house for six years before you moved in." She reached across the seat and touched his inner thigh. "I'll miss you, but I'll be fine. Between the alarm system and my gun, I feel very secure."

She slapped the boot cast on her foot. "I'm actually looking forward to beginning rehab. I'll be a lot more mobile when I can get around without a cane."

Pete smiled, relieved. Abby's confidence was returning as the trauma of the home invasion slowly receded. He was uneasy, though, that no arrest had been made. More disturbing, there were no active leads in the case. Recently, the Seal Point police chief privately admitted that the investigation had reached a dead end. John Lombardo was their only lead. If he was not responsible for the housebreak, the likelihood of making an arrest was almost nil. Based on his own law enforcement experience, Pete suspected the case might never be solved.

Perhaps it was just as well. Abby's life was returning to normal as she regained her usual optimism and confidence. Teaching and an active social life would help dim the memory of that horrible July discovery.

Chapter Forty-Eight

Pete entered the campus security office on the first day of fall classes, ready for a briefing on his assignment.

Security chief Craig Edwards waved him to a seat at the conference table. "Before we get started, how is Abby? Is she ready to get back into the classroom? And how is her foot? Still hobbling around with a cane?"

"She's fine, chief. Her confidence is back and she's looking forward to teaching. The boot cast came off last week," he went on. "Six weeks of rehab and she'll be good as new."

"Excellent. Now, how about an update on the housebreak. Has Buchard dug up any new leads?"

"Unfortunately, no. Our prime suspect, John Lombardo, has a rock solid alibi and our leads have dried up. We're still waiting for DNA test results on a few stray hairs the police picked up in the house. They might not belong to Abby or me, but that's a long shot. If the analysis doesn't produce anything interesting, the case is cold. We may never know who trashed her house."

Have the Seal Point police checked across the state for similar break-ins?"

"Yes. There have been a number of housebreaks along the coast involving property theft. The trashing at Abby's home was unique because nothing was taken.

"Whoever destroyed her home displayed a rage I've never seen before," he went on. "Had Abby been home, she could have been assaulted, perhaps murdered."

"Maybe something will turn up, Pete." Chief Edwards reached for a file on his desk. "Let me brief you on your next assignment. Beginning today, you will concentrate on a possible drug link between Rick Stewart and John Lombardo."

"Right."

"Although this assignment has been ongoing, I understand you haven't had much time to deal with it. What's the current status?" Hands behind his head, the campus security chief leaned back in his chair.

"The link between those two is tenuous at best. When the Seal Point detective checked out Lombardo in New York and New Jersey, he learned that Lombardo often spends evenings and weekends at a disco in New York City. NYPD consider that club a distribution center for illegal drugs—coke, heroin, meth, Ecstasy—you name it. I'm convinced that he's a heavy user, but I can't tie Lombardo or Stewart to drug dealings on campus, at least not yet.

"Professor Stewart has been off campus all summer, consulting with the oil and gas industry. And I've been totally involved with the Seal Point police and the housebreak since we returned from vacation in July."

"Pete, we absolutely need to know whether one of our faculty members is linked to drug trafficking. We can't allow heavy drugs to gain a foothold on this campus. It could seriously damage the university's reputation, not to mention destroy the lives of some of our students. Report back to me on progress by the end of next week.

"As of today, you're officially off the Prescott housebreak. Of course, how you spend your off-duty time is your business," Edwards smiled.

"Right." Pete grinned.

* * *

Abby worked on her laptop, putting the finishing touches to the first lecture for her course in human resource management. The sounds of Beethoven's Piano Concerto No. 1 filled the study. Sunlight shimmered off the ocean producing sheets of brilliant diamonds in the early afternoon light. Absorbed in her work, the hours slipped peacefully by. She stopped occasionally, visited the kitchen and replenished her coffee. Summer was drawing to a close. She was ready for classes to begin.

Chapter Forty-Nine

Working in her office overlooking Founders Court, Abby sensed someone watching her. Her eyes widened as John Lombardo strolled into her office and closed the door. She hardly recognized him. In contrast to the fashionably cut dark hair of last semester, a tangled, greasy mass of hair extended below his collar and a dark, unkempt beard strikingly altered his appearance.

"What can I do for you, John?" she asked crisply, closing her laptop and folding her hands on the lid. He was no longer her student; his disruptive behavior no longer concerned her. The terror she'd experienced last spring was buried deep inside. She could deal with him.

"I understand your home was trashed last summer, professor," he greeted her, slowly removing the dark glasses that hid bloodshot eyes. "Sorry to hear it. I hope you weren't too upset," a fleeting smirk creased his bearded face.

"Thanks for your concern," she responded coolly. "How did you learn about it? Were you in Maine during July?" she asked.

"Oh, no," he said softly. "I was working in New York all summer and playing golf with my father on weekends. My father and some friends in New York told me that a detective from the Seal Point police department was nosing around, checking my alibi. The cop didn't talk to me directly; I could have set him straight. By the way, I hear Seal Point is a nice little town.

"Did you think I had something to do with your housebreak?" he asked.

Abby was silent. Then she said, "Did you know the vandal also trashed my car?"

"Really? Sorry about that," he repeated. The smirk on his face belied his words.

"Anything else on your mind, John?"

"Actually there is, Abby." He grinned, "I can call you Abby, can't I, now that you're no longer my professor?"

"Whatever," she said dismissively. "Why are you here?" she asked, rapidly losing patience, wanting him out of her office.

"We still need to deal with my grade in your course last spring. Remember that grade you gave me?"

"Yes, I remember it very well. It was an F," she said firmly. "So, you're back again to discuss your grade," a thin smile crossed her lips.

"I deserved a B, professor. Shame on you for failing me," he chided. "You know I didn't fail that course. Whatever got into you to screw up my academic record like that?"

"Thanks to your father's intervention, your grade was changed to a C a week ago. Have you checked your record?" She sat back in her chair, outwardly calm, but her heart began to race as she struggled to control rising anxiety.

"I'm still not satisfied," he said.

"I can review your performance one more time, in case you've forgotten," she offered calmly.

"Why don't you do that, Abby?" he said.

She raised her index finger. "First, you failed the three examinations in the course."

"Not a big deal," Lombardo retorted.

"Second," she continued, "you plagiarized the final research paper, a very serious academic offense. And your plagiarism wasn't very clever. I found the exact paper for sale on an internet site for $100. The paper's content was an adequate effort. Too bad you didn't research and write it.

"You're lucky I didn't file an academic dishonesty petition against you," she went on. "In case you haven't read the student handbook, you can be dismissed from the university for plagiarism."

Lombardo leaned forward, about to interrupt.

She pointed a finger at him. "I'm not finished, John. Finally, your disruptive behavior during lectures angered your classmates and annoyed me. You didn't earn any credit for class participation."

She leaned back. "The failing grade I originally issued was appropriate."

"Details, details," Lombardo waved his hand dismissively. "I needed a good grade to maintain my academic standing here at dear old Reid University. My father wasn't happy with the F you issued."

"Apparently, you haven't been in touch with your father recently," Abby said. "I understand from the president that your father wanted your grade changed to a B. At the president's request, I finally agreed to change your grade to a 'gentleman's C,' although you don't deserve it and you're certainly no gentleman," she retorted angrily, her voice rising.

"Of course, I'm sure you are aware that there was more at stake than your grade in this course," she continued, quickly regaining control.

"You're referring to the $90 million gift the family pledged to the university? Apparently, $80 million is still outstanding," Lombardo raised an eyebrow.

"Yes."

"So you could say that I bought a C in your course for $80 million," Lombardo said.

"Reach any conclusion you wish," Abby snapped.

"How much will it take to change that grade to a B? How about another $5 million on top of the original gift? I can arrange that, you know," he offered.

Abby shook her head. She stood and leaned toward the student, her hands gripping the closed laptop.

"Forget it, John. The grade stands and this conversation is finished. Don't visit my office again. And if you happen to see me in the hall or around campus, don't bother to say hello."

"How unfriendly, professor," he sneered.

"Get out!" She pointed toward her office door, anger overcoming fear.

"I'm not finished with you, Abby," he taunted, slowly rising from the chair. "Not until you change that grade to a B."

"Get out *now*!" she shouted.

Lombardo suddenly reached out, twisted her arm in a bruising grip, and pulled her across the desk, his bearded face inches from her own, his stale breath sickening her.

"I'll be back, Abby," he promised, his face an ugly mask.

"I'm warning you, don't call campus security. Don't discuss this meeting with anyone—not the president, not the dean, not your live-in boyfriend or your faculty buddies. Got it, Abby?" He released her arm, angry red welts visual evidence of his assault.

He sauntered to her office door, turned and raised his right arm, his thumb and index finger extended.

"Bang, bang, Abby," he said softly. He closed the door and disappeared down the deserted hall.

She collapsed in the chair, her heart racing, hands shaking as she speed dialed Pete's cell number.

Chapter Fifty

"What happened, Abby!" Pete shouted, his cellphone breaking up as he passed a dead zone on the interstate outside Portland.

"Lombardo threatened me again! He just left!" she screamed hysterically.

"Calm down," he ordered, his voice steady. "He's probably already left the building."

"If I had my gun right now, I'd use it on that bastard," she cried.

"Abby, listen to me. Lock your office door and call Jen. If she's on campus, go to her office and wait for me. I'll be there in half an hour." He floored the SUV and raced under the green interstate sign indicating an exit ramp a half-mile ahead. Weaving through heavy traffic, he cut off an 18-wheeler, pulled into the exit lane and entered the long ramp at sixty miles an hour.

"I can't call Jen," Abby cried. "He grabbed me, warned me not to tell anyone about his visit. He's insane."

"I know this is tough, but you've got to calm down." Pete blew through a red light on the secondary road, raced down the entry ramp and merged into traffic heading north toward the campus.

She sank into her chair, phone glued to her ear. Pete's reassuring voice helped control her panic. She gazed out the window at the peaceful scene on Founders Court below. Students strolled hand in hand along the broad sidewalks, clusters of coeds lounged on blankets, cell phones and iPods close at hand, relaxing in the warm September sun.

"Maybe he was high on drugs," she said, panic finally receding.

"That's possible. It's not important now."

Someone knocked loudly on Abby's office door.

"Oh, God! Somebody's at the door! He's back!" she cried, instantly terrified.

"Abby, are you okay? I heard a door slam down this way," Jen Carpenter waited anxiously outside the door.

Abby opened the door and pulled her friend inside.

"Pete, Jen is here now," she said into the cellphone. "What should we do?"

"Go to her office and lock the door. I'll be there shortly."

Flooring the heavy Toyota, Pete raced north toward the campus, switching lanes around slower cars, hoping the Maine state police were patrolling elsewhere. Twenty minutes later he exited the interstate onto Route 1 where traffic slowed to a crawl. After what seemed an eternity, he reached the wide thoroughfare leading to the campus entrance. Ignoring the fifteen mile per hour speed limit, he tore through the handsome gates at the edge of campus and braked to a stop in a handicap spot near the entrance to the business school. Taking the broad steps two at a time, he opened the double glass doors, and raced up the stairway to the fourth floor and Jen's office.

"Abby, Jen, open up," he ordered.

Jen cautiously opened the door.

He strode past her and took Abby into his arms. Shaking, she began to sob.

"Okay, okay," he murmured, stroking her hair, "let it all hang out."

Moments later, seated on Jen's office sofa, Abby recounted every detail of her confrontation with Lombardo. Pete listened without interruption, hurriedly scribbling notes on a pad.

"He said he isn't done with me until I change that damned grade to a B," Abby concluded. "Can you believe this sorry episode goes back to that stupid grade? He's obsessed."

She laughed shakily. "I think he really intends to kill me," she said, no longer frightened now that Pete was at her side.

"Put that out of your mind, Abby," he said sternly.

"Take a look at the bruise on my arm. Lombardo turned violent instantly. He needs a lot more than anger management counseling," she said.

"This is the most bizarre episode I've come across in all my years of teaching," Jen said, relieved that her friend had regained control.

"I forgot to tell you, his appearance has changed," Abby told Pete. "When he came into my office, I hardly recognized him. His eyes were scary, wild and bloodshot. His hair is much longer and doesn't look like it's been washed in a month. And he's working on a full beard."

Pete pocketed his notes and turned to Jen. "Please don't discuss this with anyone except Rob. We may need him to deal with some legal issues. I'll report this threat to chief Edwards and he can inform the president and your dean, Abby."

"No! He warned me not to talk to anyone!" she protested.

"We're ignoring that warning," Pete said firmly. He pulled Abby to her feet. "I want both of you to leave campus now. Stay with Jen while I deal with matters here."

"Excellent idea," Jen said. "Our cars are in the campus garage; Abby can follow me home. We can have dinner together tonight. It'll be like old times when you stayed with us while your home was repaired."

"Thanks, Jen," Abby said, relieved that she would not be facing her empty house alone. "I'm sorry to impose on your hospitality again."

"You're not imposing," Jen assured her. "This is what friends are for."

"I'll walk you to the garage," Pete said, switching off the lights and opening the office door. "I shouldn't need more than an hour to file a report with the chief. He can decide when to notify your dean and the president."

"Is this nightmare never going to end?" Abby cried. "Will I ever be rid of this guy?"

"Trust me, I'm looking forward to dealing with John Lombardo," Pete said grimly.

Together, they walked across Founders Court to the campus garage. "Stay alert," Pete advised. He kissed Abby and watched as the two women started their cars and drove to the exit. Heading to the campus security office, he failed to notice the bearded figure lurking in the shadows near the garage's exit ramp.

Chapter Fifty-One

"This is Craig Edwards, Martha. I need to see the president as soon as possible. It's urgent," he said, seated at his desk in the campus security office.

"Let me see what's available." Roger Smythe's administrative assistant pulled up the president's appointments calendar on her computer.

"How about tomorrow afternoon at three? You'll have fifteen minutes."

"Martha, this issue can't wait," he drummed his fingers impatiently. "What's available this afternoon? And I'll need more than fifteen minutes."

"Sorry, Craig. The president is meeting with potential donors for the new Environmental Sciences building in Boston. He won't be back until after five o'clock. Do you want to see him after normal hours?"

"That's better than tomorrow afternoon. Can you leave a message on his phone? Tell him I need to see him today."

"I'll text message him right now, see if he can see you late today."

"Thanks, Martha. I owe you."

"Glad to help, Craig. This had better be urgent," she warned. "He hates interruptions when he's off campus fundraising for the university."

* * *

"What's the problem, Craig? Martha's message said your call is urgent."

"It's extremely urgent, Roger, but I can't discuss it over a cellphone. Can you meet me late this afternoon, or perhaps early this evening?"

"I should be in my office around six o'clock. Do you want to meet then?" the president asked.

"Yes. See you at six. Thanks."

* * *

The president wheeled his Mercedes into its reserved parking space in front of the administration building at five-thirty and speed-dialed his security chief.

"Meet me in my office in ten minutes."

"I'm on my way."

Smythe retrieved his briefcase and suit jacket and walked into the administration building.

"What problem is so urgent that it can't wait until tomorrow?" He greeted Edwards minutes later.

He listened without interruption as his security chief summarized the most recent threat to Abby Prescott, reminding him of Lombardo's threats last spring and her home invasion more than a month ago in a crime that remained unsolved.

"You're telling me the son of our chairman of the board actually went back to her office and threatened her again?" The president was incredulous.

"Exactly. Furthermore, he grabbed her arm, got in her face and ordered her to change his grade again. According to Pete Byrnes, Prescott's arm is badly bruised. Technically, she can bring assault charges against Lombardo.

"Finally," he continued, "as he was leaving her office, Lombardo raised his arm like he was pointing a gun at her and said, 'bang, bang.'"

The president grimaced. "Stupid juvenile behavior."

Edwards shook his head. "I don't agree, Roger. This is serious harassment. She may be in physical danger."

"Aren't you exaggerating?"

"No," Edwards responded stubbornly. "I'm convinced the guy is dangerous."

"I disagree," the president shook his head. "Besides, this so-called violent behavior really boils down to her word against his." The president raised his eyebrow.

"I'd rather come down on the side of caution when someone may be in physical danger. Late this afternoon I asked one of my plain-clothes officers to check out Lombardo as he left his last class today. He confirmed that his appearance has changed drastically since he enrolled here last spring."

The president chuckled. "Really, Craig. Since when do we get excited about a student changing his appearance?"

Edwards handed the president two photos from his file. "On your left is Lombardo's student ID photo from last January. The other photo is a digital image my officer took this afternoon. Lombardo's hair is long, he's working on a full beard, and looks like he hasn't taken a shower or changed clothes in weeks.

"Pete Byrnes thinks Lombardo may be into drugs. Symptoms of drug use include a radical change in appearance and violent outbursts. Lombardo certainly fits the profile."

The president examined the photos carefully, then tossed them on his desk. "If you hadn't told me this was John Lombardo, I wouldn't have identified him," he admitted softly. He sank back into his chair, tired from the hasty drive from Boston, and now facing a potentially serious problem. He was silent for several moments.

"Craig, this is a very delicate matter. You know Lombardo's family has just pledged $90 million to the university."

"Yes."

"Only $10 million has actually been received; the rest will be paid over the next five years. The cash in hand plus the five year pledge allow us to borrow additional funds and build the Environmental Sciences building over the next two years."

"I was not aware of the financial details," Edwards shrugged, wondering what was the point.

"The university can't risk losing the pledge."

"Don't tell me the Lombardo family can back out of the deal."

"Unfortunately, they can," the president admitted. "It's complicated—all part of the fundraising game universities play to secure large donations.

"You might as well hear the rest of this sorry story. When Lombardo flunked Prescott's course last spring, his father phoned me and demanded a grade change. In fact, Robert Lombardo implied that the rest of the gift would be in jeopardy unless the grade was changed.

"I recently had a very unpleasant conversation with Abby Prescott. She reluctantly agreed to change the grade to a C. The elder Lombardo had suggested a B. Today's threat was probably brought on by her refusal to give Lombardo the grade he wants."

"This is unbelievable," Edwards said, appalled. "The threats against the professor last spring and perhaps the trashing of her home in July are because Lombardo wants a higher grade? Now I am convinced he's insane."

"Clearly, this young man has problems," Smythe reluctantly agreed.

"Unfortunately, the stakes are very high. The university can't afford to lose the Lombardo Foundation gift. We cannot build our Environmental Sciences Center if we lose the lead donation. Our vision to become a world-class university would be dead. And personally, I'd be the laughing stock of the academic world," he shuddered.

The security chief glanced out the office window as dusk began to fall. "Now I understand the stakes, Roger," he said sympathetically. "But more than money and reputation are involved here. One of our faculty members has been threatened, not once, but twice. Abby Prescott is at serious risk."

"I can't believe Lombardo would harm a faculty member," the president responded.

"I disagree. Based his actions on campus and our background check, I'm convinced he is capable of physically harming her." Edwards refused to back down.

"What are my options?" the president asked grimly.

"We have several alternatives," the security chief said, relieved to have an opportunity to recommend a course of action.

"Let's hear them," the president ordered, glancing at his watch.

Edwards handed a two-page memo across the desk to the president.

"Let me summarize," he pointed to the memo. "First, we can do nothing. Lombardo stays in school and we risk possible violence against the professor or someone else he might decide to attack. Obviously, I don't recommend that alternative."

The president leaned back in his chair. "What else?"

"Second, we can use the university's student disciplinary procedures to dismiss him. The problem remains in-house without much publicity. We wouldn't notify outside authorities. I don't recommend this option, either."

"Why not?" the president interrupted.

"Because Lombardo probably would not go quietly. He's well aware that a lot of money is at stake. I think he'll threaten to influence his father to withdraw the pledge, and the university will lose money already committed to a new building."

"I hope you've got an option you're willing to recommend," the president said sarcastically.

"I do, but there are risks."

"Go ahead."

"I recommend that the university seek a restraining order directing Lombardo to avoid Abby Prescott. A local judge could issue the order. That will keep him out of her office, away from her classes, and protect her off campus and at home.

"In my opinion a legal restraining order is essential to assure the professor's safety. It would also protect the university from legal problems if Lombardo violates the restraining order. He would be allowed to remain a student unless he violates the restraining order ."

"I don't like your recommendation, Craig," the president said immediately. "Even if the order doesn't become public, Lombardo surely would tell his father, which could jeopardize the university's gift."

"I believe it's our best alternative. I'm responsible for campus safety, Roger. I can't risk Abby Prescott's personal safety."

Smythe silently mulled over the options. Then he stood, his decision made.

"Craig, you're over-reacting. Implement your first option. Do nothing for now."

The security chief shook his head, dismayed. "If that's your decision, I'll carry it out. But I think we will regret allowing this student to remain on campus without a restraining order."

"She will be perfectly safe while she's on campus. Lombardo wouldn't dare harm her here. And Pete Byrnes is already assigned to keep an eye on Prescott, isn't he?" Smythe asked.

"Yes."

"Isn't Byrnes living with her now?"

"Yes," the security chief acknowledged.

The president smiled. "Then she is protected off campus, too, which isn't our problem anyway.

"Do not seek a court restraining order against Lombardo. That's final," he said firmly.

"You need to know that Byrnes recently has been reassigned some additional duties that will keep him working twelve hour days."

"What else is he doing?"

"During the summer I assigned him to investigate a potentially serious drug problem here on campus. He can't guard Prescott all day and work the drug problem at night. If anyone can nail a drug distribution ring on campus, he's the guy. Doing both jobs requires him to work twelve hour days indefinitely. That's asking too much."

"Work it out. That's why we pay you a six figure salary," the president smiled dismissively.

"I hope you'll read my memo and reconsider your position," Craig pointed to the memo on the president's desk.

"I've made my decision," the president retorted. "I repeat: Do nothing now. Cover us by assuring that Abby Prescott is not harmed while she's on campus. What happens off campus is not our concern. However, you might talk to the Seal Point police; perhaps they will keep a quiet eye on her."

The security chief walked to the president's door. "I'll call chief Buchard over in Seal Point before I leave," he said over his shoulder.

Back in his office, angry and frustrated, Edwards turned on his laptop computer and wrote a memo detailing the conversation and the president's directive. He saved the memo in a password-protected file and backed it up to his memory stick for safekeeping. Then he phoned the Seal Point police chief.

Chapter Fifty-Two

Pete watched John Lombardo exit the School of Business building and walk to the campus parking garage. He lingered near the stairwell until the student entered the garage elevator, then raced upstairs to the second floor.

"Going somewhere?" he asked quietly, his hand on the BMW's door handle, blocking Lombardo.

"Huh?" Surprised, he confronted Pete. "What's it to you? Take your hands off my car or I'll break your arm."

"I don't think so. I've got a message for you."

"I know you," Lombardo snarled. "You're a campus cop. What's your message, Mr. Byrnes?" He began to sweat, wiped his hand across his face. "If you've got anything to say to me, maybe it's because your girlfriend, Abby, ignored my instructions."

"Bingo, John. You really didn't expect her to keep quiet about that confrontation in her office two days ago, now did you?"

Lombardo shrugged. "She's dumber than I thought."

"So you don't deny you threatened her."

"I didn't threaten her," he protested heatedly. "I told her to change my grade in that damn course."

"That's not all you did," Pete retorted. "The professor has some nasty bruises on her arm. You threatened her when she ordered you to leave her office. In my business, we call that assault."

"I didn't hurt her," Lombardo whined. "I left when she told me to go. And she still hasn't changed my grade."

"That grade won't be changed—not now, never," Pete retorted. "Let me give you some important advice, John. Leave professor Prescott alone. Stay away from her office. Don't approach her on campus, or anywhere else. Consider this the best advice you've gotten since you arrived at this university."

"Oh, wow, I'm terrified," Lombardo waved his arms, full of bravado. "That sounds like a threat. Are you threatening me? You're a security officer; you should know better than to threaten a student," he sneered.

"I'm not threatening you, just offering some friendly advice. Don't go near the professor."

"And if I don't take your advice? What are you going to do about it?" His dark eyes gleamed in the gathering gloom as a light rain fell outside the garage.

"You won't enjoy the consequences and neither will your father."

"Oh, now you're threatening my father. Explain yourself."

"Let me clue you, John. Your father provided your alibi a couple months ago when the professor's house was trashed," Pete said. "I'm betting it won't hold water when we look more closely at your whereabouts on that July weekend."

Lombardo laughed. "Dream on, asshole. I was in New Jersey and you can't prove otherwise. Now, get lost before I call campus security and charge you with harassment."

Pete walked away and exited the garage. He waited patiently in the rain until the BMW came down the ramp and through the exit gate. Lombardo gave him the finger through the open window as he gunned the engine and headed for Route 1.

*   *   *

"I can't believe the president is ignoring Lombardo's latest threat," Pete complained. Horizontal sheets of rain beat against the windows and high winds whipped the trees on Founders Court, as a strong nor'easter pummeled the Maine coast.

"Believe it," Craig Edwards said grimly. "I recommended a comprehensive court restraining order but he wouldn't buy it. He won't even authorize a disciplinary hearing through the student affairs office. Nothing," he said resignedly. "I guess he can't handle the possibility of losing a $90 million gift.

"By the way, when I notified chief Buchard over in Seal Point of the latest threat, he offered limited patrol coverage of Abby's house when you are working nights. You need to give Buchard a schedule of your hours."

"Did he mention the test results from those hair samples we gave him weeks ago?" Pete asked.

Edwards shook his head. "I asked about that. He said it will take another week."

"I don't understand the delay."

"Along with the usual backlog at the state crime lab, Buchard sent the samples to a private testing lab in Massachusetts to check for possible drug residue in the hair."

"They won't find any residue in the samples Abby and I supplied. If they find anything positive in the other hairs, we may have a slim lead. The case may not be dead yet." Pete sounded a little more optimistic.

"How is Abby dealing with this latest confrontation and the president's decision to do nothing?" Edwards asked.

"She was livid initially; then she calmed down when she considered Smythe's position. She understands the financial implications for the university if the Lombardo Foundation withdraws its donation. Obviously, Abby's personal safety is not the president's top priority. She's resigned to providing for her own safety."

Pete smiled. "All in all, she's doing okay. I think anger and defiance are finally overcoming fear. She has come a long way. Abby is not going to let Lombardo control her life.

"Of course, installing a high-end security system in her house has increased her sense of security. If the alarm goes off, the Seal Point police can reach her in ten minutes.

"I finally convinced her to take some measures to protect herself. We've been target shooting at an indoor range in Portland. She's become a surprisingly good shooter," Pete related, "and I'm confident she can defend herself if necessary. Chief Buchard has expedited her application for a permit to carry a concealed weapon. Her license to carry should be approved shortly.

"Abby also now believes that Lombardo wouldn't dare harass her again."

"Why?" Edwards asked, surprised. "Based on his past behavior and your suspicion he may be into drugs, she may continue to be in serious danger."

"I have a small confession to make, chief."

"Oh?" his boss raised an eyebrow.

"I ran into Lombardo this afternoon in the parking garage and told him in no uncertain terms not to approach Abby or he'd have to deal with me."

"Pete, don't tell me you threatened him."

"We had a nice polite conversation. No threats. Just some friendly, but firm advice. He knows I'm a security officer and living with Abby. He also knows Abby has told me exactly what happened in her office."

"Stay away from him, Pete," Edwards ordered. "Let's not create any more problems than we already have."

"Right," Pete agreed with a smile.

The chief reached for a slim folder on the corner of his desk. "Where do we stand on your drug investigation?"

"There's something else you should know, chief," Pete said quietly.

"What," he asked, absorbed in reviewing the file's contents.

"Abby is aware of the bare essentials of our drug investigation."

Edwards looked up, annoyed. "Why? Drug investigations are as confidential as we get at Reid University; you know that."

"She deserved an explanation because I'll be working nights and some weekends," Pete said defensively, "and she will be alone."

The chief shrugged. "You're probably right. You warned her not to discuss your assignment with anyone else?"

"Of course."

"How much longer until you wrap this up?" Edwards pointed to the folder.

"I don't know. Linking Lombardo and professor Stewart to drugs won't be easy.

"The latest development is that Stewart recently bought a new plane, a twin engine job that can fly to Miami with only one refueling stop. And Stewart's wife apparently spends money far in excess of a professor's salary. There's evidence that he has come into a lot of cash in the last six months. I'm trying to trace the source of his money. It may be completely innocent, of course."

The chief gazed at Pete across the desk. "That's interesting, but very thin. What else have you got?"

Pete shrugged. "Lombardo and Stewart hang out together, often in the weight room at the Athletic Center. Of course, he was a student in Stewart's Environmental Science class last spring. They may have an innocent faculty-student relationship.

"I'm more interested in Stewart's involvement with a female student, Judy Perkins, who works at a branch bank just off campus," Pete went on.

"There's an outside chance that she is helping him launder cash. Again, it may simply be an extramarital affair. I'm following up."

"Maybe it's time to contact the DEA and the Treasury. If you have enough evidence to call in the feds, I can make the call today," Edwards offered.

"That's still premature. Let me work this a bit more."

"Focus on this investigation. If you need more resources, let me know. We'll never stamp out recreational drug use on this campus, but we can't allow hard drugs to gain a foothold. Come back to me when you have more to report."

Chapter Fifty-Three

Rick Stewart taxied to the end of the Palmetto Regional runway amid the clutter of early Sunday traffic. Readying for takeoff, he scanned the cockpit instruments and waited for clearance from the tower.

What a difference a year makes, he mused. His chance encounter with Carlos Munoz in a Miami disco last summer led to the most lucrative consulting assignment of his life. Granted, hauling cocaine and crystal meth from Florida to New York wasn't exactly the consulting assignment he'd envisioned when he plotted his career as a professor and part-time consultant to the oil and gas industry. Nonetheless, consulting offered the perfect cover and cash payoffs that exceeded his wildest dreams.

Every other week over the past six months Rick made the round trip from Maine to Florida in his new plane, a turbocharged twin-engine Baron discarded from Carlos' fleet of aircraft.

Rick jumped at Munoz' bargain price and offer to finance the $200,000 loan needed to swing the deal. Rick refurbished the interior with leather seats, upgraded his navigation instruments and hired Carlos' mechanics to build a concealed space beneath the cabin floor for his illegal cargo. His new plane had been accepted without comment at the Seal Point airport, although faculty members did little to conceal their envy.

Rick's weekend run from Florida to northern New Jersey and then home to Maine had become a lucrative milk run. His cover story, consulting with a south Florida power company, explained the wealth he flaunted on campus and around Seal Point. In less than three months he'd repaid Munoz' loan with cash from his drug runs. Then, with Judy Perkins' assistance, he laundered his growing cash bounty into a Cayman Islands bank account. He waited for takeoff permission, silently acknowledging his debt to Carlos, the Columbian drug lord who had become his new best friend.

He mentally reviewed the day's plans. Because he would fly under visual flight rules, he didn't file a flight plan and would exercise his judgment in blending in with local traffic along the route north. At the small airport in New Jersey, he would offload this week's cargo, one hundred kilos of pure uncut cocaine from Columbia plus another fifty kilos of crystal meth from Carlos' Mexican superlab.

With his plane's longer range, Rick could fly nonstop from Florida to New Jersey. From there, he could either refuel and fly on to Seal Point in a single day, or lay over and visit his parents. Thus far, the flights from Florida to the New York area were as uneventful as Carlos predicted when Rick signed on to the job last summer.

He expected to reach Maine this evening, in time to visit Judy. He smiled in anticipation. She had become an integral part of his dual life. Her banking expertise was invaluable in establishing and maintaining his Cayman Islands tax-free bank account.

Waiting for takeoff permission, Rick mulled over his future plans. In three months, he would resign from Reid University and divorce Sue after providing for his two kids. If Sue harbored any suspicions regarding his new wealth, she never let on. Delighted with her virtually unlimited budget, their marriage mellowed as Rick's wealth increased.

Last month, when he and Judy ran into Sue in a Portland restaurant, the encounter had not aroused suspicion. Rick introduced Judy as the bank officer handling his business interests. Sue merely greeted them casually, introducing them to her tennis pro from the Seal Point Country Club. She didn't care what he did as long as the money continued to flow.

In less than a year Rick had become a wealthy man. Today's $300,000 payoff would bring his Cayman Islands stash to more than $4 million dollars. His parents' legacy was no longer an issue, merely icing on the cake, funds he would tap to support Sue and the kids.

The tower controller's voice interrupted his reverie. "November four three five Juliette Kilo, you are cleared for VFR departure with a left turnout."

"Five Juliette Kilo, we're rolling," Rick acknowledged.

He eased off the brakes, set the nose on the runway's centerline and with a final scan of the instrument panel, nudged the throttles forward. He loved the surge of power at his fingertips as the plane accelerated down the runway and reached takeoff speed. Gently pulling back the control column, the plane leaped into the air. He gained altitude over the Atlantic, and a few minutes later executed a 90-degree left bank, quickly reaching his cruising altitude.

Keeping the coastline in view on his left, he set a course for northern New Jersey where the now familiar van would be waiting to transport his cargo into New York City. He settled back, made a cursory sweep of the airspace around him, and engaged the automatic pilot. For the next couple of hours, his biggest problem would be a lowering cloud cover from a low-pressure front west of Delaware. Over southern Virginia, he would head east to avoid the storm and air traffic around Washington.

Hours later Rick disengaged the autopilot, began a gradual descent to 5,000 feet and turned east to avoid the weather ahead. Ten minutes later, preparing to reset the autopilot, he spotted an abnormal oil pressure reading in the left engine. Unconcerned but alert, he monitored the instruments closely. Over the next several minutes the pressure continued to slowly drop until it hovered just above the red warning line.

He swore as a jolt of adrenaline fueled by rising panic surged through his body. At that moment, the left engine backfired, belching oily, black smoke. Seconds later the engine misfired again, and he watched a thin tail of flame snake through the smoke. Shit! This couldn't be happening! Not today, not with drugs on board.

Mind racing, he struggled to control his panic. Finally, years of training in aircraft emergency scenarios took over. He quickly feathered the engine, shutting off the fuel and starving the fire. He watched the propeller slowly rotate to a stop. He increased power to the right engine, and adjusted the rudder trim, working desperately to maintain altitude and speed.

Rick considered his options. He was confident he could limp into New Jersey on one engine, but why take the chance? The better alternative was to land, identify the problem and make the necessary repairs. He was confident his illicit cargo, securely hidden under his feet, would remain undiscovered while the engine was repaired. There would be a delay, but no need to ditch the plane and forfeit his $300,000 paycheck.

Decision made, Rick tuned his radio to the international distress frequency, 121.5. "Mayday, Mayday, Mayday, Baron 435 Juliette Kilo has a left engine fire," he radioed.

Immediately, he received a response. "Baron 435 Juliette Kilo, Virginia Beach Approach. Squawk 7700 and ident. Say altitude, fuel and souls on board."

Rick punched 7700, the general emergency code, into his transponder and pressed the 'Ident' button. On the Virginia Beach Approach screens Rick's radar return blossomed, instantly separating him from the other radar traffic. Then he pressed the NRST button on his panel mounted GPS, which responded with a three letter identifier, OCS, the heading,

290 degrees, and the distance to the nearest airport, Oceanside, which was seven miles away.

"Four three five Juliette Kilo squawking 7700 with three hours of fuel and one soul aboard."

"Baron 435 Juliette Kilo you are radar contact fifteen miles southeast of Virginia Beach at 5,000 feet. Confirm that you are declaring an emergency at this time."

"Roger, Baron 435 Juliette Kilo is declaring an emergency," he acknowledged.

"Baron 435 Juliette Kilo, Oceanside is at your ten o'clock and seven miles away. You may descend at your discretion. Winds are three zero at five, altimeter three zero one five. You are cleared to land any runway and stay with me this frequency."

Rick banked to the left and headed toward the coast, using all the piloting skills he could muster. The plane began to lose altitude as he struggled to maintain level flight with only one engine.

It was a losing battle. The low silhouette of the Virginia coastline appeared through a layer of haze. Slowly, the shoreline loomed larger. He took a deep breath. With luck he would not ditch in the ocean. If only he had a co-pilot to dump the cargo while he was over water. In an instant his life had morphed into a nightmare.

Now less than one hundred feet above the water, he realized that an emergency landing at Oceanside Airport was impossible. Low scrub and pines bordered the beach and extended inland. He would try to pancake in an open area, set fire to the plane if it failed to ignite on impact and make a run for it.

"Baron 435 Juliette Kilo, radar contact lost, do you have Oceanside in sight?"

"Negative, Virginia Beach. Searching for an open area. Can you send equipment please?"

Off his left wing he spotted a clearing, an area possibly large enough to set down in. It was his only alternative. He banked sharply and headed toward the meadow, bracing for a gear-up controlled crash landing, fighting the cross wind from the ocean as he turned south. The open field was a mile away. It would be close.

A second surge of adrenaline delivered a rush of heightened awareness and clarity of purpose. He cleared the low pines on the field's north edge and cut the fuel to the right engine, fighting to maintain level flight. With the stall warning screaming in his ears, he shut down the master electronics switch. Instant silence. Rick lost control when a strong gust of wind lifted his left wing as the plane neared the ground. He hung onto the controls and braced himself.

The nose dropped and the plane augured in at a shallow angle, lurching through the underbrush, plowing a furrow in the sandy soil. Hurtling across the field at more than fifty miles an hour, the twisted mass of metal skidded violently toward the trees at the edge of the meadow. Rocks, heavy brush and scrub pines shredded the fuselage and crushed the front windshield.

The plane careened to a final resting place against a huge dead pine. A massive branch punched through the broken windshield, trapping Rick in the wreckage, severing the left carotid artery in his neck.

Thirty seconds later the shattered remains exploded in an oily, fuel-driven ball of fire. The first rescue vehicles reached the crash scene thirty minutes later, long after the plane had become a barely recognizable charred hulk, Rick Stewart's funeral pyre.

* * *

"I can't believe Rick Stewart was hauling drugs!" Abby exclaimed to Pete over dinner the next evening.

"Believe it," Pete said grimly. "Sniffer dogs from the Virginia investigating team found drug residue in the charred wreckage.

"Give him credit—his consulting activities offered a perfect cover. He apparently was an important cog in a distribution network into New York City. Of course, it's possible the drugs were destined for Maine—we'll never know for sure.

"No wonder Rick was able to buy a larger plane," he continued. "According to the Portland papers, his drug flights probably generated a few million dollars in cash over the last six months. And someone at the bank, a young lending officer, apparently was helping him launder the loot to an offshore account. By the way, the lending officer is a student at the university. She is now under arrest for money laundering."

"So I heard," Abby nodded. "Judy Perkins was a student in my class last spring. She and Lombardo also were enrolled in Stewart's class at the same time.

"I sympathize with Rick's wife and kids. Sue supposedly knew nothing about his drug activities or his extramarital affair. Apparently, he wasn't planning to share his illegal spoils with his family.

"This must be the biggest scandal in the school's history," Pete remarked.

"Yes. And Roger Smythe is taking some heat because of Rick's association with the university. The media constantly report that he was a faculty member here. They never fail to editorialize about how pervasive the drug culture has become on campuses across the country. For most of our students, though, alcohol and pot remain the drugs of choice."

"You sound pretty casual about drug use on campus."

"Not at all," Abby shook her head. "That's just the reality on every American campus."

Chapter Fifty-Four

"I have some interesting news," Buchard said, seating himself on the sofa in Abby's newly furnished living room and accepting a fresh cup of coffee.

"Fantastic. Are you finally ready to make an arrest?"

"Sorry, not yet," he cautioned.

"I've received the analysis of the hair samples lifted from your house." He took a bound report from his briefcase.

"Don't keep me in suspense. What have you found?"

"John Lombardo's hair samples were among those lifted from your house after the home invasion," he revealed. "Did he ever visit your home while he was a student in your class?"

Abby shook her head. "Absolutely not. I never invite students to my home. My phone number is unlisted and most students have no idea where I live."

"This could be significant. It means he was in the house at some point," Pete observed, seated beside Abby.

"How confident are you that the hair sample is Lombardo's?" she asked.

"He has a prison record; we matched the DNA sample from your home to a Justice Department database," the chief explained.

"Are the samples evidence enough to charge him with the break-in?" Abby asked.

"Unfortunately, no. However, I have more information that will interest you. All hair samples, including yours and Pete's, were sent to a lab in Massachusetts for analysis of drug residue. As expected, your samples proved to be negative for drugs."

"No surprise there," Pete chuckled.

"Chief, I thought a urine test, not hair analysis, is used to detect drugs," Abby said.

"That's the usual method," the chief agreed. "The urine test is inexpensive and generally accurate. However, there are a number of ways to beat that test. Some frequently tested athletes and others have devised rather clever ways to falsify urinalysis.

"Hair analysis is more complex, expensive and time consuming. When the DNA test indicated Lombardo's presence in your home, I ordered the hair analysis because you suspected that he might be a drug user. That test explains the delay in reporting back to you."

"What are the lab's findings?" Pete asked.

"Lombardo's analysis initially came back positive for meth amphetamine and cocaine. At that point, it's standard procedure to confirm the finding through a GC/MS analysis."

"What's that? Can you explain in more detail?" Abby asked.

"I'll do my best, professor. Chemistry wasn't my strongest subject in college," the chief smiled.

"First, a caution. The positive result for meth amphetamine in his hair sample merely indicates that Lombardo ingested that drug at least a week prior to our finding the sample in your home.

"The drug gets into the hair follicle through the bloodstream, and that takes time. Hair grows at the rate of half an inch a month. After a drug is used, it takes a week to ten days for the hair containing the drug to grow out of the scalp enough to be cut. Our test sample was nearly two inches long, which works out to around four months' growth of hair. According to the testing lab, it's generally accepted that when a sample tests positive, the drug in question must have been used several times or more within the window of the test."

"Now I'm really confused. What does that mean?" Abby asked.

"It means that meth and cocaine were taken more than a week prior to our obtaining the sample. We can't prove that whoever trashed your home used meth in the week just before the break-in."

"I see," Pete interjected. "It only indicates drug use during some period in the past."

"Exactly. And there's an additional limitation," the chief said. "Some prescription diet pills contain either amphetamine or meth amphetamine. Further, amphetamines are sometimes prescribed for ADHD. Finally, Ecstasy, currently one of the most dangerous illegal drugs, also is in the amphetamine class of drugs. You probably are aware that Ecstasy is widely distributed in bars and discos, places where Lombardo is known to hang out. It also can be identified at confirmation."

"What do you mean by confirmation?" Abby asked.

"Unfortunately, so-called 'false positives' can occur in the testing process, and all positive results require confirmation. That's where GC/MS comes into play. The term refers to gas chromatography/mass spectrometry. It's an additional analytical tool. I can't explain the details—I don't understand them myself.

"The bottom line is that if amphetamines are found in a hair sample, then meth amphetamines will also be present. The same is true for cocaine use. If cocaine is found, the metabolite for cocaine, benzoylecgonine, will be found."

"That's enough chemistry for me," Abby laughed. "I'm thoroughly confused. What's the bottom line?"

"In plain English," Buchard said, "someone whose hair was found in your home—perhaps the person who trashed your house—had residue of both meth amphetamine and cocaine in the hair sample tested. That residue indicates drug use at least a week prior to obtaining the sample. The positive result was confirmed through the GC/MS analysis.

"John Lombardo's DNA was identified in that hair sample," Buchard said.

"Although he can't be charged based on the DNA and hair analysis, he is back on our list of persons of interest. Unfortunately, he's the only person currently on that list. And he has an air tight alibi for the period under investigation."

Buchard regarded them pessimistically. "While I'm personally convinced that Lombardo trashed your home, we don't have enough evidence to arrest him. The district attorney would refuse to prosecute."

"One thing is certain," Abby shook her head resignedly, "he was in my home and he certainly wasn't an invited guest."

"I'm sorry, professor. Although we lack evidence to bring charges, I've assigned two officers to continue the investigation. Maybe we'll get a break." Buchard stood to leave.

"Chief," Abby sighed, "I'm convinced that Lombardo's behavior goes beyond anger management problems. He's insane. And because his father is chairman of the university's board of trustees, the president won't press charges. He is untouchable because his family's charitable foundation has pledged $90 million toward a new building on campus."

"I understand that the president refused to seek a restraining order, which would offer you some protection. Fortunately, you have installed a very good security system in your home and Pete is here to protect you most of the time. Now that you can handle firearms, you can protect yourself if Lombardo ever tries to enter your home again. You are safer than many women threatened by a stalker.

"We've made some headway. Your case isn't dead."

Abby shook her head. "I wish I felt as confident about my personal safety as you and Pete."

Pete accompanied Buchard to the door.

"Please coordinate your work schedule with our office. I'll have an officer check Abby's property every couple of hours when she's here alone," Buchard said quietly.

"Thank you, chief."

"What is the status of your campus drug investigation?" Buchard asked.

"I'm wrapping it up. Rick Stewart's death ends my work on the case. I'll be reassigned to duties during the day on campus where I can keep an eye on Abby and John Lombardo.

"Professor Stewart's apparent involvement with transporting drugs was a real surprise," the chief remarked. "We casually checked him out after he acquired that new plane. His parents definitely are very wealthy. Although Stewart was living way above his faculty salary, his family wealth explained it. And Stewart's frequent flights to Florida and Georgia appeared legitimate."

"His drug involvement surprised everyone," Pete admitted. "I began an investigation when I observed Rick and Lombardo hanging out together on campus. I wasn't able to link the two to drugs on campus. His flashy lifestyle fit with his family wealth and the supposedly lucrative consulting contracts he constantly bragged about."

"Well, Stewart won't be doing any more consulting," the police chief concluded.

Pete accompanied Buchard to his cruiser. "Thank you for keeping an eye on Abby. This property is remote. It's a gorgeous, private location, but it has its drawbacks when there's a lunatic on the loose.

"By the way, are you aware that Lombardo's appearance has changed dramatically? He looks more like a homeless person prowling the streets of Portland than a multimillionaire's son."

"Yes, I know. Craig Edwards sent me a recent photo."

"I'll get back to you with my new work schedule." Pete promised. He watched the chief back down the driveway.

He returned to the house and found Abby in the kitchen. "How about dinner in Portland and then an early movie? I'm not working until ten o'clock or a little later. What do you say?" He kissed her neck.

"How about some bedroom time before we go," she countered.

"That's the best proposition I've had all day. I'm up for it if you are."

*   *   *

She lay in Pete's arms, drowsy and content as soft afternoon sunlight etched geometric patterns on the sheets. "We probably should go to dinner and take in that movie," she whispered lazily.

"We don't have to go out," Pete said, his hands caressing her breasts. "I'll fix dinner here. You can relax, have some wine, and watch me cook up something simple. How about steak on the grill, a Caesar salad, and some garlic bread?"

"Wonderful. I just want to cuddle with you, maybe watch the Red Sox beat the Yankees on television before you leave for work."

"The cuddling part sounds appealing," he smiled, "but the Red Sox game is postponed. There's a hurricane heading up the coast, remember?"

"Pete, I completely forgot about the storm!" Abby sat up in bed. "Too obsessed with Lombardo, I guess. The hurricane is still way south of Boston. It probably will head out to sea. We rarely get hurricanes this far north."

"Forecasters can be wrong, of course. The weathermen are warning this could be the worst storm to hit New England in decades. After work tonight, I'm taking off the next two days to prepare for the storm. We shouldn't take any chances," Pete said.

"I need to secure the boat even if the storm doesn't make landfall. And I'll take care of boarding up and taping your windows facing the ocean. You don't need another round of damage to the house."

"Do you mind working on the house tomorrow?" Abby asked.

"Of course not. I've already ordered a stack of plywood from Home Depot," he murmured. "I'll pick it up in the morning." He leaned over her and kissed her breasts, his hands gently probing her inner thighs.

"Pete," she gazed into his eyes, "don't tease if you can't perform!"

"Check me out. I'm ready if you are," he whispered.

*   *   *

She sat on a stool beside the center island in the kitchen. Elbows on the counter, she watched contentedly while Pete opened a bottle of Penfolds shiraz and poured the deep burgundy liquid into their wine glasses.

"Cheers." He leaned across the counter and kissed her.

Chapter Fifty-Five

"Professor Prescott, the president would like to meet with you as soon as possible. Can you come by the office this afternoon?" Smythe's administrative assistant asked.

"When can he see me?"

"How about three o'clock?"

"Perfect. My last class ends at 2:45," Abby checked her calendar. "Three o'clock it is."

* * *

She hurried across Founders Court to the Administration Building in the gathering gloom of an approaching thunderstorm, prelude to the unusual September hurricane heading for Maine. Slowly gathering force, the monster storm lumbered along at five miles an hour on a northeast track, converging with a front southwest of New England, roughly tracking the infamous 1991 storm later dubbed the Perfect Storm.

A category three storm, Hurricane Melinda was forecast to reach coastal Maine within the next twelve hours. Boston television stations predicted winds in excess of 115 miles an hour, a damaging storm surge fed by extremely high tides and heavy rains. Melinda would be the strongest storm to hit New England in more than twenty years.

The university's facilities crews were frantically preparing to safeguard the school from the hurricane force winds and rain. Campus buildings with large expanses of ocean-facing glass were boarded up. Workers continued to tape windows, ignoring the distant lightning flashes of the approaching storm.

Abby hoped her meeting with the president would be brief. She wanted to be home helping Pete board up her sliding glass doors and windows.

"President Smythe will see you immediately. He's anxious to get home early today," his assistant greeted her.

"Me, too," Abby said. "Living by the ocean is fantastic until a hurricane comes along. Thank God they don't often reach this far north."

"You're his last appointment today. In case you haven't read your email messages, all classes are cancelled tomorrow. We're expecting power outages and some property damage. And Roger is not in a great mood," the assistant warned, knocking briefly and then opening the president's door. Abby entered, closing the door behind her.

Roger Smythe, standing behind his massive antique mahogany desk, greeted her cordially and led her to the sofa near the fireplace, seating himself in a chair opposite.

Abby had a good idea why she'd been summoned. She was prepared, her mind made up, and she suspected the president would not welcome her decision.

He got right to the point, "Robert Lombardo, our chairman of the board of trustees, called this morning. His son continues to complain about that grade in your course. He isn't satisfied with the C you finally issued. He wants a B, and his father is lobbying me about it. I need a response today."

"You know that Lombardo actually earned an F in my course," Abby reminded him firmly. "At your request, I reluctantly changed his grade to a C because of the importance of the major gift his family pledged."

"Yes, and I appreciate your willingness to put the future of the university ahead of your academic judgment in this specific case. Incidentally, I regret your most recent confrontation with the young man in your office."

"That was more than a confrontation, Roger. It was very disturbing. Chief Edwards tells me you've decided to ignore the episode, despite physical threats to me personally.

"In my judgment, a restraining order is not necessary."

"You realize, of course, that I can file assault charges against Lombardo. My attorney assures me the court would issue a restraining order," she said serenely. "My affiliation with the university could become public, creating the kind of publicity both of us want to avoid."

"I hope you won't take legal action, Abby. Apparently, there is a serious personality conflict between you two. I'm convinced that his behavior toward you is an aberration. There have been no complaints from other faculty."

"Personality conflict?" she grimaced. "His violent behavior is a lot more than a personality conflict. He shouldn't be allowed on this campus under any circumstances. His next target may not be as lucky as I've been."

"You're overreacting again, Abby."

"I'm not overreacting!" she retorted angrily. "Lombardo has repeatedly threatened me and you apparently want to sweep his behavior under the rug. He's dangerous, perhaps psychotic. Have you talked to him since the semester began?"

"Of course not. I don't have time to talk to students," he snapped.

"You should call him into your office, get acquainted with him. Lombardo is a physical wreck; he's lost a lot of weight, is on a downward spiral. I believe drugs are the root of the problem."

"Abby, please don't make serious drug charges against any student without proof," he warned her.

"Fine." She sat back, struggling for control. "Why did you want to see me today?" she asked.

"I'm asking you to change John Lombardo's grade from the C that is on his record now to a B," the president said directly.

Abby was furious. "Not a chance, Roger. I've changed that grade for the last time."

"If you refuse to change the grade, then I'll direct your dean to make the change," the president responded coldly.

"That would be a mistake," she said, not about to be bullied. "If anyone changes that grade, I'll email every faculty member on this campus and disclose every detail of this sorry episode. I'll make public the threats Lombardo has made against me personally. I'll reveal your continued efforts to force me to change the grade or direct my dean to change the grade. And I'll also tell the faculty that you refused to seek a restraining order to protect me, an action that was recommended by the chief of campus security."

His face beet red, Smythe attempted to interrupt. Abby would not be silenced.

"I hoped this problem could remain confidential—in the family so to speak," she seethed, anger overwhelming caution. "You are refusing to deal with serious threats by a student against a faculty member because you're afraid of losing a major gift. And you are deliberately violating the university's academic standards," she accused.

"If that grade is changed, you won't be able to bury this sorry episode. When the faculty learns the details, the local newspapers and television outlets will pick it up. And your role in this incident will become public." She finally paused to catch her breath.

The president's carefully controlled professional façade vanished. "No faculty member can speak to me in those tones," he roared. "Get out of my office. This discussion is finished."

Abby reached for her briefcase and calmly walked to the office door. She turned. "I'll never change that grade, Roger. And I suggest you notify your chairman of the board that his son cannot manipulate the academic standards of this university." Adrenaline surging, she was outwardly in complete control.

"You might also urge him to examine his son's physical and mental health," she continued. "I believe John Lombardo is close to a complete psychotic breakdown. He needs help. His family is facing a far more serious problem than the resolution of a grade dispute."

Without waiting for a response, she closed the door and made her way through the president's deserted outer offices. She took the stairway to the ground floor, hurried across Founders Court to the parking garage and ran up the stairs to the third floor. Hands shaking, she fumbled for her car keys.

Backing out, she failed to notice the lone figure seated in the late model BMW three cars away. Both cars exited the garage, the BMW staying well back of Abby's Lexus. Lights on and wipers running, she merged into heavy traffic on Route 1 as rain and wind battered the car. The BMW kept pace several cars behind. Thirty minutes later Abby entered the village of Seal Point, followed by John Lombardo.

* * *

Head in hands, Roger Smythe sat at his desk in his darkening office. Reluctantly, he placed a call to New York City.

"Hello, Robert. I understand that New York caught the fringe of the hurricane. We're expecting a direct hit early tomorrow."

"I hope the campus is battened down," Robert Lombardo said.

"We're ready. Our facilities people have been working nonstop since last night. Of course, the weather forecasts may be wrong. With luck the storm will be downgraded before it reaches us." He leaned back in his chair, nervously twisting the phone cord in his hand.

"Robert, I'm not calling to discuss the weather. Let me bring you up to date on the issue of your son's grade in the business course he failed last spring."

"John is extremely angry about the way his instructor has treated him."

"I've just reviewed the grade with his professor. She absolutely refuses to change his grade from a C to a B. Indeed, she argues that your son's correct grade was the F she originally issued."

"I see."

The president waited through a long silence at the other end of the line.

"Roger, I'm tired of dealing with this," Lombardo said finally. "My son is twenty-five years old. Maybe it's time he took responsibility for his studies. Actually, I was disappointed with his work habits in my company during the summer. He seems more interested in hitting the New York bars and disco joints than learning the business and putting in a solid day's work. Frankly, I'm a little worried about him."

Smythe breathed a silent sigh of relief.

"I appreciate your understanding, Robert. As president of the university, I am ultimately responsible for the academic integrity of our programs. Evaluating students and issuing grades are among the faculty's most important responsibilities, and they resist administrative interference in the process.

"You will recall that recently I convinced the professor to raise your son's grade from an F to a C. She agreed very reluctantly, and only because I pressed her personally. This afternoon she absolutely refused to make any further adjustment. I'd like to consider the matter closed," Smythe concluded.

"All right," Robert Lombardo said finally. "I'll call John and read him the riot act. No more whining about grades. He'll just have to meet the academic standards of the university or suffer the consequences. Maybe a little tough love is in order.

"Deep down, John is a good kid," he continued. "However, he has been a real challenge to his mother and me."

"I'm sorry to hear that," said the president sympathetically.

"Several years ago John became addicted to a very bad drug, crystal meth amphetamine. You may be familiar with it," the senior Lombardo revealed.

"I understand it is a dangerous drug," the president replied. "We don't tolerate hard drugs on this campus, and our security people enforce the policy very aggressively."

"Let me tell you a bit about John's drug problems. Crystal meth—called ice on the street—is far more dangerous than cocaine or heroin. It triggered a family crisis and nearly destroyed my son."

"How did you deal with it?"

"We sent him to an excellent rehab center for three months. During his stay the medical staff identified a serious mental problem. The diagnosis was borderline schizophrenic. Fortunately, he's able to function normally as long as he takes his meds.

"His mother and I hope the university environment will help John turn his life around," Lombardo continued. "We made a special effort to spend quality time with him this summer, golfing every Sunday afternoon at my club, and taking a sailing vacation on my yacht. John grew a beard and let his hair grow. He claims the look is cool among the college crowd. I think it's disgusting, but that's a father's opinion," he chuckled.

"Reid University may be John's last chance to succeed in school. I believe he is on the right track, although he obviously needs to develop better study and work habits. He's still very immature, Roger. I hope you'll keep a personal eye on him."

"Yes, of course. My wife and I will invite him to dinner soon, get to know him better."

"Thank you," the board chairman said, concluding the discussion.

"Robert, on another matter. I'd like to meet with you in early October to discuss plans for the new Environmental Sciences building. I think you'll be impressed with the architect's preliminary ideas. I'll have my administrative assistant get back to you later this week to set up a visit."

"Fine. And Roger, please ignore my earlier remarks implying that the foundation might withhold funds for the new building. The financing will be available as agreed. I won't disappoint you."

"Robert, thank you. You are an important friend and benefactor of the university and I personally value your friendship and generosity."

The president hung up and let out a deep sigh of relief. Gazing out the window at the gathering storm, he noted that the university's principal benefactor had failed to mention his son's prison record on drug charges.

Perhaps Abby's assessment was correct. John Lombardo might be back on drugs. He jotted a reminder in his appointment book to invite the young man to dinner soon. A personal evaluation might be useful. In the meantime, Abby Prescott would need some stroking to bring her back into the fold. There would be plenty of time to deal with her later.

He switched off the desk lamp and left the office.

Chapter Fifty-Six

Abby pulled into the driveway, touched the garage door opener and eased her new Lexus into the space beside Pete's SUV. She gathered her briefcase and entered the kitchen where she was greeted by the aroma of Pete's spaghetti sauce simmering on the stove.

"Hi there," Pete kissed her and then reached for a bottle of Merlot. Abby watched him pour generous portions of the wine.

"I really need this," Abby said as they touched glasses.

"How was traffic on Route 1? Any problems?"

"Not really," she said, reaching across the counter for a breadstick. "Heavy but moving along. The rain is just beginning. What's the latest forecast?"

"According to the National Weather Service, Melinda is still a category three hurricane. Storms this powerful rarely reach this far north, especially so late in the season when the ocean waters have begun to cool."

"Looks like we're in for some excitement."

"The storm should make landfall somewhere north of Portland around midnight. There's nonstop weather news on every television station; the Portland and Boston stations are comparing Melinda to the Perfect Storm of 1991. Of course, they may be exaggerating."

Pete turned up the volume on the small LCD television set resting on the granite counter. They watched silently as radar images of the huge storm filled the screen.

"Wow, this is a monster storm," Abby said soberly. "Are we ready?"

"Ready as we'll ever be."

"What about your boat?"

"It's secured with double anchors away from shore in a relatively sheltered spot. The harbor is well protected; the boat should be able to ride out almost anything."

Abby wandered into the living room, glass in hand. "Pete, you've really been busy. This place looks like plywood heaven," she said, checking the sliding doors facing the ocean. She closed the drapes, concealing the raw plywood Pete had hastily nailed up during the day. He joined her, bottle in hand and replenished their glasses.

"With a little luck, we'll ride out the storm with minimal damage. At least I hope so," he said optimistically.

"We'll probably lose power, Abby." He shook his head ruefully. "I should have persuaded you to buy a generator when you were repairing the house last month."

"Too late to worry about that now," Abby said philosophically. She kissed him lightly. "Thanks for all your preparations on the house. I owe you. I wouldn't have known where to begin.

"According to the car radio, people along the coast north of Portland are being urged to seek shelter inland."

"You definitely should leave," Pete advised firmly. "Seal Point Regional High School out by Route 1 is our local emergency center. Take the Toyota. The road to town will be passable for another few hours before the full force of the hurricane hits. I'd feel better knowing you are safely in a shelter."

"What about you?"

"I'll stay here, look after the house and try to minimize damage in case the sliders give way or we lose some windows."

"Then I'm not leaving," Abby said decisively. "We'll ride this out together. I've never been in a hurricane before. It could be exciting." She circled her arms around his waist.

"This isn't my kind of excitement," Pete said soberly. "I was in a hurricane years ago as a kid in Boston. I thought it was cool until trees started crashing around our house."

"I'm staying here, Pete. That's final."

He shrugged resignedly. It was nearly impossible to change Abby's mind and he understood her reluctance to abandon her home, despite the risks.

"Wind is the big unknown. The highest winds will come from the northeast and if we're lucky, the garage will take the brunt of the storm. At least there are no windows on that side. However, if the sliders or glass panes break, we could have a lot of water damage," he warned.

"I picked up extra batteries for the radio this afternoon, along with an ice chest and a bag of ice. The extra batteries and several flashlights are in this drawer." He pointed to a drawer below the center island counter. "We can store the frozen food in the chest for perhaps a day.

"This house was designed to withstand nor'easters, except for all the glass doors and windows. We'll wait and see how it survives a category three hurricane."

"You've thought of everything, Pete. It should be a wild night."

"Is the campus ready for the storm?" he asked, standing at the sink, filling a large pot with water for the pasta.

"I think so. Maintenance crews worked all day boarding up the windows facing the ocean and duct taping a lot of others."

"And you haven't told me about your day."

"I'll fill you in during dinner," she promised casually.

*　　*　　*

"Abby, way to go. You didn't knuckle under to the president!" Pete saluted her across the candlelit dining table as gale force winds shook the house. "So he is still trying to get that grade raised. No doubt he's feeling the heat from Lombardo's old man."

"Now I really appreciate the value of lifetime tenure. The president can throw me out of his office, but he can't fire me. And I tossed out a few threats of my own. Of course, Roger controls promotions. I'll probably never be promoted to full professor," she said glumly.

"Don't worry about another promotion. By the time you're eligible for full professor, Smythe may be long gone from Reid University."

"I doubt it, Pete. He's a born and bred Yankee. He's not going anywhere."

Abby rose to clear the table when the kitchen lights flickered once and then died.

"Damn, there goes the power. That's probably it for the night."

Pete reached for the wall phone. "The line is dead. Not surprising."

"What about our cell phones?" He took his phone from its belt pouch, speed dialed Abby's cell number and waited.

He shook his head. "There's no reception. People are probably overwhelming the system."

"Let's check the radio," Abby suggested, standing beside the candlelit counter. Pete tuned to a Portland station and turned up the volume.

He held up the tiny radio. "This is now our only link to the outside world. Let's hope the stations don't get knocked off the air."

They listened to another weather alert. "This is WPME Portland. Based on current projections, the eye of Hurricane Melinda will make landfall shortly after midnight, passing slightly north of Portland," the announcer said.

"Sounds like Seal Point could take a direct hit," Abby said, excited and apprehensive at the same time.

"Listen, there's more." Pete leaned over the counter.

"Thousands of Maine coastal homes already are without power. Melinda is moving at ten miles an hour on a north by northwest track," the announcer warned. "Residents along the Maine coast from Portland to Bar Harbor should prepare for winds in excess of 110 miles per hour and a coastal storm surge exceeding twenty feet. Expect extensive damage in low-lying areas.

"After making landfall, the storm will pick up speed, moving along a north northwest path. Areas as far inland as Augusta could receive up to ten inches of torrential, windblown rain. The storm will lose strength quickly and probably be downgraded to a tropical storm by the time it reaches extreme northern Maine tomorrow morning.

"Officials are urging residents within ten miles of the Maine coast to seek immediate shelter inland. Station WPME will shortly announce the location of the nearest shelters in towns along the coast between Portland and Bar Harbor. Stay tuned throughout the evening."

Pete took Abby in his arms. He leaned back, searched her face. "Are you sure you want to stay here? I'd feel a lot better if you took the SUV and camped out at the high school. There's still time."

Abby shook her head. "I'm not leaving without you."

"And I'm staying right here," Pete said firmly. "I want to protect the house."

"Then we'll ride out the storm together."

"Okay," he relented, the discussion over. "Let's try to get some rest. We probably won't get much sleep when the storm finally makes landfall." He reached out and kissed her.

"Are you suggesting?" she asked, dark eyes glistening in the candlelight.

"I'm ready if you are."

They headed for the bedroom.

The approaching storm was an aphrodisiac, deepening their lovemaking. Engrossed in each other, their passion unquenchable, the hours passed. Shortly after midnight, a light sheet covering their glistening bodies, they listened to the howling wind and the roar of storm driven waves crashing against the rocks. The house shook violently.

"Melinda is close," Abby whispered.

"I should have persuaded you to take the Toyota into town," Pete said, lying on his side, stroking her muscular thighs.

She moved over him, her body molded to his slender frame. Her fingers traced the curve of his jaw.

"We'll ride this out together. Whatever happens, it beats spending the night on a cot alongside a few hundred strangers at the high school. Imagine making love all night in front of a bunch of kids and old folks," she giggled.

He kissed her deeply. Their lovemaking resumed as the storm intensified beyond the boarded up windows of the master bedroom.

*   *   *

Outside, at the end of the road bordering Abby's home, a black BMW, lights extinguished, parked on the side of the road. Buffeted by eighty mile an hour winds and driving sheets of rain, the car was invisible had Abby or Pete chanced to look out the kitchen window. Hunkered down in the car, his iPod blaring in his earbuds, John Lombardo laid out his second line of crystal meth.

He giggled hysterically as wind and rain battered the heavy car, shaking his hand, spilling the white powder onto his lap. There was plenty more in the bag. Seconds later the drug hit his brain; he slumped back and prepared to wait. He would visit Abby and her boyfriend on this memorable night, a visit they would never forget.

Chapter Fifty-Seven

The eye of the hurricane made landfall two miles south of Seal Point.

Lombardo raced up Abby's driveway to the kitchen entrance, heavy flashlight in one hand, his .38 automatic tucked in his jacket pocket. He picked the door lock with his tools, a trick he'd learned from an addict years before in Oregon. Hand shielding the flashlight, he cautiously entered the kitchen and looked around.

The battery-operated backup alarm system Abby had installed two months ago sent a silent radio signal to the alarm company. In Portland, the duty person relayed an intrusion report to the Seal Point police headquarters. The police dispatcher logged the message, concluding that the alarm was triggered by storm-related damage. She did, however, notify chief Buchard by radio of a potential problem at the Prescott home. Follow-up would await the storm's passing.

The candles set out by Pete and Abby earlier in the evening cast dim shadows across the kitchen and living room. Except for the crashing of surf on the rocks below, the house was eerily silent in the calm eye of the storm. Lombardo listened, nerves tingling, fed by the load of meth saturating his brain, ready to execute his plan.

He made his way into the living room, then headed toward the master bedroom, his right hand grasping the handgun nestled in his pocket.

*   *   *

Pete awakened suddenly, immediately aware of the silence in the eye of the hurricane. He gently eased Abby's arm off his chest and slipped from the bed. Naked, he walked into the living room, dim candles lighting the way. Groggy from lovemaking and sleep, he didn't immediately react to the moving shadow near the fireplace.

"What the hell," he muttered softly, confused. "Who's there?"

Lombardo aimed the Maglite into Pete's eyes, blinding him instantly. Pete raised both arms in a futile attempt to shield his eyes and identify the dark shadow behind the light.

"What the hell is going on?" he asked, disoriented

Lombardo giggled. "Hello, Pete. I just invited myself inside, out of the storm. Did I wake you and Abby?"

"Lombardo? Is that John Lombardo behind the light? What the hell are you doing here?" Pete asked angrily, instantly wide awake.

The intruder moved the light down Pete's naked frame. "Aren't you some specimen of manhood," he taunted.

"I've come to see your girl, Pete," he said softly. "Abby hasn't followed my orders. We need to talk about that grade one more time."

"Pete, where are you?" Abby called from the bedroom, confused.

"Move into the bedroom, lover boy," Lombardo ordered, waving the gun in the light's beam.

Pete retreated slowly into the bedroom. "We have a visitor, Abby," he said calmly. "John Lombardo has decided to join us in the middle of the hurricane." He moved toward the bed, turning his back on the intruder, approaching the nightstand beside the bed.

"Uh, uh. Don't open that drawer. Get into bed and cover your sorry ass," Lombardo ordered.

Pete reached the edge of the bed, hesitated, then slid across the sheet and put his arm around Abby, who had drawn the top sheet up to her neck, shielding her naked body from the intense Maglite beam.

"Hello, professor. Surprised to see me?" Lombardo giggled.

Stunned and disoriented, Abby didn't respond.

"Oh, let's not be so formal. I'll just call you Abby and Pete. And you can call me John," he said from the doorway. He entered the bedroom and sat down on the chaise lounge in the corner.

"Well, now, this is a lovely bedroom, Abby. Great for sex games, huh?"

"What do you want?" Pete asked, sliding in front of Abby, partially shielding her from the gun. "You can be arrested, you know."

"Shit, man. No one's gonna arrest me in this weather," he laughed. "I'm just looking for shelter from the storm. You're not being very hospitable."

He settled back on the chaise, the flashlight illuminating the bed and its two occupants, his gun cradled in his right hand.

"What's in that drawer, Pete?" He gestured toward the nightstand next to the bed. "Have you got a gun tucked away in there?"

"Why don't you come over here and find out?"

"Why not," Lombardo stood, suddenly furious. He walked to the bed, gun in hand.

Pete was ready. He lunged, head low, body stretched toward the intruder. He grabbed Lombardo's arm just as John fired the first shot. Legs pumping strongly, Pete surged forward, buried his head in Lombardo's abdomen, and wrestled him to the floor. Wounded, his strength waning, he grabbed Lombardo's gun and tossed it onto the bed toward Abby. Her hysterical scream registered in his brain as he surrendered to the black void.

Lombardo, pinned beneath Pete's unconscious body, struggled to free himself. Shoving the dead weight aside, he went to his knees, grabbed the Maglite lying on the floor and shined it on Pete's unconscious form. Blood poured from the gaping wound in his left side, a dark stain spread across the beige carpet. Still on his knees Lombardo crawled toward the bed, steadied himself and reached for his gun, lying near Abby.

She got there first, grabbed the automatic and pointed it toward her crazed student. Lombardo backed off immediately, laughing hysterically.

"Shit, Abby, don't do something stupid." He stood and raised his hands, suddenly serious. He stepped cautiously toward the bed. "That gun can be dangerous. Give it to me before you hurt yourself."

"Back off!" she screamed. "Get out of my house!" She nearly dropped Lombardo's unfamiliar gun, awkwardly clutching the handle, her finger off the trigger, the barrel pointed toward the intruder.

"You wouldn't make a guest go out into the storm, now would you?" Lombardo jeered, instantly calm and confident. He stepped over Pete's prone body and opened the nightstand drawer. Glancing down, he found Pete's service automatic nestled next to a tube of KY gel. He took the gun, checked the safety and eased the fully loaded clip from the handle. An extra bullet remained nestled in the chamber as he shoved the clip back into the gun.

Turning his back on Abby, he retreated to the chaise lounge, seated himself and redirected the flashlight beam toward the bed. Slowly, he scanned her naked body.

Her back pressed against the headboard, legs drawn up to her chest, Abby shakily cradled Lombardo's own gun in her hand, pointed across the room toward her assailant.

With her free hand, she hastily drew the top sheet up to her shoulders. This nightmare could not be real. She would awake to find Pete sleeping peacefully beside her. She stared at Lombardo's gun in her hand, and then at Pete's bloody form lying beside the bed. She struggled for control, unable to process the shocking reality.

"My God, what have you done? Is he dead?" she cried.

"Yup. I think your boyfriend just bought the farm, Abby," he giggled. "Too bad. It was an accident, of course. He shouldn't have attacked me."

Tears stained her face. She gazed in disbelief at the loaded gun in her hand—John Lombardo's gun—the weapon that had just shot her lover and best friend.

Adrenaline surged through her body, anger overcame fear and pulled her back from the edge of hysteria. Gripping the gun with both hands, she pointed the weapon toward the dark figure seated on the chaise.

"Get out or I'll shoot," she warned, despair fueling a deep, agonizing frustration.

"No, you won't," he taunted, loaded with meth, master of the universe. "We still have business together."

"Get out!" she screamed, an adrenaline-fed surge of courage kicking in.

"Don't interrupt!" he yelled, his mood instantly ugly. "It's that damn grade, Abby. I'm not leaving until you change my grade. I think a B—no, an A—is about right," he snarled.

Abby fell silent, suppressing rising panic, desperately analyzing the situation, searching for a solution. Lombardo clearly was insane, obsessed about his grade. Was the situation hopeless, or could she reason with him in his present obviously drugged condition? Was there any chance he would let her live after he had just killed Pete? She would make one last effort to save herself.

"So you're still worried about that grade?" she stalled, willing herself to speak calmly.

Lombardo's violent mood reverted instantly to calm. He settled back on the chaise, confident, in complete control, languidly waving Pete's gun back and forth in her direction.

"I'm in charge now," he said, "and I'm not leaving until you change the grade."

"John, get real. The power is out and we're in the middle of a hurricane." She slowly lowered her gun to her side, apparently surrendering, her hand resting on the gun in a fold of the bed sheet.

"Even if I agree to change your grade, I can't do it now. I can't access the university's records from here."

"But you will change the grade?" Lombardo asked, a smile flitting across his face.

Abby was silent. Her lover lay mortally wounded in a pool of blood beside the bed. Lombardo was crazy, but not so insane that he would let her live to see the dawn, no matter what she promised.

She shook her head. "That grade won't be changed, not now—never.

"And you know the reasons why," she continued calmly. "You earned an F based on your performance in the class. I changed your grade to a C only because the president asked me to, not because you earned it."

"Screw it! This is your last chance!" he screamed, instantly out of control.

"Get out, John. Get out of my house, *now*!" Abby cried.

"Here's the deal," Lombardo said menacingly. "You agree to change the grade to a B and I'll leave. Otherwise, I'll have to take drastic action— maybe hurt you."

He glanced at Pete's body lying face down on the carpet beside the bed. "Your boyfriend can't help you now. Do you want to end up like him?" He tilted his head, an insane smile on his face. His finger tightened on the trigger of Pete's gun, the weapon he had taken from the nightstand.

Abby's heart pumped wildly. For the second time, courage fed by anger and frustration overcame her terror. She raised Lombardo's gun, the weapon that moments ago had shot her lover, and pointed it across the room toward her assailant.

"I won't change that grade," she retorted, "and you won't need to worry about grades. You'll be spending the rest of your miserable life in prison."

"Wrong again, Abby. It was just an accident. Pete shouldn't have tried to grab my gun."

He rose slowly, nonchalantly, and approached the bed. Pete's gun cradled lightly in his right hand, pointed toward Abby. "Put down the gun now," he ordered calmly. "I won't hurt you—not if you agree to change that grade."

She raised her arms, cradled Lombardo's weapon in both hands. "Don't come any closer," she screamed. "I'll shoot."

"No, you won't," Lombardo taunted, unconcerned.

He stepped over Pete's body, his knees touching the edge of the bed.

"Give me the gun, Abby," he ordered, reaching out, supremely confident she would not pull the trigger.

Abby aimed at Lombardo's torso in the dim candlelight and squeezed the trigger. The deafening blast reverberated around the bedroom.

Wounded, he surged forward, one knee now on the bed.

She squeezed the trigger again, and then again. He roared as dark arterial blood shot to the ceiling. With a final gasp, he lunged onto the bed. Pete's outstretched gun smashed against her thigh.

Abby screamed and scrambled away, falling to the floor in a tangle of bed sheets. Panicked, she stared in disbelief at Lombardo's motionless form, lying facedown on the blood-soaked bed, Pete's loaded service automatic outstretched in his lifeless hand. Then she dashed around the bed, rolled Pete onto his back and searched for a pulse.

He moaned weakly, his eyes mere slits, glazed and unseeing.

"Be still, Pete," she whispered, gently cupping his face. "You've been shot. I need to stop the bleeding."

She ran to the bathroom, grabbed a hand towel and raced back to his side. She glanced only once toward the motionless body on the bed. Bed sheets now drenched in blood, Lombardo clearly was beyond help. He couldn't survive multiple gunshot wounds at point blank range.

She reached for the discarded Maglite on the floor and examined the bloody wound in Pete's side. At her gentle touch, he stirred, his breathing labored and shallow.

"Hang on," she pleaded, willing herself to deal with the crisis as rising panic threatened to overwhelm her,.

Pete moaned, eyes flickering, struggling at the edge of consciousness. Kneeling on the carpet beside him, she laid the hand towel onto the round entry wound and pressed hard, the first aid course she had taken years ago not completely forgotten.

With a quiet moan, Pete lapsed once again into unconsciousness.

Chapter Fifty-Eight

Working frantically, Abby pulled a blanket from the bed and covered Pete's body. Minutes later she gently removed the blood soaked towel and examined the wound more closely. Pressure had staunched the bleeding. The single .38 caliber bullet from Lombardo's gun had entered Pete's left side below his waist. She reached under his body, searching for an exit wound. The bullet remained lodged in his body. She ran into the bathroom, grabbed a fresh hand towel and a roll of adhesive tape. Then she gently covered and taped the entry wound and tucked the blanket securely around his comatose body.

Isolated as the storm raged outside, she was powerless, communication with the outside world severed. She left Pete's side momentarily and crawled to the bed, searching for her cellphone. During the next few hours she occasionally turned it on, praying for a signal before the battery ran down. The adrenaline charge that had sustained her in the crisis faded, replaced with despair and a deep lassitude. All she could do was wait, paralyzed by fear.

She stretched out on the carpet beside Pete as waves of panic washed over her once more. She closed her eyes, forced herself to breath deeply, fought for calm, facing a crisis nothing in life had prepared her for.

Through the fog of shock and trauma, she became aware that the eye of the hurricane had passed. Ferocious winds and rain returned, battering the house with a vengeance, accompanied by the roar of surf crashing against the rocks below the house. The backside of the massive storm had made landfall. The hurricane gathered speed, tracking on a northwest path that would soon attack the inland populated areas of Maine. It would be several hours before the winds and rain would slowly diminish. Later, she would have no memory of the long hours before help arrived.

At some point during the dark hours that followed, over the screeching winds and torrential rain, the sound of shattered glass in the living room roused her. Wind roared unchecked through the house, invading the bedroom, extinguishing the candles throughout the house.

She ran into the living room, Lombardo's light in her hand. Layers of shattered glass covered the carpet near the sliding doors. The plywood that Pete had installed bowed dangerously as windswept rain poured through cracks, threatening to expose the house to the storm's full fury. She pointed the beam upward just as the heavy panes above the shattered sliders surrendered to the howling wind and crashed to the floor at her feet.

She screamed, suddenly aware she was standing barefoot and naked, surrounded by a sea of shattered glass. She could not save the living room from complete destruction.

Abby retreated, fighting the wind and rain, pushing shut the heavy master suite door. In the dressing room, she slipped on shower clogs and donned a heavy robe. Relatively safe from the chaos in the rest of the house, she stretched out beside Pete on the bloodstained carpet. Her back to the bed and her arm cradling his body, she ignored the bloody remains of John Lombardo.

As the wind blew relentlessly through the living room and kitchen, her world collapsed. All sense of reality faded. Rousing herself occasionally, she focused on Pete's unconscious form beside her, searching for the pulse in his neck, thankful that he was still alive, praying that he would not die. The blood now staunched from his wound, she checked his breathing, shallow but steady.

Time held no meaning. Utterly alone, her mind shut down. She retreated to a hidden place, a zone in which no thought penetrated except a mantra, a prayer for her lover's life.

The hands of her watch seemed frozen in place. Inevitably, however, the minutes and hours slowly passed.

*   *   *

The wind and rain subsided as dawn crept silently into the bedroom. A distant siren pierced the sounds of crashing surf, rousing Abby as though from a deep slumber. Disoriented, she staggered to her feet.

Abandoning Pete, she ran through the kitchen and out the door. Chief Buchard's cruiser, light bar flashing and siren screaming, screeched to a stop in the driveway. He leaped from the car and raced to her through the rain. She held out blood soaked hands and collapsed in his arms.

Minutes later a dozen state and local police cruisers, sirens blaring, drew up to the house at the end of Ocean Lane.

"Lock down the house, the grounds, and that BMW parked across the road," Buchard ordered the officers gathered in a light rain outside Abby's home.

"Set up a roadblock. Extend crime tape from those trees to the rocks above the ocean," he directed, pointing to the back of the property. "Keep the damn television trucks, reporters, cameramen, and spectators at least a quarter mile away from the house. Nobody talks to reporters—television or otherwise," he gestured toward the gathering media in the distance. "And nobody views this crime scene.

"The coroner will be here shortly. Have him report to me directly. Have Craig Edwards, the campus security chief at Reid University, report to me when he gets here. Our police photographer and the state police investigator are on their way. Check picture IDs before allowing anyone you don't personally recognize beyond the crime tape."

"You going to tell us what happened inside that house?" one officer asked.

"I'll tell you this much, and keep it to yourself," Buchard warned, "we've got one body in the master bedroom. White male, mid-twenties, shot three times at close range.

"The Seal Point ambulance is taking another victim—white male, alive, but barely—to Maine Medical Center in Portland. Whoever leaks that information to the media is toast. Fired. Understood?"

The officers nodded soberly.

"Now get to work."

Buchard returned to the house and found Abby, now dressed in jeans and a sweatshirt, in the bedroom. Arm around her waist, he gently led her across the shattered living room and through the kitchen to his cruiser in the driveway. He helped her into the front passenger seat, whispered a few words in her ear and closed the door.

Over the roof of the cruiser, he motioned to his first sergeant. "Take professor Prescott to the emergency room at MMC. Make sure the ER people understand she's to be informed of Pete Byrnes's condition. He's the guy we just loaded into the ambulance.

"Stay with Prescott until her friend, Jen Carpenter, arrives. Don't let any media people near them. I'll expect you back here within an hour. Now move out," he ordered.

"Right," said the sergeant, one leg inside the cruiser, ready to roll.

Tires squealing, the sergeant switched on the light bar and gunned the cruiser along Ocean Lane. Siren screaming, the car raced past the gathering crowd of spectators, TV cameras and reporters. Carrying a silent passenger, the sergeant sped through the village of Seal Point and turned south onto Route 1.

Abby, a shrunken figure huddled in the front seat, stared vacantly out the window. The property damage and general devastation from Hurricane Melinda did not register in her consciousness. She prayed silently, desperately hoping the doctors could save her lover.

Fifteen minutes later two Portland TV remote trucks, broadcasting from the scene, reported the shooting death of one victim and the wounding of another in an expensive contemporary home by the sea in Seal Point, Maine.

Chapter Fifty-Nine

Abby climbed into her Lexus and took Highway 1 south to Portland. Traumatized two weeks ago, she had gratefully accepted Jen and Rob Carpenter's hospitality because her own home, nearly destroyed by the hurricane's winds and rain, would not be habitable for another month. On her physician's recommendation, she began treatment for post traumatic stress disorder when a series of panic attacks overwhelmed her during the days immediately following the tragedy at her home.

Concentrating on traffic as she approached the city, she took the Maine Medical Center exit and stopped at a red light. Without warning, waves of panic overwhelmed her. Heart racing, sweaty palms gripped the steering wheel as an endless mental tape of the horrible night captured her mind.

Would she ever be able to erase that memory? She reached in her handbag for the Zoloft tablets, swallowed one without water, hoping the pill would take effect quickly.

A cacophony of horns brought her back to reality. She drove to the hospital, found a parking spot and sat in the car, waiting for the medication to calm her shattered nerves. Minutes later, she entered the hospital lobby and took the elevator to the fifth floor. By the time she opened Pete's hospital door, the panic attack had passed.

"How are you feeling, Pete?" she kissed him gently.

"Fine, no pain," he assured her, glancing at the intravenous tube sending the painkiller from the bag above his head to his hand. "That juice is the same stuff I got in Iraq after the IED hit my Hummer.

"I got some good news from the doc this morning," he said, grinning. "I'm definitely on the mend and he promised to let me out of here next week."

"That's fantastic."

"It will be a couple months before I get back to work full time. I'll have time to repair the house—again," he said wryly.

Abby sat on the edge of the bed, holding his hand. "I'm meeting with the district attorney this afternoon. Maybe we'll finally have closure on this sorry mess," she said, relieved that the Zoloft had worked its magic. "Rob will be with me, and chief Buchard will also be in the room," she continued. "This will be my official statement. I admit, I'm a little nervous."

"You'll be fine. Just tell the DA exactly what happened as you remember it."

She glanced at her watch. "Before I leave, there's something you should know."

"What's that?"

"I've been having insomnia," she revealed. "The shooting is an endless tape of broken visions in my head. Pete, I killed another human being in cold blood," she said, tears welling up. "I realize that shooting Lombardo was my only option. It was him or me. Still, I'm feeling incredible guilt, even though it was in self defense."

"Sweetheart, I'm so sorry. The trauma you are experiencing is a natural reaction that will take time to recede," he said sympathetically.

"On doctor's orders, I've begun therapy," she confessed sheepishly. "I have a session with Dr. Taylor right after I finish with the district attorney."

"Good idea," Pete said. "A psychiatrist will help you work through this. I know from experience."

"You've seen a shrink?" Abby asked, taken aback.

"Yes," he admitted. "After I came back from Iraq, I experienced symptoms of post traumatic stress. It took a year of group therapy to deal with the problems."

"Now I understand why you're reluctant to discuss your tour of duty in Iraq," she said softly.

"And I don't want to dredge it up now," he said firmly. "Let's agree the subject is off limits."

"Of course," she said.

"John Lombardo was sick, really sick," she mused, lost in thought. "Sure, we all thought he was weird, possibly on drugs. If I had recognized how sick he was and gotten him medical help, he might be alive today."

"Stop, Abby," Pete interrupted her rambling. "You are not responsible for his drug addiction or his paranoid schizophrenia. He had many opportunities to deal with his problems long before he arrived on campus.

"Concentrate on putting this experience behind you. Time and some psychiatric counseling will help you heal. Trust me, a year from now, this will be a distant memory."

* * *

Downtown Portland was quiet on this weekday afternoon. Abby parked in a public garage and walked to Rob's offices where she was immediately ushered into a bookcase-lined conference room.

She dreaded the upcoming meeting with Ben McCormack, the Cumberland County district attorney. At Rob's request, McCormack had agreed to delay questioning her while Pete remained in critical condition following removal of his left kidney, the result of the gunshot wound inflicted by Lombardo.

The meeting was further delayed when Abby began experiencing symptoms of post traumatic stress disorder and Pete contracted an aggressive blood infection, an unfortunate complication of the surgery. Finally, Pete was declared in stable condition two days ago. Now that he was declared in stable condition, she could no longer delay making a statement to authorities about the September 26 tragedy at her home.

Fortunately, her statement would be taken in Rob's office rather than in the offices of the district attorney, where her appearance would quickly attract press attention and television cameras.

Rob came into the room and took a seat beside her. "How are you feeling?"

"Nervous," she confessed. "I know it's time to nail down the details for whatever legal procedures I'm facing. The television stations and newspapers are having a field day speculating about how Lombardo died."

"You'll be fine," Rob reassured her. "This procedure should take less than an hour. Ben McCormack is a good man; you need to relate what happened that night in detail. You'll finally be able to bring closure to this nightmare.

"I'm confident the DA will conclude that you acted in self defense in the face of repeated threats during a home invasion. They need your statement to wrap up their investigation.

"Pete has already given his statement. Of course, he was unconscious much of the time. Because he was a victim, no charges will be brought against him.

"I'll be here to represent you and a court steno typist will record your statement," he concluded.

"Try to relax, Abby. Just answer each question as clearly and concisely as you can. Remember, this is not an adversarial procedure."

Abby looked up as the conference door opened and the district attorney of Cumberland County entered, followed closely by Roland Buchard and a short gray-haired woman carrying a tiny machine mounted on a tripod.

Tall and slim, Ben McCormack shook hands with Abby and Rob, and stepped aside while Buchard gave Abby a bear hug. The steno typist set up her machine in a corner of the room near the conference table.

"Where would you like us to sit, Rob?" McCormack asked.

"Abby and I will take seats at the head of the table. I suggest you sit on one side and chief Buchard take the other side. We can begin whenever your steno typist is ready."

Abby stood and McCormack swore her in. After she seated herself, he immediately began the questioning. The others sat back and listened.

"For the record," he began formally. "Let me summarize the facts of this case, which are the subject of this deposition. The gunshot death of John Lombardo and the wounding of Peter Byrnes occurred in the early morning hours of September 26, 2009 at the home of Abigail Prescott in Seal Point, Maine.

"Our purpose today is to obtain the statement of Ms. Prescott. During the past two weeks statements and evidence have been gathered from numerous sources. We have reports of the coroner and medical examiner, statements by the family of John Lombardo, by Roger Smythe, president of Reid University, by campus security chief, Craig Edwards and by police chief Buchard and other officers who arrived on the scene around 7 a.m. on September 26. Yesterday, I took a brief statement from Peter Byrnes at Maine Medical Center here in Portland. Let us proceed."

* * *

Thirty minutes later, the district attorney neared the conclusion of his questioning. "Ms. Prescott, will you please summarize in your own words exactly what happened immediately after Mr. Byrnes was shot by Mr. Lombardo."

Abby took a deep breath.

"Lombardo's gun ended up in my hands," she began, her voice shaking as she relived the shooting. "Pete somehow grabbed the gun during the struggle and tossed it toward me on the edge of the bed. When he was shot, he fell directly on top of Lombardo, momentarily pinning him to the floor.

"There was a little delay while John got out from under Pete, who was unconscious and bleeding. During those few seconds I grabbed Lombardo's gun, which Pete had tossed toward me.

"When Lombardo saw his gun in my hand, he didn't seem frightened. He casually stepped over Pete's body and opened the nightstand drawer beside the bed. He found Pete's loaded service automatic, waved it around a bit, then backed away from the bed and sat down on the chaise lounge in the corner of my bedroom."

McCormack interrupted. "Let's be very clear here, Ms. Prescott. Please describe exactly your location, Mr. Byrnes's position and Mr. Lombardo's position."

"Pete and John struggled briefly, then Lombardo shot him," she repeated. "Pete fell on top of Lombardo, but managed to grab the gun and toss it on the bed. They were both on the floor. I was on the bed—a king bed—as far away from both of them as I could get. At that point I thought Pete was dead." Abby shuddered.

"What happened next?" the district attorney asked quietly.

"Lombardo shoved Pete aside and got to his knees. Despite the fact that I had his gun, John took his time, crawled to the nightstand beside the bed and found Pete's loaded gun in the drawer."

"At that point, you had Lombardo's gun and he had taken Mr. Byrnes' loaded service automatic from the nightstand drawer. Is that correct?" asked the district attorney.

"Yes. I was fumbling with the gun; it probably looked like I didn't know what to do with it."

"Go on," McCormack urged.

"Lombardo backed away and sat down on the chaise across the room. He was cocky, not at all concerned about Pete, and not worried that I was pointing his own gun at him. He started talking about changing that damn grade in my course. He finally said he wouldn't hurt me if I gave him a B."

"Do you believe Lombardo's housebreak during the September 26 hurricane was over a disputed grade in a course you taught last spring?" McCormack asked.

"Yes," Abby nodded emphatically.

"Then what happened?"

"At first I tried to reason with him. Very quickly it became obvious he was beyond reason. Finally, despite the horrible circumstances, I found the courage to tell him the gentleman's C grade would not be changed—not now, never. Those were my exact words. In retrospect, I have no idea why I didn't simply agree to change the grade to the B he wanted. After all, there was a gun pointed at me."

"You also had a gun pointed at Mr. Lombardo," McCormack reminded her quietly. "You were not defenseless."

"True," she admitted. "Although I was terrified, I remember telling him he'd already murdered one person, and he'd spend the rest of his miserable life in prison. At that point I thought I was going to die, too. I assumed Pete was dead and Lombardo would kill me next. The situation was hopeless."

Abby was silent, reliving the scene, her head down, her eyes staring unseeing at the mahogany conference table. No one spoke.

She took a deep breath and resumed. "He ordered me to give him the gun," she said, her voice barely above a whisper.

"No. Let me go back," she said more strongly. "Right after Pete was shot, I screamed and told Lombardo to get out of my house. He actually giggled, like he was enjoying the situation."

"You pointed the gun at him and ordered him to leave?" McCormack repeated.

"Yes, I distinctly recall ordering him out of my house at least three times. The first time was immediately after he shot Pete. Then I yelled at him at least twice as he came toward the bed a few minutes later."

"All right," McCormack leaned forward. "Let's go back to the point where you told him his grade would not be changed. What happened next?"

"He went crazy, screaming and yelling, waving the gun around. That's when it all fell apart. He started walking toward the bed. He ordered me to hand over the gun.

"Pete's service automatic was in his hand, pointed at me. That's when I warned him twice to get out of the house or I would shoot."

Abby stopped, her voice broke and she teared up, lost in the horror of that moment two weeks earlier.

The group waited patiently.

She gathered herself and continued. "Lombardo kept coming toward the bed. I gripped my gun—Lombardo's gun—with both hands, and aimed it toward him, the way Pete had taught me at the shooting range."

"For the record, let me clarify a point here," McCormack interrupted. "I understand you have a valid Maine handgun license issued by the Seal Point police shortly after your home was trashed. You had completed a firearms safety training program under the direction of Mr. Byrnes. Is that correct?" McCormack asked.

"Yes, that's right."

"Go on. Lombardo was approaching the bed and each of you had a gun pointed at the other," McCormack prompted.

"I warned him again. He just kept coming." Abby shook her head, tearing up again, her head down. Her voice dropped. "I told him to get out again. A few seconds later he reached the edge of the bed. His arm was outstretched toward me, gun in his hand, no more than a few feet away."

"What happened next?" McCormack asked.

"Then I squeezed the trigger," she whispered.

"I'm sure the first bullet hit him somewhere in the torso. But he just kept coming." Abby began to sob. "He was reaching for my gun. I was absolutely certain he was going to shoot me." She turned away, embarrassed, unable to hide the tears streaming down her cheeks, devastated by the images of that horrible night.

"I must have fired two more shots, although I don't remember them," she resumed, struggling for control. "I understand the police found four spent cartridges in the bedroom—all fired from Lombardo's gun, the gun I was holding. Obviously, Lombardo fired the first bullet, wounding Pete. I distinctly remember firing the second shot just as he reached the bed."

She was breaking down. "I must have pulled the trigger twice more. I'm sorry, I just don't remember firing those last two shots. My mind is a blank. It all happened so fast," she cried.

Rob Carpenter interrupted. "I think we need a break here."

"Of course," the district attorney agreed. "Ms. Prescott, I know this is very difficult for you, but your statement is crucial to our investigation."

Abby composed herself. "I understand. I want to finish this."

She bit her lip and resumed. "After the first shot, when Lombardo kept coming toward me, I was certain he was going to kill me," she repeated.

"I remember the noise, the awful sound of a gunshot in my bedroom." She collapsed completely.

McCormack stood. "Everyone, take a fifteen minute break," he ordered. "I am sorry for your pain, Ms. Prescott. Your ordeal soon will be over." He led Buchard and the steno typist into the law firm's outer office.

"Abby, I'm sorry you have to relive this," Rob said, leaning over and offering her a handkerchief.

"I'm so embarrassed, Rob. I just need a few minutes," she wiped her eyes.

"Take all the time you need."

He left the conference room and led Ben Cormack and chief Buchard into his private office.

"I regret putting Ms. Prescott through this ordeal, but her statement is essential to closing the case," said McCormack.

"She'll be fine shortly. She needs a little time," Rob assured him.

"What do you think?" He regarded Ben McCormack soberly.

The district attorney was silent for several moments. Finally he said cautiously, "Based on Ms. Prescott's testimony and the forensic evidence, this appears to be a case of self defense. That's preliminary and unofficial," he warned. "My office will review the evidence and the statements of all the parties."

"This is a textbook definition of self defense," Rob Carpenter pointed out, pleased with the district attorney's tentative decision. "Abby Prescott experienced a brutal home invasion in which Pete Byrnes was shot and nearly killed. She was forced to defend herself after ordering Lombardo out of the house multiple times. She had no other option."

Chief Buchard turned to the district attorney. "These two people have suffered enough. I hope you'll expedite this case."

The district attorney did not respond and the group returned to the conference room.

"I have no further questions for you, Ms. Prescott. Is there anything more you wish to add for the record?"

Abby, poised and in control now that the ordeal was ending shook her head.

"No."

"I will forward a copy of your transcribed statement, probably late next week. You and your attorney can review and suggest corrections," the district attorney told her.

"Mr. McCormack, I'm terribly sorry that I have no recollection of the shooting after I fired the first shot. I'm also embarrassed that I can't remember much about the hours after the shooting when I was waiting for the hurricane to pass and help to arrive."

Abby shook her head. "I simply don't remember."

"Your reaction is understandable, Ms. Prescott. We have other means to reconstruct the five hours while you awaited rescue. I will seek a statement from your physician regarding the depth of the trauma you experienced and your inability to reconstruct the shooting in more detail."

McCormack prepared to wrap up the interview.

Abby took a deep breath and then asked Ben McCormack the question that had haunted her for more than two weeks.

"What happens to me now? Will I be charged with a crime?" She looked up at him.

"Based on the information you have provided and the earlier statement of Mr. Byrnes, my preliminary and unofficial conclusion is that the death of John Lombardo was a case of self defense," McCormack said quietly.

"There will be an inquest before a judge, probably within a month. If my final conclusion is that this is a case of self defense, I will ask the judge to so rule and that will end the legal issues surrounding this tragedy."

Chief Buchard turned to Abby. "The trashing of your home last July is a crime that may never be solved," he said, "although it may be related to the events of September 26. Without proof and with the possible perpetrator dead, I think we will let that sleeping dog lie. Dead men don't face charges in Maine."

"Was Lombardo really high on drugs the night he died?" Abby asked.

"Yes," the chief replied. "We found a significant quantity of meth amphetamine in his car. And according to the autopsy report, his body was loaded with crystal meth. There is additional evidence that he was a heavy user. The drug may have contributed to his violent behavior, aggravating his known paranoid tendencies.

"Unfortunately, Abby, you became the focus of his paranoia. I'm personally amazed that a student would be willing to kill someone over a grade in a university course. His obsession is a good indication of his impaired mental state.

"I interviewed his parents recently in New Jersey," Buchard went on. "They are victims, too. They tried to help their son. God knows, John Lombardo had all the advantages of wealth, plus two loving parents. Despite their efforts, they couldn't cope with his mental and drug-induced problems. That young man was in drug rehab at the best clinic in the country and he still couldn't kick his coke and meth habits.

"I have other news for you," Buchard continued. "This morning I received a phone call from Roger Smythe informing me that the Lombardo Foundation has pledged $2 million to establish a foundation in the name of John Lombardo. Its objective is to develop a drug education and rehabilitation program for the citizens of Maine, focused on young people from grade school through university level."

Chief Buchard glanced at his watch. "That's enough news for now."

McCormack and Buchard shook Abby's hand, nodded to Rob and left the conference room.

Rob Carpenter hugged her. "You were great, Abby. Everything's going to be fine. It's over. You and Pete have your life back."

"I'm heading off to see my psychiatrist right now," she said, gathering her handbag. "Then I'm going back to the hospital to tell Pete about the interview. Tell Jen not to expect me for dinner. I'll eat hospital food with Pete."